"A sexy, dark, and (well, yes) biting story told by a wizard of sleight of hand: episodes erotic, poignant, ghoulish are revealed like a cardsharp's quick wins— hands comprised of flash cards, police ID, and several aces of hearts. Barlow writes with semaphoric speed, managing to unfurl an urban legend both intelligent and romantic."

—Gregory Maguire, author of *Wicked* and *What-the-Dickens*

"Lean, gripping. . . . A hip, quick moving thriller."

—Jonathan Gibbs, *The Independent*

"I like this book—lycanthropy indeed begins at home."

—David Mamet

SHARP TEETH

SHARP TEETH

Toby Barlow

HARPER

An Imprint of HarperCollins*Publishers*
www.harpercollins.com

HarperCollins books may be purchased for educational, business, or sales promotional use. For information, please write: Special Markets Department, HarperCollins Publishers, 10 East 53rd Street, New York, NY 10022.

Grateful acknowledgment is made to reprint the following previously published material:

Lines by Robert Frost taken from March 15, 1963, issue of *Vogue*, copyright © 1963 reprinted by permission of the Estate of Robert Lee Frost; lines from "Werewolves of London" by Warren Zevon, Leroy Marinell, Robert Wachtel. Copyright © 1978 Zevon Music. Used by permission; excerpt from "Theses on the Philosophy of History" in *Illuminations* by Walter Benjamin © 1955 by Suhrkamp Verlag, Frankfurt a.m., English translation by Harry Zohn © 1968 and renewed 1996 by Harcourt, Inc., reprinted by permission of Harcourt, Inc.; lyrics to "Cassidy" by John Barlow © 1972 Ice Nine Publishing Company. All rights reserved. Used by permission, "The Werewolf" written by Michael Hurley © 1965, 1993 (renewed) SNOCKO MUSIC (BMI), administered by BUG. All rights reserved. Used by permission, "As It Happens" (excerpt) by Denise Levertov, from *Poems 1960–1967* © 1965 by Denise Levertov. Reprinted by permission of New Directions Corp. *The People's Almanac* by David Wallechinsky and Irving Wallace © 1975. Used by permission. Lines from "The Hungry Wolf" written by John Doe & Exene Cervenka © 2001. Published by Pacific Electric Music Publishing, Inc. Used by permission.

FIRST EDITION

Sharp Teeth was first published in the UK in 2007, in slightly different form.

Designed by Leah Carlson-Stanisic

Illustrations by Natasha Michaels

Library of Congress Cataloging-in-Publication Data is available upon request.

ISBN: 978-0-06-143022-0

08   09   10   11   12   OV/RRD   10   9   8   7   6   5   4   3   2   1

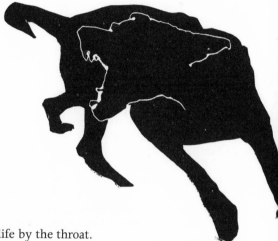

Poetry is a way of taking life by the throat.

ROBERT FROST

book one

There is no document of civilization that is not at
the same time a document of barbarism.

WALTER BENJAMIN

His hair was perfect.

WARREN ZEVON

I

Let's sing about the man there
at the breakfast table
brown skin, thin features, white T,
his olive hand making endless circles
in the classifieds
"wanted" "wanted" "wanted"
small jobs little money
but you have to start somewhere.
Here.
LA
East LA
a quarter mile from where they pick up the mariachis
on warm summer nights
two miles from La Serenata de Garibaldi's
where the panther black cars pause on their haunches
while their blonde women eat inside
wiping the blood red
mole from their quiet lips
"wanted" "wanted" "wanted"
he circles the paper
then reaches for the phone
breathes deep, begins.

"nope, sorry"
"job was taken already, good luck"
"you got experience?"
"leave a message"
"forgettaboutit"
"you sound Mexican, ola, you Mexican?"
"call back Monday"
"mmmn, I don't know nothing about that"

"no"
"no"
"no"

Then his barbed hook catches. A thin gold vein
is struck. Buds of hope crack through the dry white earth:
"oh sure, come on by, what's your name?"

Dogcatcher.

His father was not a man but a sleepy bull
with sledgehammer hands and a soft heart.
He once brought a dog home from the pound
for Anthony.
Sipping coffee by the phone now
that little yapping note of hope still rings in his ears.
Anthony smiles, remembering the way
the puppy sat between his father's strong legs
as they stood looking down like gods
at the cowering little creature.
They laughed. The pup relaxed,
wagged its fat tail.
His father was kind to the dog, to the kids, to his wife
until a week later when he went through the windshield
on Sepulveda. Hit so hard
it didn't matter where he landed.

And after that nothing was kind
it was every man for himself
and there were no men
just a widow, some kids
and a dog who went back to the pound,
taking his chances with no chance at all.
C'est la guerre.
Pondering his path,
Anthony wonders now,

if maybe that dog
wasn't just some real bad luck.

"Packs of thirty or forty at a time
wander loose
like gauchos in their own damn ghost town.
They come from the hills, up from the arroyos.
We don't know how many, estimates vary,
but each time they come in
a few house dogs go back with them.
Anytime you got toy poodles breeding with coyotes
it's gonna get interesting."
Calley is so white, he's red
with blanched features pickled and burned.
He shows Anthony how to wrangle, how to pull hoops, slip a wire.
They sit at the firing range. "You'll be shooting tranqs,
but might as well practice with live rounds." Calley shows
bite marks on his hands, legs and arms.
His breath bites too: coffee, cigarettes, and just plain old rancid.
"I'll ride partner with you for a bit, but with all the cutbacks
they're making us all ride solo now."
"What happens if I hit a pack?"
"Hit a pack, hit the radio." Calley pauses, draws on a smoke
the red in his eyes almost matches the
blood vessels spidering across his face
It's a foggy, milky, bloodshot stare,
but it still holds a mean light.
He rasps, "You like dogs?"
"Yeah, sure."
"Mmmn," he nods. "You won't."

The "animal control" logo makes Anthony wonder.
Animals have no control, they run, they fuck, they eat,
they kill to fuck, they kill to eat
and they sleep in the noonday sun.
Anthony's not afraid of the dogs,

he's not afraid of the work,
he just hates the other guys.
He sits apart, trying to stay clean.
Perhaps over time he will become like them
with their permanent stains and bitter dispositions.
But Christ almighty, he thinks,
I hope not.

II

There's blood everywhere,
but it's the creatures at the edge,
licking the corner of the ruby pool,
that hold your curiosity.
So get this straight
it's not the full moon.
That's as ancient and ignorant as any myth.
The blood just quickens with a thought
a discipline develops
so that one can self-ignite
reshaping form, becoming something rather more canine
still conscious, a little hungrier.
It's a raw muscular power,
a rich sexual energy
and the food tastes a whole lot better.

Imagine,
sleeping with the pack
the safety, the loyalty,
the protection.
Imagine
the elemental comfort.

Bone, love, meat, gristle, heat, anger, exhaustion, drive,
    hunger, blood, fat, marrow.
Fifteen men lying in one house.

Listen to the night as
they softly growl
someone chases something in his dreams
desperate for satisfaction
then silent.
There's one woman here.
There's one leader here.
The pack does what he says,
she comes and goes
as she pleases.

Lark was challenged
that night there was no moon.
The pack had seen and felt it
coming and building.
Lark was a man when it started,
wolf when it ended.
Con tried to cut him with a knife
coming in through the front door
but with perfect liquid grace,
Lark slipped past the weapon's edge
grabbed Con's hand and bent it back.
The blade flew through the Ruscha.
Teeth gleamed bare and sharp
muscles tore through jackets
Ted Baker shirts were shredded
blood striped the walls
sweat soaked through.
A Tag Heuer watch flew off
what was once a wrist.
Con was a man when it started,
he wasn't much by the time it was done.

Some of us have problems.
They still talk about Bone and what the grease does to him.
He can't go into fried chicken places

the smell, the scent, turns his blood right away.
They say he took out a Popeye's once.
It made the news, unsolved.
It took him an hour.
He walked in, just to pick up a bucket.
The smell hit, the change happened,
and the whole place had to go.
Chicken, customers, biscuits, and gravy.
Lark says control is everything.
There's no percentage in hating
your nature, it's just in the blood.
That was about three years ago,
there was some buzz,
press says gangs,
people wail on television
then, not surprisingly
life just keeps moving on.

Between money, work,
and the day to day
Lark never loses track of
the long range.
The pack never questions
his intentions,
if they did, they sense
there would be no answers.
So they follow his lead
and they stay quiet,
they drive their 7 Series the speed limit
and Bone gets his chicken from the drive-through.

They do their best to stay clean.
They still talk about the last one who tried something.
Baron, down at a party in Irvine,
thought a couple of lines might be fun.

Press says gangs,
people wail on television
but it was just Baron.
There are some problems
but, mostly, life just goes on.

Lark has a woman.
He says every pack must have one.
The pack has needs
but Lark says its not about that.
He says control is the path.
As she lies there among them,
her curves lines of delicate torture,
the tension can snap so tight,
that each one of the pack
feels like a piano wire pulled taut.
Lark says the desire pulls the pack together
calls it the Ukan path.
The pack follows it because here
inside the circle
they taste the fresh, wet meat of success
while outside the circle
lies nothing but coyote darkness.

Blood, fat, marrow, grease, sinew, muscle, guts, hide, fur, sleep.

They may twitch in their dreams when they sleep
but they sleep deep.

III

She rides alone,
a route that brings her
down by the beach
which takes her back,

her memory flickering
as it does
to what had been.

She's supposed to be going straight to the bar,
to see if he's there.
Lark sent her, it's a simple plan,
a slow-working plan, to what end, who knows,
Lark protects her from the dogs, keeps her safe.
He says it's a three-week job, easy.
She trusts him.
But she still has time to swing past the beach.

Back then, back before,
she hated the punks, goth shit was geek drama
she was clean then
she loved strong boys
she felt pure with the athletes
and she wanted nothing but another green day
with no need for anything deeper or more profound
    than the phrase
junior college.
There on the sandy beaches and
the lush green sod of the quad she had only three loves:
Chad, so kind, a surfer, easy smile and a pirate's tooth
his hands roamed her body, then his body up and roamed.
Easy heartbreak, must not have been so deep.
Enter Mike, sweet Mike, his body arched
over volleyballs nets, he was tall, tall, tall,
but when he stopped coming by,
and she felt that heartache
cut deeper into her ribs,
she could still walk it off,
she knew something better was coming.
Then Pete. Oh, Pete,
basketball, lacrosse, blue eyes that seemed swimmable.

She smiled so brightly at him, her teeth practically chimed.
He could kiss her anywhere, touch her anywhere,
anything for Pete, everything ached and opened for him.
When he touched her thigh,
she was anchored to the world.
She drew pictures of him while he slept,
she hummed along when he sang.
Nice.
But then something
was sprung, she doesn't remember
how the dark sparked but
one idle daiquiri day
she slipped out some small thoughtless words,
stupid jealousy, nothing really, but
the day paused and
everything vibrated wrong.
And then Pete answered back
with something much worse.

The moment seemed
slow but Pete
had her flying
arcing across the room
her head knocking hard against a wall
just like that.
Pete was looking down at her
and she was so weak and small
it didn't take much
to throw her across the room again
and then again.
No bruises to speak of,
only
her sense of tomorrow
all smashed and jumbled
like a pool of paint lying on the floor
after all the bright colors bleed together

into a simple
shit brown.

That was long, long ago right?
only yesterday, right?

She sleeps now with Lark
surrounded by a dozen or so men
who could do terrible things
to anyone who ever tried to touch her
but she doesn't need the men
she could do plenty of damage
all by herself.
She has the blood for it.

Driving forward, looking back,
she finds there is only the loosest bond
between time and pain
some things don't pass,
the injuries don't heal
they merely find a place in our guts
and in our bones
where they fitfully rest,
tossing and turning between our knuckles and ribs
waiting to wake
as the shadows grow long.

Pete lives with a wife
down near the beach.
Lark says he can't be touched. Not yet.
She listens, but she knows
what a girl like her could do
to a fellow like Pete now.

IV

The only reason to get up is the dogs
Anthony feels cold to the job itself.
The men are all pricks
they smell like cleanser
they want him to be one of the gang
Calley, Mason, Malone.
Watching them
as they beat the dogs down
Anthony stands at the edge, smoking, thinking
that hatred and love emanate equal distances
inside and outside the flesh,
which is why kind folk
are said to have good hearts
while bastards like these
just smell bad.

Some carne asada tacos,
six bucks he can't spare
split three ways in a kennel
on three dogs who seem to know
they're about to be put under.
None of them warm to Anthony's small gesture
they just wolf it all down.
Anthony pets the brindled one
who won't look up. Anthony glances over
hearing a yelp as
Calley kicks a dog.
"Life's a bitch, and then you die," says Calley.
I hate this fucking job, thinks Anthony.

Anthony sips his beer at the bar,
wishing the subject would change.

But his new occupation is a social trip wire
because everyone and without exception everyone
has a dog story to tell.
Most seem to focus on the cruel and sudden demise:
the bus, the pickup truck, the drunk teenage driver,
the electric fence, the unfortunate incident on the tracks,
the rat poison, the sudden debilitating illness, the heart attack,
the slow flatulent decline.
The bartender tonight is saying something
about a big Afghan something dog,
one she had back in the seventies,
"before the dog food they sold was any good," she says.
Boy, thinks Anthony, how does she know that?
But in all these tales the dog is the innocent shooting star
we all wish upon
until it burns up, aging fast and disappearing
behind our jagged horizons.
Each dog marks a section of our lives, and
in the end, we feed them to the dark,
burying them there while we carry on.
Which somehow reminds Anthony that maybe
it would've been nice
if that car had hit the dog
instead of his dad.
Nother round. Nother round. Nother round.

Or, hey, it's tricks,
"why he could run with an egg in his mouth, play Chopin,
root for vermin and felons, dance a hula, predict the weather,
smell a liar, sort the mail, lead the blind, cry real tears."
But nobody seems to recall
the sublime form of a dog as she lies
curled up like a comma
in the cool forgiving summer shade
there beneath the bed.
Or the absolute satisfaction

performed with quiet muscular grace
of a dog roughly going at a good meal.
Or the joyful dance in a dog's eyes
as she sits alert watching,
waiting for you
to do
that something
she wants you to do.
"Do it," she says. "Do it now."

In the corner of the bar
Anthony notices
a woman, dark hair,
with nicer shoes than this place deserves
sitting alone.
She seems slightly familiar to Anthony.
But she isn't.
Not yet.

Back over in the white cinder blocks and the cages
word is Mason hasn't signed in for three days.
Someone finally gets around to calling but there's
no answer on the cell or at home.
He lives, no surprise, alone.
The crew talk about it over lunch
Calley says Anthony should go with him
check up on the missing man.
"I need the kung fu kid."
"Judo," Anthony corrects.
"Whatever, let's go."

They drive over. Already they have little to say to one another,
Calley's radio is broken. But the man can't sit with silence.
"You got a woman?"
Anthony thinks about not answering,
then mutters, "No."

* * *

Judo is unnecessary when they get there as
Mason is quite gone, and it doesn't look like
anyone is going to find him.
Anthony wonders
where so much blood could possibly
come from.

Now he just wants to be home
or at the bar
or back at work
not talking to this cop Peabody.
Anthony tells him
how he pulled up to the house with Calley
how there was no answer at the front
so they went around to the back
where they found the bay window smashed
and christ, gagging,
breathing deep, gagging, he
dialed 911 on the cell
while Calley puked in the bushes.
The forensic guy interrupts
coming up from behind,
he's a creepy-looking guy—
—christ, everyone here looks creepy—
though this guy's plastic gloves don't help.
What's he saying?
"Did Mr. Mason have a dog?"
Big red prints on the patio, on the floors,
see there, tramping blood on the small patch of
    green grass,
fading into the alley.
"No," says Calley. "He hated dogs."

The cops finally test and confirm,
"His blood."

And with so much of it gone
it almost doesn't matter where his body went.

Calley doesn't say much
to the cops or anyone else.
He stares down blankly at the concrete.
When Anthony finally drops him
in front of the liquor store
it's still a bright day, the reflection of everything
glaring in the blinding light of LA.
"See you later."
Anthony watches Calley walk through the open door
and disappear into the pitch-black hole called
forget this fucking day.

Back at the office
a sudden shortage of staff
buys those three dogs in the cage some time.

V

Lark tells the team to wrap up the contract
today.

The pack follows four rules in its negotiations,
eloquently explained by Baron.
"We don't have to meet them halfway.
We can always walk away from the table.
We don't have to say a word if we don't want to.
And the last rule is simple:
if they think we might kill them,
if they sense that in their balls
and feel it tugging at the base of their brain,
then, guess what,
everything's up for negotiation."

* * *

They have three lawyers in the pack,
including Lark.
Every negotiation includes one of the lawyers
along with two others from the pack.
You'd be surprised how intimidating
three silent men,
men of strength,
can be.
So quiet,
the pack can hear every heartbeat.

In two hours
they get their opponents down to 1 percent.
The pack's cut is high,
but there are never any complaints,
not from the studios, the unions, the trade associations
or anyone else who hires them.
The clients who sign on with Lark's team know two things:
the price is quite high and the victory is quite sweet.

After the negotiations
they head to the office.
Besides the pack,
there are eight other senior employees,
capable lieutenants, white, starched
and hell-bent on bonuses
with no idea who they serve.
The senior director, Jill,
grew up in Barbados
went to Stanford, Harvard Law
kickboxes and rides horses
all with a composure that carries
the warmth of Tiffany crystal
and the instincts of a hit man.
Lark thinks they could make her
governor in ten years

if they wanted to,
but he can't quite see
how that would help.

The mail room guy
they share with the publicist across the hall
has a metal band.
Lark knows the pack could make him big too
but then they'd have to listen to his music.

"Hey, where's Lark today?"
"Up in Pasadena."
"Damn, again?"
Lark's new game.
The Pasadena bridge club.
He never played, none of them did
but he now insists they all tournament,
a decision that makes them bristle.
This is what pissed off Con
and look what happened to him,
so they play, making their grand slams.
Two of the pack, Cutter and Blue,
are good, fun to watch as they awaken
to a dexterity Lark never expected.
The pack smiles, leaning around the card table,
drinking Evian and laughing
as these two prodigies pull in win after win.
But when the match is over, the mood shifts,
Lark can sense it. An uneasiness ripples through the group.
The pack doesn't see the path and so
wonders, in whispers and muttered undertones,
if this new game is part of
Lark's grand plan or if he's just
making them bide their time, wasting their strength on trouncing
puffy blue hairs and preppie scholars
with nothing but spades and clubs.

So much potential violence sitting pretty
in stale club rooms with the dead air
and bleached-out carpets.
Perhaps, they say, he's trying our patience,
distracting us, programming us for something.
Nobody knows what.
No one can see where this angle leads.
Eventually they relax,
the red meat and the deep sleep reminding them
that while the plan may be Lark's
the money in the bank
and the food on the table
is all theirs.

On warm nights
when the Santa Anas are blowing
they drive out to the eastern deserts
with ice coolers packed with San Pellegrino
and sirloin.
Shutting off the engines
they crouch beside the car's warm bodies
tense up
ignite the change
muscles ripple and the fur and teeth
and then they run through the night
racing fast, playing, bouncing over one another,
wrestling, nipping at heels and coats, rolling in the dust
running it out till their coats are wet and
their tongues dry.
Any plan that gets you that
is something more
than all right.

She has been gone more of late
comes in when they're all asleep.
She lies next to Lark

murmuring in his ear
as he strokes her side.
The pack trusts Lark when he says it's not
like that
with her.
The truth being,
they probably couldn't stand it
if he did cross
that line.
They have a discipline,
they've learned the way.
The runs they take through the night
quench the desire and drain the hunger
from their blood,
but some deeper needs still ache.
Discipline control power.
The goals are simple but
the path is hard.

Lately
she's gone by dawn.
The pack feels something's up
things feel different, shifted,
and the vibe is that
it's got nothing
to do with cards.

VI

The cop Peabody is back
talking to the pound's janitor
stiffening with recognition
as Anthony comes in.
Anthony instinctively straightens too.
He doesn't want any more of this.
"Your buddy Mason was three days late

why didn't you call him earlier?"
whatsthisshit, thinks Anthony
but he answers the rote questions
already hating the suspect and Columbo dialogue
and wondering why he feels suspicious.
He's not a suspect.
He just didn't like Mason
and now he feels guilty
because he's not sad he's gone.
So he feels like a suspect.
Or maybe his head is just spinning for nothing.
Every death should feel important, profound
but, honestly, this one is only a little bit weird.
Really, thinks Anthony, I'm innocent of everything
short of hate or indifference.
And who isn't guilty of that?
He focuses on the cop and his questions.
"He wasn't my buddy."
"Why did you go over?"
"Because Calley wanted me to."
"Are you Calley's friend?"
"Not really."
"Then why did you go?"
"Because I knew judo, Calley asked me to."
"Why would you need to know judo to check up on a
    friend?"
"I thought he was just kidding."
"Judo. Okay. So, how long have you been working here?"
"Five weeks."
"Who did you replace?"
"I don't know much about him. A guy named Turner."
"Where's Turner?"
"They say he just didn't show up one day."
"Did anyone go over to his house?"
"Beats me."
"Why the attitude, Anthony?"

"What?"
"Why the attitude Anthony?"
"I don't know what you're taking about. Honest."
"Okay, I'll be in touch."

Anthony drives his rounds
two calls come in about mad pits.
He corners one in the park
it's not mad, but it's not nice either.
The lasso goes on, the pit's in the truck.
He calls it in but doesn't get an answer,
no one is minding the desk. Moments later,
reports come in of a pack chasing a bitch
up near the observatory,
scaring the hell out of the mountain trail joggers
who have just been reminded
that they are merely
warm and scented flesh.
And slow flesh at that.
He radios in for help on that one,
if they can corral the bitch they might be able
to herd the others, but no men are available—
the office is already stretched thin
and Calley is a no-show today.

So that pack gets to run on through the heat undisturbed
while Anthony keeps driving.
It's tedious, cruising around, covering 100 miles
without leaving LA. He stops at
the Yucca Taco Hut, gets his carne
asada tacos sans salsa for the three back in the cages
and heads in.

As the security gate opens he glances
and sees a girl parked behind a car
watching the entrance, yes,

she looks familiar now.
What the hell is this? Seriously, what the hell.
He hasn't had a date in a dog's age
so, it's worth thinking about,
along with the fact that she seems to be a stalker.
Damn, rock stars have them
but do normal relationships ever start like that?
Who knows, maybe
in a way
every relationship begins with a stalker.
He feeds the dogs.
They seem happier tonight
maybe they heard about Mason
maybe sitting there behind their cages
days away from the needle
they think they're fine.
His mind darts back to the girl.
Yeah, it's been a while since he had a girl
walking around inside his head.
The cop Peabody crosses his mind too.
Where were those questions going?
There's not a lot making sense these days,
but he knows one thing
cops and women
lead to little rest.

VII

You want to know about
Lark's arithmetic?

fact

he knows there are two other packs
though as far as he can sense it

they don't know about him.
He caught the scent of one while reading the paper,
stories about odd crimes leaving clues and marks
only someone who knew would notice.
That's in Long Beach, near the docks.
He dug up a rumor
of someone running a gray market
down in the warehouse district,
a gang that sometimes had a lot of dogs around
and other times didn't seem to have any.

The other scent more vague
down near San Pedro
just something he's noticed in the police blotter.
Too many reports of loose dogs wandering around
that vanish before the cops get there.
Probably nothing.
Worth a look.

Lark has sent Penn down to follow the trail.
Penn came back, says it smells funny.
Lark sends him back again,
keep hunting.

He figures the Long Beach pack
is running off the import trade's
darker markets.
While he has no idea about San Pedro,
Lark is about 100 percent certain
the Long Beach pack is real.
He sends Baron south, tells him to
slide into whatever's there.
Root around, dig up their numbers,
their plans, their structure,
their means for growth.

* * *

Meanwhile, Penn returns from San Pedro with nothing.
Not that there necessarily would be much to know.
Ragtag dogs come along every ten years or so,
some stray from a distant pack
pulling together a gang to make a go of it,
thinking they can carve out a niche in this town
until they cross the Russians or the Crips or
anyone else with a sense of territory.
Wolf or dog or man, they all answer to bullets
and disappear with
no one the wiser.

Lark keeps thinking. Even if they're both real,
nobody but him is playing the white collar,
nobody but him is touching real money,
nobody else has anything in the north part of town,
and nothing comes close to
Lark's plan for what's next.

It's okay.
The slow plan seeps forward,
he's sending Baron's kid brother Bone down to town
to make that kennel job stick this time.
Things are getting a little fractured
no one likes playing three games at once
but it's nothing to worry about.
The slow game will keep playing slow
so long as he just
pays attention.

fact

he knows that one out of five
people in Los Angeles have a dog,
a real dog, making the canine population

equal to all the people
living in Atlanta.

fact

he knows that it's impossible to tell a wolf
from a man if
he keeps his chin up
and his teeth clean.

fact

there are powers in this town
even more invisible than his.
Someone had been asking about a pack of men
who could do some rough work, these questions
came with more questions, about dogs.
Lark's smelled the leads,
tried to follow them but got nowhere.
The questions died down, the rumors floated away,
making Lark think that whoever was asking
must have found something like an answer.
Somehow, that didn't feel so good.
So he kept digging,
tracking them until he came up against
clubs no one can join
with tournaments no one can play.
But there are ways in, he's sure,
he keeps prodding.

One clue came
from a concierge who dealt in,
among other things, children.
Wealthy pedophiles picked up what they needed from him,
along the way he picked up dirt and secrets he could sell.
Lark listened to the concierge chatter on

as they sat in a canary yellow hotel suite.
Something about a strange man
with a large silent partner.
"This man, this little man, he is quirky,
he wanted to know about fighting dogs,"
said the concierge, tapping his fingers on the chair's armrest.
"I say to him, 'man, that's the one thing I don't sell.
I hate dogs. I love drugs, any drugs,
I love pussy, young pussy, you know, but not dogs. No way.'
The little man was asking about a girl too,
someone specific, mid-twenties, blonde,
I said hey, welcome to Southern California.
I mean, good luck, right?"
Lark smiled, pressed on, chatted and pretended to barter,
picked up what more he could.
Then excused himself to hit the john.
Going in, he left the door slightly ajar.
There, while listening to the concierge whistling
some popular song.
Lark took off all his clothes
and changed,
then nosed the door open
and trotted back into the suite.

The concierge left the world
bloody and scared.
He was cleared away without a liquid trace,
the room licked clean, more pristine than
any maid could make it.

Lark follows the clue to a card game.
He sent the smart ones, Cutter and Blue,
to ask around, study the players, get into the room.
There's something up there.
It's tedious but worth sniffing out.
He knows it will come, he feels it, he waits.

As someone once said,
"paciencia y barajar."
So just hold on to your patience
and keep shuffling the cards.

Wolf packs,
loose packs,
domestics.
That's a lot of untamed territory.
And to make these moves with assurance,
Lark has to have his pack tight.
That's why he lured Con into taking him on
showing him signs of weakness,
Sun Tzu bullshit, easy stuff,
Con took the bait and was buried in the yard.
Poor fucking Con, he was strong and he was proud,
Lark liked him fine but the pack is stronger now,
they're solid.
"Thank you, Con," he thinks to himself
as he puts on cuff links, straightens his tie.
He never stops,
he always thinks to himself,
and right now he's thinking

fact
something unknown
nips him with worry.

VIII

Calley wakes up
if it could be called that
hits the phone, calls in sick
turns on the TV
lays still in the bed
opens a bottle

and wishes someone would come
and put a chain saw through his gut.
Why the hell not.

IX

It's at the same bar, the first one, the dark one,
Anthony is sitting there sore as hell
he wrestled a Saint Bernard today
it would have been funny
if the thing hadn't been so strong
he doesn't mind it though
he sensed the dog wouldn't bite.
He is beginning to know
these sorts of things.
"Is this seat taken?" she asks.
There she is. Dark hair. Cautious blue eyes.
Great.
She looks at him a little too intently,
a subdued version of the look you'd expect to get
when you finally met
your stalker.
"No, hey, no, here. Make yourself at home."
"I've been meaning to talk to you."
A strange opening bit, but, well,
he'll take anything, let's see where this goes.
"Yeah, I've seen you around."
"You work at the pound?"
"Mmmn-hmmm."
"I hear there's a job opening up there."
"Word gets around."
"Look, you don't know me, but, well, one of my brothers,
Bone is his name,
he's looking for a job,
would you mind meeting him?"

"Bone's his name?"
She pauses, smiles, "Nickname."
"Oh, well, sure, yeah, I'd be happy to meet him."
A small silence.
He's desperate for a word, a thought.
His head feels like straw at the very moment when
he could sort of use a brain.
"Look, I'd buy you a beer but—"
"No," she says. "I'll buy, let me, please, as a way of saying
    thanks."
His pride kicks in funny.
"Well, normally I'd say, um, I dunno, you know?"
He squirms a little, scratches his neck.
"What are you saying?" she asks, her hand now resting on his.
He looks at her hand, looks into those eyes, smiles and replies,
"I'm saying I think we could use a drink."

The mixture of liquor and beauty and time
lend three hours in a bar
their own delicious alchemy.
She doesn't say much,
asks a few questions,
"So, what do you like?"
"I like the ocean."
"We're in LA, that's an easy answer."
He smiles, shrugs. "Easy and true."
She likes that phrase, easy and true.
She nudges him on
here to there, says some things, but mostly
listens some more
and pretty soon
Anthony has said it all.
It's like she's got every number
to his master lock
and now he's wide open.

His job, the guys there at work,
Mason's death, a cop's questions
he unveils more, his father going,
his mother, self-medicated out of existence,
his brother, little better, long gone,
she listens, he puts a life on the table there.
He listens too, she grew up
near the beach, later he'll remember that her father
was Italianish, her mother Mexicanish
just like him.
He fills in the rare pauses with more of him,
he tells
how he feels working with the dogs
like they're each playing a role
every dog wanting to be wild and Anthony
just there to rein them in.
It's animal control and
there's a song playing in the bar
a woman singing of wild winds,
they're drunk enough now that
Anthony can ask her to dance
so he asks and she smiles yes
they dance slow in a place that's empty
save for the old soldier with the broken piano key teeth
who's murmuring doggerel to a man in a wheelchair.
The old man's laugh crackles,
but the dancers don't notice,
they just sway together toward the end of the song.
She looks up at Anthony,
her stalker eyes are twin blue moons looking sympathetically
    down
on his briar-ridden world.
"You're very nice, Anthony," she says
holding him tightly
for a few more breaths,

before gently pushing off and
walking out the door.

He would follow. He would, honest,
but when he held her, dancing,
everything felt good but
not everything felt right.

X

She knows Lark is watching her,
but he shouldn't worry.
This is an easy job, three weeks.
Then that's it, time to pick up,
move on, get out.
Maybe just swing by her old beau Pete's
before she disappears up 101
maybe Seattle, Spokane,
or some nothing town.
She's said this before
but now there's something in the air,
some hidden sense that's telling her
she better get going, because
it's getting late.

She likes the dogcatcher
yet that's a pointless thing,
like a candy comic
better to crumple it up and move on.
She'll stick to Lark's plan for now
play the dogcatcher for what he's worth
get Bone in the door
make Lark happy
help the pack
then go.

* * *

She doesn't need the dogcatcher
she just needs some sleep.
She likes Anthony.
Tomorrow she'll take Bone down to meet him.
Pieces will fall into place, just like Lark says.
Three weeks, tops.

She doesn't need the dogcatcher,
and the only thing that bothers her
is that she's thinking about him
a little more than she should

like for instance
right now.

XI

Two days later and now the cages are really short on men,
downtown may have to get involved,
and nobody wants those suits
sorting things out.
Anthony has to call Calley.
The guy answers the phone weeping.
Jesus, he's slobbering too.
"Come on, pull it together," is Anthony's general message,
and he's not even sure why he bothers to say it.
All he hears in return is
"udde phlub bubba turner sob, fucking turner, wha."
"What? Turner?"
The phone goes dead
as everything seems to these days.
This is definitely
one lousy job.

"Hello, dog pound, dispatch section."

"May I please speak to Anthony Silvo?"
Anthony recognizes the cop's voice.
"Detective Peabody? This is Anthony."
"Anthony, yeah, I called to tell you about Turner."
"Turner?" Anthony doesn't like the timing,
first Calley is gurgling the name and now
only an hour later, it's on the cop's lips.
"Yeah, Turner, the last guy who had your job,
we can't find him."
"What?"
"Yeah, apparently, the week before you started
he disappeared."
Anthony keeps listening.
"He's not anywhere, Anthony, not with relatives,
not in the morgue, he didn't have any friends,
he had even less money, he's gone."
Anthony asks if the cop has any theories.
"Maybe the guys down there are dealing drugs,
or maybe they're selling dogs.
I don't know Anthony,
but something is going on."
"Selling dogs?"
"To fight leagues maybe, to gangs who pit them against one
    another."
Anthony looks around the kennel's bright fluorescent room,
he can easily see this crew doing something like that.
They already stink of being that low.
"Okay, Anthony, all I'm saying is
keep your eyes open. Something about this situation
feels a little odd."
"Are the police going to help?"
"You know what the city dollar is like these days,
we're stretched thin. Hell, I can't even get a new partner."
"We're stretched here too," says Anthony. "But thanks for the
    warning."

XII

She told Lark what he needed to hear
that the man would help Bone get the job
that the man was worth keeping
and could be helpful
while the rest were simply trash just like Lark suspected
and that the plan was proceeding
according to plan.
Lark seemed to be waiting for something else
as she talked.

She's speaking too fast.
When she's done, when she pauses,
Lark reaches over and
gently touches the spot
above her collarbone, there
where the flesh sinks in
toward the heart.
All he says is,
"Be careful."

He was the one who had brought her in.
She had met him sitting at a table on Abbott Kinney.
"Is everything okay?" he asked,
his eyes tracing the line of salt
where the tears had dried on her face
hours before.
He was a kind expression on hard features,
they had coffee. He listened for hours,
his patience becoming the bedrock
she could rest her fears upon.
They walked along the canals,
mostly in silence, Lark waiting

and patient, until she finally
opened up, choking out
the sad story
of life with Pete,
how almost every day came with
its habitual tumble of humiliation.
Lark didn't react,
just walked her back to her house
told her to wait
while he went in to talk to Pete.

Fifteen minutes later he came out
with a duffel stuffed full of her things
then drove her to his house.
To this day she doesn't know
what he said to Pete
she only knows
considering Pete
it must have been something
pretty strong.
She's leaned on Lark for so long now
you'd think it was love.

The house was empty that first night
looking back, the boys must have been
on a desert run
where they often disappeared,
chasing one another for the weekend
sometimes stopping in Vegas
to feed unquenched appetites.
So there she was, alone with Lark.
He gave her a room
she slept solidly for fifteen hours
woke up and it was night again,
just a scratch of moon in the sky.
She found Lark sitting in the kitchen

with a small knife, some bandages, a bottle of wine.
Now it was his turn to talk.
"The way I see it, you have to find your own way," he said
as they drank.
"You can't trust anyone else for your strength,
you've got to find it inside yourself."
He said many things as
the night wore on
and she slipped down
into the soft crook of his words.
"What I'm offering is something
that will change you completely.
Its strangeness will seem like a dream
but it comes with a certain power.
With this power, maybe you take back some of what you've lost."
The talk went on until the moon disappeared,
and she bit her lip and looked down and knew that
whatever it was, she would agree.
But he kept talking,
until she finally wanted it so bad,
she could feel the night's darkness
vibrating inside her.

Unfolding the knife, he slowly cut himself
along a well-worn pink-and-yellow scar
that ran the length of his last finger.
The knife cut through the lines
of quieter fortunes.
She shook her head,
leaned back wary, a little nervous.
Gently, he took her by the wrist
and paused for a moment,
until a glint of confidence returned to her eyes.
Then he cut into the small piece of fat beneath her thumb,
and pressed his bleeding palm against hers.

"It's okay. It's for you," he said, wrapping the tape
and binding their hands together.
She looked into his eyes now, watching
as his pupils dilated wide.
She looked down to where
blood flowed across the kitchen table
a red line coolly sliding across the tile.
Three beats of the heart later it hit her.
What followed was messy,
the quick spasm, the doubling over
while her stomach clenched and heaved.
White bombs exploded through her muscles
adrenaline and heat flooded her system
she felt the red rush to her cheeks.
A piercing shriek shook the windows
and she passed out.

Unconscious on the floor
twitching and morphing,
she could not see
the silent wolf
lapping up the spilled blood
in a quiet and diligent manner.

She woke up with the sleeping pack
lying all around her like waves in a strange ocean.
She wondered how many days she had missed
as the sun slipped down again behind the hills.
All she knew was that this was a different world.
She breathed a deep
sigh of relief.

Dog or wolf? More like the one than the other
but neither exactly. Standing on four legs in her fur,
she is her own brand of beast.

She could play in your yard, but
you would not want to find her
crossing your trail in the twilight.
And were you cornered by her,
eye to eye,
you would see that
there are still some watchful creatures
whose essence lies unbound by words.
There is still a wilderness.

XIII

Over time, the intensity of the days
plays on Lark's nerves.
One rival pack is a new thing.
He needs to be careful.
Two rival packs is downright bad news.
And three games to play. Damn.
Napoleon had only Wellington and Blucher.
Roosevelt had Europe and the Pacific.
Augustus had the Gauls and his wife.
But Lark has three games.
Ah, to hell with it.
The cards have been dealt
and no matter what
everyone's in.

So pay attention.

He sends her down with Bone to get the dogcatcher's job.
He calls up to Pasedena.
Cutter and Blue sound frustrated and bored.
They keep moving up in the bridge tournament.
They're naturals, good with numbers and they can smell
their opponents' moves.

But this isn't exactly the life these two dreamed of.
They can do a thousand sit-ups and run fifty miles without
      pausing to rest.
They can make a man disappear without a trace.
They can turn into dogs in a little over twenty seconds.
But now they're just ticking away time
counting clubs and diamonds
like bored officers in some dusty corner of the empire.
Lark says "Keep your eyes open. Tell me what you see."
Cutter says, "Shit, it's a handful of blue hairs, an odd French
Canadian couple, a bald guy who won't stop talking about
      Tampa, and a lawyer from Hillside."
"Keep an eye on the bald guy," says Lark.
Probably wrong, he knows,
but he has to keep Cutter interested somehow.
All he's certain of is that these days,
everyone has to be
on their toes.

XIV

She walks into the kennel, everyone looks up,
nothing that lovely is supposed to be in here.
Anthony spots her right away and moves toward her.
She's with a guy.
The guy with her doesn't look like any kind of relative
but hey, who knows.
"This is Bone."
He nods at Bone and sizes him up,
a lean fellow without much warmth,
but fuck it, he seems better than Calley, Mason and the rest.
Anthony hands him the paperwork and
they wait as Bone fills it out.

Her eyes are dancing, nervous.
The dogs are yapping in the cages

wild right now for some reason.
Anthony feels a little anxious, a little awkward,
he just wants to get her out of here.
Finally, they all head out the door,
while the sun on the pavement is as bright as a blinding
    mirror.
He shakes Bone's hand, thanks him for coming down.
He shakes her hand too, holding it for a second longer.
Squinting in the light, he tries to catch her eye,
tries to read something in her look.
"Would you guys like to get some lunch before you go?"
"No, no, but . . ."—she pauses,
watching as Bone goes round to the passenger side—
then, in almost a whisper she says,
"I'll meet you at the bar, later, okay?"
He nods
hell yes.

XV

Lark's been exploring the San Pedro pack for a month now.
He has his dog in there now. Baron slowly earned the trust.
Packs are tough to crack, once you share your blood
they think you're theirs.
Baron's been playing it straight, in deep.
Baron has been getting phenomenal tattoos.
He's been tossing in the lots with the other dogs.
He's been studying their family, their moves, their lines of
    business.
It's gray market on a good day, black on the rest.

Lark drives through an In and Out.
He gets eighteen burgers and throws them in the back
Then he drives down to the piers,
pulls into an open lot, and waits for Baron.
Baron says he's got news.

Lark gets there early.
He likes having the time to think.
Things seem too loose these days
even with Con gone and the pack tightened.
It's not the girl
that's hard to control
but that's not it.
Something is making moves
plates are shifting.
Pay Attention.

Lycanthropes first came out of the native tribes
in the Northwest,
born, legends say, from a native thirst
for a superior warrior.
But when the weather turned,
their packs were wiped out
knifed and skinned in fear
as native American witch hunts
took on their destruction
as a sacred, healing mission.
On a hundred nights, surrounded and fighting mad,
pack after pack were driven into drought-dry woods
where they were all burned
down to smoldering stumps.
The howling shook leaves in distant trees
and rolled through the valleys
like the screams
of lost birds
echoing the thunder.

Small packs survived, waited,
roamed the endless wilderness
met the trappers and shared raccoon fat
and maple sap, sucked the marrow of crow and buffalo bones.
This is when boundless nature

seethed in the untamed wilds,
bushels of game birds, barrels of fur
could be found in any glen.
They taught the lone trappers, guided the coon-skinned scouts,
riding on, through the expansion,
keeping things low
building new codes
to match the manners of the whiter world
which is to say, live on the invisible side
and if you kill
kill the unmournable:
deserters, wanderers, rustlers, rum runners, drug dealers,
men who will never be missed. Life goes on.
The light asks little from those who send the darkness away.

Wolves don't have to take blood,
but when the change happens, well,
control can be tricky and
there is that
certain hunger.
Now, better technology, wider surveillance, and safer streets
make every change more complicated.
The blood sugar fever still survives
but invisible becomes more difficult.
It's either retreat
or adapt.
They stepped deeper into the shadows.
Nobody saw them.
Rumors became legends,
ghost stories became TV shows,
while outside, in the dark, the packs wandered on.

They still travel together.
Without a pack, they're called coyotes
by those who know.
And though it's true that

real coyotes fill the hills
with the endless barking
of their own restless packs,
it's also true
that it's not easy to
survive as a coyote
when you're all alone.

Lark checks his watch.
Baron's late, should have been here already.
Each second now undoes itself, unraveling like a fraying thread.
Lark clenches his jaw, reaches in the back, grabs a burger,
the crinkling of the paper wrapper scratches at the silence.
His eyes dart through the night's shadows as he chews.
Lumber and spooled wire, an old broken boat
up on blocks, and there in the corner
one shadow moves.

The hair on his neck is up now.
He gently puts the burger down.

He fires up the ignition,
hits the gas
hits reverse
the car sweeps back
his headlights arc into the space
catching four big hounds.
Circled and frozen midstalk, a plain attack,
even if he changed, they could take him
easy, there are four of them.
But he's not changing,
he's driving.
And cars
tend to win.
Drive now. Fast. Thud. Bump. Reverse.
He swerves in the dirt and catches one on the fender side.

Another jumps on the hood,
but gassing it pushes the car forward and
that one slips off, landing on its side.
Back fast brake forward again now,
catching that one solidly against the bumper,
smashing it against a piling.
With the wet crack and cry
out goes one headlight.
He spins the car back
to see the two other dogs
peeling off into the dust and dark.
They are smart enough to run.

While the engine idles
he eats the rest of his burger
and thinks.
Trapped in the car, he would have been done in seconds.
Strategically perfect.
Where is Baron?
And whose pack was that?
What else do they know?
Probabilities begin to dawn on him.

He hits the gas,
hopes that no cop stops him for his headlight,
and prays for speed.

XVI

This is what Calley sees when he opens his eyes:
a small man, sitting by his bed, skinny, white hair
in a black suit, money tie.
Calley sits up, what's this guy doing in his room? What—
Another man steps out of the shadows
The guy is big and round as a planet.
An islander? Samoan?

This whale kicks Calley forcefully and then
with pure flashing pain
Calley is left holding his hand, numb and probably broken,
And so, Calley being Calley,
he sits back, swollen with fear and flesh
exposed and waiting for whatever comes next.

"Sir, please, stay seated." The man has a lisp like a twister and
moves through the room like he has been there a thousand times.
"Sir, do you remember when you took the dogs?" the man says.
Sir?
"What?" Calley's head throbs and his brain sweats
somehow he felt something odd like this was coming,
a premonition brewing in his rancid gut, stewing for weeks now.
"Sir, you took the dogs, with your friends Turner and Mason,
up to the hills. The fighters.
You sold them, you do remember that, yes?"
"What?"
"How much did you get for them, sir?"
Calley tries to remember. Like six hundred bucks.
But who the fuck is this guy? "Who the fuck
are you anyway?" Calley nurses his dead hand.
The Samoan's slap stings, blood fills Calley's mouth.
"The dogs, Calley, I'm asking about the dogs you took."
He remembers way back. Eight months?
Someone had come round looking for dogs, it happened some-
     times.
They didn't want nice ones.
And Turner and Mason had just the curs,
two nasty coke fever junkyard psycho dogs,
drugged and beaten to be worse than bad
found in a drainage ditch on the south edge of town
where they'd been guarding over a third.
It took six tranqs to shut them down.
The vet had stitched them up and then
seeing a market opportunity,

Turner and Mason had moved them to two cages
they kept in Turner's dark garage.
The dogs woke up pissed, impossible to contain,
and were about to be shot by an itchy Turner.
But then the opportunity knocked, someone
was looking for something fierce
and fast.
Nobody asked where they were going.
Maybe they were going to be used for fights.
Maybe as guard dogs.
Nobody cared.
Calley was only in because they needed help handling the dogs.
They took a fire road up to the drop-off.
It was hard work, the bitch bit Calley's hand.
But on the hill they met four dark men built like fire plugs,
pierced and tattooed all to hell,
and one older Mexican, standing at the edges,
who paid them cash.
Said little, worked fast.
Calley waited by the cars,
nursing his bleeding palm.
He tells this to the man in the suit and the Samoan
Calley didn't know anything about the Mexican or his friends.
All he knew was that he drank that money fast
thinking there would be more
but nobody ever called back.

The little guy in the suit gets up. He picks up an empty bottle.
His voice is syrupy, maybe southern?
"Liquor is a funny thing," he says.
"It can make a wise man an idiot and then,
almost magically at times, it makes an idiot wise."
Calley eyes him. How did these guys get in here anyway?
The man goes on,
"Yes, liquor is the thin white coat of paint
you wash over the cracks in your foundation.

Makes any rotten house livable for a few hours.
Sometimes even days."
Calley rolls his eyes and says, "Okay, asshole,
　　do you want a drink or not?"
The man stops talking, looks at him for a minute, nods and
in less than a second the Samoan's standing, one foot on the floor
the other squeezing Calley's throat,
the smell of leather and blood
up in Calley's nose,
the shoe pressing Calley's skull against the wall.
The fat dogcatcher is flailing pink, gasping
while the little man speaks.
"One, most of the men you sold the dogs to are dead.
The dogs got them.
Dogs can work fast, and if they're fast and large and smart,
and if they work together, well. . .
of the five men you met
four are dead.
Only the old Mexican you mention
remains unaccounted for.
The forensics were fascinating.
These were good dogs. Dogs trained in the south.
They gnawed out the men's throats
ate their guts.
The men weren't dead,
they were dying slow
the dogs didn't want them dead.
Because, of course, the dogs wanted
to eat them alive."
The little man turns his head sideways and looks
into Calley's bloodshot, terrified eyes.
"They chewed off their hands
snapped their Achilles tendons,
these big men, these fire plugs you mention,
they wanted to scream but
like I said

their throats were gone.
The dogs bit their toes down to the nub.
You remember these men, right?
Big strong muscular fellows.
And as these men crawled across the dirt
screaming without voices.
The dogs ate slow.
These were good dogs.
And now Turner is gone,
to the same dogs no doubt,
And Mason, well, you saw that.
Leaving you and the old Mexican.
Now, we don't know where to find him,
but, thankfully,
you're listed in the phone book."
He pauses, walks over to the window,
plays the dust on the pane with his fingers.
"I must say, your foundation looks weak, Calley.
The cracks are showing."
Calley is silent, his breath shallow.
He doesn't dare say a word.
"But perhaps it's too late. Because honestly, Calley,
from the little I've seen,
it seems like, in many ways,
you have always been dead."
The man puts the bottle on the floor by the bed.
"Relax and enjoy this, Calley, we'll be back.
It's too bad you couldn't be more helpful.
But don't worry. I don't want you,
I just want those dogs."
And the man and the Samoan walk out.

Calley rolls his eyes to the ceiling,
he's feeling like he's drowning.
He reaches for the drink.

book two

A room is, after all, a place where you hide from
the wolves. That's all any room is.

JEAN RHYS

I have seen where the wolf has slept by the silver
stream,
I can tell by the mark he left you were in his
dream.

JOHN PERRY BARLOW

I

Lark pulls in to the driveway
headlights play the preview of a bad movie.
He's jumping out and moving fast.
It's a little past 2 a.m. and
nothing smells good.
The lights are all on,
the front door is open.
Far off he can hear sirens.
He's inside
facing too many pieces of news
for him to process in the time he's got.
Three steps into the house and he's already seen
the two dead dogs in the living room.
The house is empty.
Sirens are getting louder.
There's blood everywhere.
"Like a Jackson Pollock valentine," he thinks,
quickly bolting the front door.
Moving through the rooms
with the fluidity of water,
he turns out every light.
Bedroom. Kitchen. Living room.
Then he rolls the dead dogs in a rug and
slides them behind the couch.
Pauses. The sirens.
He heads downstairs to the small workroom tucked
into the back of the basement.
There are three security cameras on the property
and a monitor here. He turns it on and fires up the laptop.
The screen reveals the patrol car
pulling into the drive.
He clicks at the laptop, logging onto his accounts.

On the monitor, the patrolmen are getting out.
One stays by the car.
Nobody has touched the accounts.
"Whoever they are," Lark thinks to himself,
"they aren't that smart."
A patrolman is at the door now.
He hears the bell, ignores it.
Lark transfers the balance to an old, unused account.
The doorbell rings again.
Was there any blood on his car?
The patrolman moves around the house.
Lark switches to camera two, watches the cop
flash his light across the shrubs.
The phone rings,
Lark picks up quickly.
"Hello?"
"Mr. Lark Tennant?"
"Yes."
"This is Atlas Security. We have reports of a disturbance
at your house. Is everything okay?"
"As far as I know, yes."
"We've sent patrolmen up to the house."
"Oh, well actually, I'm not there. I have my phone forwarded,
    I'm in the desert."
"Do you have guests staying there? The patrolmen reported—"
"—oh, actually, I can probably tell you what happened."
"Yes?"
"My sister came by to get the dogs, she's dog sitting, sometimes
    they get upset."
"Well, that makes some sense, one of the reports mentioned dogs
    barking."
"One of the reports?"
"Oh, everyone in the neighborhood called."
"Boy, well, thanks for looking into it."
"That's our job."
Lark hangs up, leans back, and exhales into the dark room

watching the cameras as the cameras watch
the patrolmen murmuring into their radios as
their car pulls slowly away.
Lark waits and waits. Thinking. Figuring.

When he went to meet Baron there were eight in the house.
Cutter and Blue were up in the Valley
playing in a two-day bridge tournament.
And he doesn't know
where she was.

II

She's lying next to Anthony,
naked, exhausted,worried.
What do you tell a man to whom
you can't say everything?
As much as your bones muscles tendons
ache to open up, the truth still lies
curled and buried beneath your tongue.
So, instead of revealing all, she makes jokes.
"I guess you'll give my brother the job now, right?"
"Is that what this was all about?"
He kisses her,
and a rush of warmth fills her blood.
"Kiss me again." She reaches in the dark.
She feels the hunger awakening inside her
she wants to hold him closer,
just as she did
when they first danced.
She knows people can only
stand so close
for so long
but her body tries to hold as much of him as she can find
as her mouth measures the length of his neck,
the width of his shoulders.

There in that embrace, she feels something
shuffling around, moving warily
fumbling through the dusty rooms of her heart,
and, one by one, turning on the lights.

III

Peabody the cop wakes up
because his three-year-old
is vomiting.
It's nothing serious.
There was a birthday party earlier
cake, ice cream, soda.
But still
it's vomit
at four
in the morning.
Damn.
An hour later
the house is asleep again.

IV

Calley hasn't had a drink
in twenty-two hours
he hasn't slept either
not since the last visit.
He tries to remember the other guys
Turner and Mason.
Was he better than them?
Did he deserve to live?
Twenty-two hours is enough
there's some vodka in the freezer.
He looks out the window again.
There's a dog sitting there,
on the lawn across the street.

Watching him.
Calley's not so social
but he's been around long enough to know
that's not the neighbor's dog.

V

At the end of a card day
Cutter calls the pack
no one picks up,
Blue says fuck it.
Two days of silence has got their fur up.
"It's like we've fallen off the map,"
says Cutter,
feeling a little like the Pasadena Hilton
is a spaceship and they've lost contact
with planet Earth.
What the hell?
They're three rounds up in the western regional
kicking ass.
Blue took the Mormons down
on a hand that played like pure rockabilly.
The fat ass Fresno cracker fell
to a perfect finesse that made his eyes tear up.
So long sucker.
Lark knew they could do it
But they've surprised even themselves.
Celebrated with three pizzas,
four cheeseburgers, some buffalo wings,
and a couple of steaks.
Yeah.
They call the house one more time
hoping to find a pack to howl along with them
to celebrate like brothers would
but nobody answers.
No cells answer either.

It all puts a certain pall
on the festivities.
Whatever. Time to call room service.
Time to eat.

VI

Bone wakes up in a new pack.
With a new code.
Slowly coming back from defeat.
Still feeling the teeth on his neck from back in the house.
He had been outplayed and out-fought that night
and wound up lying wild-eyed on the living room floor
an invading dog's teeth stretched across his neck.
Then he heard Baron's voice. "Don't kill them."
Realizing then that Baron had somehow
betrayed them all.
Who knows why.
Life's filled with tough choices.
For instance at that moment
when Bone lay there on the floor
his neck still caught between his attacker's teeth
that was a moment of choice.
A breath, a decision,
"I'm with you Baron."
Baron kneeled down
and looked directly into Bone's eyes.
"Smart move, bro."

"Lark is dead to me," thinks Bone.
"Pretty soon, probably dead to the world."
Rising from his mat,
he looks through the warehouse's open door,
feels the sunshine waking the neighborhood,
smells the morning's sweetness.
"This day is nice," he thinks.

"Tomorrow will be nice too,
and I'll do whatever I have to do
just to keep 'em coming."

VII

Lark IDs the dead dog he knows,
Zack, a rough wild one.
Lark remembers that the kid wasn't
much of a fighter.
The other's unknown.
He has to mop, bury, plan,
But first, a pause, a reconstruction.
As the light comes over the mountains,
Lark's reading the blood on the wall,
his senses unfolding the tale
of what must have gone down.
He traces streaks of red with his finger,
thinking, intuiting, guessing
how it must have been.

It was early in the night,
perhaps twenty minutes after he left.
They came up, his pack had just eight here.
She wasn't in the house. Where was she?
Bone was here, she should have been too.
The other side arrived, bringing fifteen.
Yes, he smells Baron.
The surprise must have been complete.
And perhaps his pack wasn't as ready as it should have been.
He didn't build them to fight like this.
The way he had it organized, the Ukan path, focused on lying low,
on avoiding wars. It was easier to infiltrate the enemy
isolate them
and then take them out one by one.
He hadn't foreseen the assault.

Lark wonders how much else he missed.
Three games. Did he blow them all?
His head spins. He stomach feels hollow.
It's the feeling that hits a world-class chess player
when he finds he's not in the game at all.

He touches a small pool of blood.
There was probably a courier, a delivery
anything to get the door open.
Zack answers, the moment of defeat lying right there.
The first rush brings eight or so in, taking out Zack first.
He barks the warning as he goes down,
and the others pour into the room to help
teeth ready for skin, fur up and set to fight.
One of the invaders lunges forward, spitting for blood,
but two of the pack take him down,
one cutting his throat so fast
the assault is thrown off for a stroke of time, the surprise
pushing them back on their haunches, as
blood from the torn artery arcs across the room.
But then the attackers surge forward again,
through the raining blood
which glistens on their coats
and flicks in their eyes,
only raising their adrenaline.
Their numbers are too good
and Lark's dogs are too unsettled.
In the breath of moments, it's over.
Three lie with their throats
caught between three jaws,
all ready to cut.
There is a bark. A man enters. Words are spoken.
A long pause. A jaw tightens.
A submissive nod from one of Lark's wolves
and then the conquered head off, tails between legs,
delivered into a new world.

VIII

Her cell rings again, for the sixth time.
"Maybe you should answer this time," says Anthony.
She pulls the sheet around her body and
takes the phone to the living room.
"Hi, Lark."
"Are you all right?"
"Yeah, I'm fine." She takes a breath.
"Lark, I'm not coming back."
There's a long silence before he answers,
"I'm not sure there's anything to come back to."
She waits for him to say more.
Nothing but the sound of traffic through the phone line until
finally he speaks again. "The house is gone, the pack is gone."
His voice sounds hard
but not angry,
"Christ, Lark. What? What happened?"
Another long pause.
She can't tell if he's feeling anything.
There's only gravity and heaviness on the phone.
Then his tone changes, sounding almost casual.
"I'm going up to Pasadena for a while.
I don't know when I'll be back.
but do me a favor, okay?"
"What's that Lark?"
"Just answer when I call."
"All right, Lark, I'll answer."
She hangs up realizing he never asked
where she was.

IX

A new pack, a new path.
The Ukan way was something Lark believed in.
Discipline from the inside, a tension holding the pack together.
The new pack follows a different form,
nobody has a name for it,
but it's a rough way of life.
They drive in three vehicles, six to a black Econoline,
Bone rides in the lead group. Sasha sits up front next to Ray.
She's stripping down, pulling off her black jeans and
the T-shirt that reads LOVE HONKY.
She's got hair that is jet-black,
marble white skin and an attitude of pure assurance.
Bone marvels at that, watching as she changes
into a black dog whose motions
still carry hints of her human rhythm.
Nobody notices how transfixed he is, the rest of them
are too busy changing themselves.
Bone doesn't have to change. Ray has other plans.
They pull into a suburban sprawl and hit the lights.
The other vans follow suit and they cut the engines, gliding in
    dark.
Getting out, Ray and Bone are men, the rest dogs.
The dogs vanish around the house except for Jackson and Sasha,
they trot alongside the men, large animals with a quick gait.
All according to plan.

Stepping up to the tract home, Ray rings the bell. No answer.
Ray rings it again. They hear footsteps,
the door is opened a little more than a crack.
A woman pokes her head out, looking like she hasn't slept in a
    thousand years.
Small scabs cover her cheeks and chin.

Ray is polite, using a cowboy voice, "'Scuse me, ma'am,
are you missing—Whoa!" Sasha darts forward, bursting in,
"Get your fucking dog outta here!" the woman shouts.
distracted just enough so she doesn't see Ray's gun
until he hits her with it.
"Shut up." Two moments later and Bone has her arms pinned
back as Ray puts duct tape over her mouth,
her eyes bulging. They hear a man's voice shout,
"Whose damn dog? Margie?"
Ray holds the front door open as Jackson runs in.
Then the snarl of the attack and a man's scream.
Ray goes back and hits the light, a hallway door to the garage is
    open.
The man's cries grow louder.
They enter and find a homemade lab.
Blood is everywhere, the man's stomach ripped open.
Sasha and Jackson settle in next to the body, attentive.
Ray scratches Sasha behind the ear, Ray surveys the room.
"Two here, one's missing."
He duct tapes the man's bloody mouth.
"Bring the woman in here, we'll wait."
Bone drags her back in from the kitchen, she doesn't fight.
He hits the lights, the six of them sit in the dark.
The man wheezes through his tape.
They wait.

Bone looks around. Clearly, the lab is making something,
speed, crank, crystal meth, who knows.
All Bone has been able to piece together is that Ray
is paid by someone unknown to hit these home cookers.
No one talks about who is paying for this and
he really doesn't care.
They've been swooping down on mom-and-pop shops
all over the Valley, spilling blood,
intimidating them with fierce displays of the damage
a dog can do. The woman lying at Bone's feet is scared now,

her eyes swimming wide and panicked.
She doesn't have to wait long before she hears
footsteps and keys fumbling.
She makes grunting noises through the tape
but it's not enough.
The missing man comes through the door and
his shopping bag full of milk and egg
takes Ray's shotgun blast.
As the pack moves out, stepping
over the spilled groceries and blood,
the dogs pause to lap the yolk and white from the floor
then scamper to catch up to the pack.

It's bloody muscle work, Bone thinks,
it's not the way Lark would have done things.
Lark believed the tension of the threat
was more powerful than the blood of the action.
But this is Ray's pack now.
Enough said.

X

Morning and she's sitting in the bright kitchen
wearing his robe, stirring her tea.
How is it? How is this so? How is she here?
Her body worn delicious in exhaustion,
wrapped in wisps of his scent.
But wondering how long it can last.
We are all china barely mended,
clumsily glued together
just waiting
for the hot water and lemon
to seep through our seams.

She takes a sip, running through the questions.
What next?

What if he knew?
She's wondering how to unknot all that's bound within her
when his fine, fit body carries the rest of him into the room
and pours himself some tea.
"Morning."
Soft kiss, like dream trains coupling at the station.
Soft kiss again, like pleasure should be.
"Hey," she says, "How do you, um . . ."
"Excuse me?" kiss on neck, ear,
there, where the current hits the soul.
"How do you, um," pausing. A little laughter.
She tries to begin somewhere, "um,
how do you feel about getting a dog for the house?"
Now he stops and looks at her a little funny,
she can't tell if it's uncertainty or
just sleepiness. It was a clumsy question, not even close
to what she really wants to say.
He stirs to answer but his phone stirs too, vibrating
with a request for help
from a strained and understaffed kennel.
In the timeless war between work and love,
chalk another one up for work.

XI

The cop, remember the cop, eats toast with
too much butter on it
and double-checks paperwork.
His phone rings, he picks up to find
an odd voice
a man's voice,
"Mr. Peabody, Detective Peabody?"
Instinct makes Peabody look at the picture of his kid
and his wife on the desk.
As his old partner used to say,
sometimes you can feel it coming

before it ever begins.
"How can I help you?" says the cop.
"Well . . ." purrs the voice "I was wondering about
the dogs and the pound case."
Peabody sits up. Because
that's simply not how the case is known,
there isn't even a case to speak of, except
inside his own head.
"How can I help you, sir?" Peabody asks again.
"Well . . . it seems you might want to talk to a Mr. Calley."
This guy is just creepy. What he's saying is stupid, rote stuff.
But his voice makes your bones hum like everything is off.
"Calley? I have spoken with Calley," says Peabody, but adds,
    "Is there anything specific I may have forgotten?"
"No, no," says the voice. "But the perception, by people
who are watching these things, who are perhaps responsible,
they might be interested in your interest."
"People who are watch–?"
"Please, Detective, let me continue.
If you would pay closer attention
then the people who are watching this,
and I'm sure they are watching,
well, they will become unnerved,
then these interested parties will make moves,
present you with opportunity."
Peabody sits back at his desk.
"So, you want me to talk to Calley,
to get some pieces moving?" he asks.
"Yessssss," answers the voice. "Let's just see how they move."
There is a click. No good-bye.
Peabody looks at the picture.
His kid. His wife.

XII

Lark knows he doesn't have much time.
He's been moving some money around for a couple of days.
Cutter and Blue he has covered.
"Stay up there," he says. "Look for the odd man,
the man who was asking about men and dogs."
Meanwhile, every account has been flipped,
    tracks wiped clean.
He called the office and told Jill to shut the place down,
sending her a severance envelope that made her smile
along with a note saying, "Prague would be good."
She got the point, got the ticket, got gone.

The problem with being alone is simply
that it doesn't work.
Everything about being what Lark is
now involves risk.
Dogs hate you, people don't trust you,
eventually you're run out or found out
winding up with a belly full of bullets
or the sleepy needle death.
The only way it works
over the long haul
is to lie as low as possible,
your belly pressed to the earth,
until you can find
someone else who can watch your back.

Alone and exposed.
He knows he could go
hang with Cutter and Blue
in their hotel suite.
But Lark wonders

who in his pack has pieced together his strategy,
who was watching well enough to see the big picture?
It isn't quite clear. So he avoids all traps
works out a new plan,
and tries to bring it home.
Hell, he thinks, for most people
that's called everyday life.

For now Lark's sleeping in a motel off the Pacfic Coast Highway,
just far enough away from the game to make him feel safe.
He sits on the beach weighing possible moves.
"Hi, do you want a sandwich?" a blonde girl asks,
perhaps thinking he's homeless, or just being nice,
but he doesn't answer and keeps his eyes set on the sea
while deep calculations fire like storm lightning
in the canyons of his mind.

He runs through options. Precedents. Ideas. History.
He's studied every pack, every discipline.
He knows there are infinite paths out there.
And one, he knows, is something
called the hide-and-seek.
He thinks about going to the dogcatcher
and getting the girl.
She could use some protection.
But perhaps she wouldn't want his help,
maybe she's happy.
And it could be dangerous,
too many knew something about Lark's kennel plan.
She's probably less safe than she could ever suspect.
He can't worry about her,
he's just got to shift ground and keep thinking.

Anyway, there's always the Pasadena plan.

XIII

The new pack takes another ride,
the vans packed tight.
Bone spends a moment missing
the luxury of the cars he rode in with Lark.
But these days won't stand
for such sentimental thinking.
He drives on.

It's late when they pull up at a farm just outside
    Oxnard.
Doors open and out of the ten passenger vans leap
a crowd of angry K-9s.
A few steps later and they've already leapt the ranch gate.

Ray and Sasha head up to the big house,
The rest have strict orders:
stick with Jackson, cross the fence
kill everything in the field.
They charge the thin lines of the electric fence,
meeting the jolt head-on.
The current just gets them going.

The wet grass feels cool beneath the paw.
Bone hears something big shudder across the dark lawn.
Four animals stand there.
Stupid big llama or camel-like beasts,
their eyes awash in alarm.
He remembers these. They're called alpacas.
Moving in fast, he bares his teeth, aiming for the knee
where he bites down quick to force the break.
His cousin in Colorado used to raise them for their coats.

The animal is down, screaming, but with the broken knees
it can't hold him off.

Bone circles round, thinking
about how his cousin made a lot of money with a female, a
    breeder.
He's never eaten alpaca. But as the fur flies
and screams of other animals break through the night,
he finds that while it's not exactly a delicacy,
it is different.

He's back in the van within twenty minutes
again never quite learning what that trip was all about
though suspecting the folks in the house met a similar fate
as the poor, dead beasts of the field.
Then again, in the end, thinks Bone,
we probably all wind up meeting
something like what they got.
Until then, count your mornings.

An hour later, as the van rolls on,
Bone is thinking about Lark, still out there.
Hiding or hunting?
And what then?
He almost doesn't want to find Lark.
But Ray does. Sasha does.
He can tell, whenever the subject comes up,
it nags at them,
like an untied shoe that's taunting you
while you're trying to get out the door.
They'll find him.
Coyotes never last.

That night, they stay in the Realto bunker,
one of a handful of warehouses the pack has
spread out around the docks.

Bone tries to sleep but can't
and listens instead to one of the crew fucking Sasha.
Her clumsy lover moans like a dying ox while she, in turn, is quiet.
The bastard skulks off, and another approaches.
Bone tries to sleep. He knows he doesn't rank a turn with her.
Finally, Ray barks
everyone scurries
Sasha moves to curl up next to Ray.
His lips nip at her chalky skin.
She gives him a small smile.
Bone turns over and tries to sleep.
The alpaca is not settling well.

Ray pays the dockworkers for rumors
the pack hauls in stolen containers
strips 'em out and sells off the contents
furniture, key chains, tires, stoves, coats.
Simple bread-and-butter work.
If they find drugs they hand them over to the mob,
no questions asked. Ray's known well enough.
The other missions, the smashing of the small labs,
two or three times a week,
that's work they do for a client Bone still hasn't seen.
Maybe it's vigilante justice,
neighborhood watch gone horribly awry,
but Bone suspects some darker plan.
Lark didn't reveal his plans either, thinks Bone,
but there was at least a sense of some greater end.
Here, they move, attack, eat, sleep,
the lucky ones fuck, but they are all
ever unsettled and edgy.
These creatures may be among
the most superior predators in the world
but in the end,
as any toothless soul will tell you,
it's a dog's life.

XIV

Calley opens the door, sees the cop standing there
looking clean as a preacher, surrounded by the white light.
"Hell, what are you here for?" Calley says.
"I thought you might be able to help me," says Peabody,
stepping into the mess without invitation.
"Why not call?" Calley gestures
with an open beer. It's ten thirty in the morning.
"Well." Peabody shrugs. "I've got questions too,
like why aren't you at work?"
Peabody doesn't think he can bear to stay long,
the place smells like chemical puke.
"Fuck all, and fuck you," mutters Calley.
Peabody smiles warily.
He's not sure what he's doing here. Or
why he came.
But Calley has aged ten years in ten days,
and somehow that's an amusing sight to Peabody.
We are strange creatures, he thinks,
finding dark humor in shady corners.
"Listen, can you tell me anything else about Mason?" he asks.
Calley grimaces, says nothing.
"What about Turner?"
Tears well up in the corners of Calley's eyes, but he shakes his
    head no.
"Okay, Mr. Calley, do you have any more information? Anything
    at all?"
"Nah." Calley wipes his eyes. He looks like a liar all the time,
which makes him tricky to read.
Peabody presses a bit. "Nobody has contacted you? Nothing has
    happened?"
"Um, one second please." Calley looks at his feet, he holds the
    wall for support,

then looks at his hand. "That fucking Samoan," he mutters.
"What's that?"
A moment passes, Calley won't meet his gaze, just rubs his hand,
when he finally looks up, what was pale before
is now the flesh of a drowned man.
"Nope, nothing. Sorry. Indigestion," Calley lies.
Peabody nods, leaves his card.
Getting into his car, he drives around the block,
then pulling back so that he can see down the street,
he parks
and watches Calley's place. Nothing.
Inside the apartment, Calley is now
on his knees in front of the toilet
vomiting and thinking about how
he'd like a drink.
That fucking cop. Why did that cop have to show up?
Calley's wrist still hurts from the fat man's heel.

Outside, Peabody doesn't know what he's looking for.
There's nothing around, a few parked cars.
Then a dog comes out, unleashed, no owner in sight.
The dog sits at the corner and looks at Calley's house.
Everything is quiet on the street.

Calley is drinking from the whiskey bottle
like a linesman chugging Gatorade.
Tears stream down his cheeks.
Why not tell the cop about the weird man
and the big island dude?
Why not tell him what the weird man said about Mason?
This is a lot of fucked-up shit. So much. Too much.
When did everything get so muddy, guilty, and wrong?
He squeezes his eyes shut.
More and more, faces of dogs he once reined in
come flashing back in waking dreams,
snarling angry or cornered in fear

just like they were when he first found them.
He thinks how many he put down,
pressing their necks against the floor while the vet
searched for a vein.
Most of the fight was already gone at that point
their wildness worn out by the cage.
So many walked to their end with a kenneled resignation,
most not even looking up when the needle came,
their spirit long departed before their last breath.

Out in the car, time passes, Peabody watches.
The sitting dog hasn't moved.
Finally, Peabody pulls out the radio.
"Yeah, get me animal contro—"
He hears the shot. Loud. Sharp. Close.
"Shit, correct that, shot fired, Midvale and Woodbine. Over."
He gets out of the car, weapon in hand.
For some reason, there's not the usual adrenaline rush,
instead every move feels clumsy and slow.
Coming around the corner on foot
he sees the dog sitting in the same spot.
Peabody climbs the front steps and
bangs on the door. Nothing.
Through the window he can see Calley's body.
Blood flows out of it like from a burst pipe.

Shoulder to the door does the trick.
Nothing is built solid out here.
Once in, there's little to be done.
He sees the metal of the pistol
hanging from the mouth.
Peabody's first thought is how
his old partner used to call this type of exit
"A little eat and sleep."
Peabody goes out onto the street to look for the backup.

He sees the dog hop up into the bed of a truck,
which promptly rolls away.
Nothing strange in that.
But thinking of that lisping voice on the phone
Peabody takes out his pad and writes
the license number down anyway.

Why not.
Nothing to do here
till the coroner comes.

XV

Anthony in love is unlikely
in its grace,
like a drunk with a magic trick.
There's no reason it should work,
but it does.
Sitting at the kennel, driving in his truck, handling the dogs,
he's a man in a musical.
He steps light on the balls of his feet, moving
to a melody that oils his joints, loosens his stride.
Just watch him open a door or turn a key, it's that evident.
He doesn't think much about the missing dogcatchers,
new guys come in who are the same as the old ones
only younger, a little dense,
but not yet bitter.
He spends his extra time in the kennel where
he's quietly moved the three dogs off death row
over to some cages for "medical observation"
still feeding them tacos and wishing
they knew their good luck.
He doesn't worry about money.
He's got a job and a girl and a slight smile
which doesn't even disappear

when they call the staff into a half circle
to report what happened to Calley.
Suicide, well, so long,
he barely even registers it, just
sips his bad coffee and
keeps an eye on the clock above the door
counting each tick till the end of the day.
Punching out, he leaves
still smiling.
Anthony in love is home
and she is just coming in
with a slight difference on her face
that makes him pause.
Look, she's wearing a small shadow on her expression
but, there, see, it fades, his smile chases it off
just as the sun
chases away the mournful moon.
These days things are stupid
and good like that.

His hands are sore from all the back rubs he's given her
his stomach full from all the meals she's cooked.
Their love is just about the weight
of the casserole she's taking out of the oven right now.
Their love is eternal because time
seems to have fled, embarrassed
to be sharing such a small apartment
with so much dumb affection.

XVI

Lark sits. He's tired.
He's been trotting around this neighborhood
trying to look loose and aimless.
The green lawns of Pasadena hiss with wealth.

At the moment, he's an unleashed dog
prowling around,
causing horns to honk
as he crosses against the lights.
Circling school yards
he eyes the children
and waits for someone to call the cops.
Where is the concerned citizen?
Lark takes another rest,
looking around impatiently,
his nose full of the cut scent
of fresh grass and money.
He waits.

The Pasadena Animal Shelter is said to be
the Four Seasons and The Ritz combined.
The woman who funded it was rich enough
to distrust
all who approached. Nephews, nieces, cousins,
were turned away as she
found her only comfort
in the soft fur of her terriers' coats.
When she died, alone, she gave to those
whose loyalty was most easily earned and hardest lost.
The Pasadena Animal Shelter has a spa. It has more vets
than the local clinic has doctors,
it has a dietician and
a masseuse.

Lark waits. He barks. A stray can't get arrested in this town.
Finally, not seeing any option, he goes and takes
a dump on the green grass of the open plaza.
Then he does a little dance,
it's one of the peculiar canine habits
he wishes more people would adopt.

He could have gone downtown
wound up in Anthony's shelter,
but Anthony's is a city kennel
and city kennels have a policy
of neutering strays.
And if there's one thing Lark is not signing up for
it's that.
Pasadena's shelter is private and of a sweeter disposition
when a beast comes through the door
they don't take a knife to its balls
first thing.

As if he needed a second reason, he suspects
the girl's near that kennel
with her dogcatcher, and if so, they have worries enough.
He doesn't know what that other pack is up to.
But again there were a lot of pieces of his plan
just lying out there in plain view
for Bone or Baron or any of them to put together.

In any case, his untethered wandering seems
to have finally sparked some interest.
Questions ripple through the park.
"Hey, is that your dog?" The man's holding a cup of
    Starbucks.
"No," says the woman with the yoga mat.
They briefly consult and agree,
the man goes to find a cop.
Lark sits.
He'll eat well. Sleep. Have some time to think.
One nice thing about Pasadena, he thinks, is that
nobody's hunting dog in this town tonight.

The man is back, he couldn't find a cop.
He calls 911 on his cell.

The woman waits with him.
They flirt. Lark is amused to eavesdrop.
"Oh yeah, he's a beautiful dog."
"Looks like he's got some shepherd in him."
"Or wolf."
"Yeah, he's big. I had a dog sort of like this once . . ."
Lark listens to them come together,
their mutual problem solving
leading to small chuckles, nervous smiles.
Lark wonders if way back when
the first bonds, the first community
didn't really begin
with the same simple question
"What are we going to do
with all these wild animals?"

XVII

Close by
Cutter and Blue are in a tough spot.
Two old sisters from La Jolla have them down, cornered,
The boys haven't won a hand in hours and
they're just a few points away
from being utterly wiped out.
Damn.

They shouldn't be slammed like this.
But there have been some late nights of late.
The last time they talked to Lark he said
it would probably be a while till they heard from him again.
He sent them new credit cards linked to new accounts
told them to lie low and not answer the door.
He told them to keep playing.
Then he was gone.

Since then it's been cases of Mountain Dew and mountains of
    Domino's pizza.
They have been doing well, rising slowly in the various local
    tournaments.
And when the claustrophobia gets too bad
they drive out to the desert and run,
hunting for the occasional feral cat.
They like to think of it as a community service,
after all, house cats that escape into the wild
survive on local birds, threatening the blue jays and warblers.
So hunting the felines down does protect the biodiversity,
but actually, they only do it
because dogs hate cats.
Later, in the car again, they change and they drive,
racing the dawn
back to the hotel.
When the valet greets them
they look ruffled and unkempt, their eyes burning.
They hit the beds
Two hours of sleep and they're back to the tourney
where things had been going just fine until they met these two.

The sisters are from La Jolla, both married real estate,
worth a mint, they dress and smile like dolls.
Cutter imagines that they were lovely once.
But now they're just quaint little grins.
He looks at the one on his left
what a biddy, who would think the gray matter
would be that sharp at that age. And then,
for a flicker there,
mischief glints in her eyes.
Is there something going on?
Cutter tries to step outside of himself
seeks a broader perspective on the game
using his imagination to walk around the table
to watch it cold

thinking it through,
looking for the solution to the puzzle.
Now there's a game within the game.

The sisters sit erect, their posture polite,
their bidding perfectly pronounced through pursed lips.
No hidden messages there.
But Cutter keeps watching
their serene faces, their well-timed and courteous smiles.
They hold their hands straight up, as erect as their backs.
They fan out the cards, ordering them just so.
Perhaps there's something there.
Usually, someone holding a hand
holds it the same way, game after game,
but a cheater can signal, there—he sees it—
the sister bidding holds her cards up with not just her thumbs
but with a stray finger tucked back there too,
while her sister holds her cards in a normal fashion.
They are ahead in the bidding
but Cutter's not going to give it to them.
If they win this they win it all.
He overbids the girls with no cards to support.
Cutter and a mystified Blue go down hard.

But Cutter has bought some time.
The next hand is dealt.
Now we shall see, he thinks, he waits, he waits,
the girls each organize their hand, moving the cards about.
Watching, out of the corner of his eye,
he sees one suavely tuck two fingers behind her hand
while the other sister nestles one finger back behind the cards,
and props the cards up with her thumb.
It is a casual, smooth, and practiced move,
but it makes Cutter's pulse surge,
because it's so clearly a signal, a cheat.
Cutter smiles, he likes these girls.

And this time he has some cards to play,
even with their slippery ways, they can't beat his hand.
He bids low, holds the win. Then asks to take a break.

The girls sip bottled water in the corner of the stale lounge.
Blue is in the men's room.
A club secretary approaches the ladies.
"There's a call for you at the front desk."
Crossing the room together, one lifts the receiver while the other
    watches.
Cutter's voice growls into her ear,
"If you cheat again this match, lady,
I will chew off your fingers with my teeth
while my partner gnaws the flesh off your sister's skull."
He hangs up.
She hangs up.
She shakes her head, looks at her sister
and sighs. "Oh my."

Blue and Cutter pull it out,
    trouncing the ladies in a surprise comeback.
Over at the next table, the losers
    are a couple from Ventura County
while the winners are a small man
    who could pass for Truman Capote
and a large man who could pass for a Samoan.

XVIII

Ray vs. Sasha,
Sasha vs. Ray,
day in
day out
real chaos for the whole pack to bear.
Skulking to the sides like children
as the metal gets thrown around the kitchen the dogs listen

along with the occasional shattering of glass.
The dogs shake their heads, after all
Ray has made this bed,
he wants Sasha to keep the pack in line
but he wants her too. As his own.
She calls bullshit on his attitude every few days.
Things get physical. Both of them kick
and scream and bite.
She's not afraid to put her fist into his face,
though she pays for it.
The back-and-forth goes on.
Blood spills on the floor.
The tussle sometimes comes when they're wolves
sometimes when they're just another couple
trying to make it in LA.
This fight isn't supposed to be mortal,
merely cathartic, a bleeding of the bitterness.
They fight till they are spent, breathing heavy,
Sasha's black hair wet with sweat,
Ray heavy in his breath like an old wrestler
and then the balance returns.
She licks his ear.
He quietly reaches out and holds her, kissing
the bruises on her arms and shoulders.
Like so much of the trouble in the world,
it simply ends with exhaustion.

Bone is watching, thinking, trying to get out from the bottom.
He stands against the wall quietly observing
as Ray sits at the center of the warehouse, listening
to Penn.
Penn is telling him about some other pack that might exist,
a San Pedro pack that he had investigated a while back for Lark.
Ray is rocking back on one leg of his chair.
Bone hopes Ray is smarter than he looks
which would be a good thing

'cause he looks about as dumb as a rock.
Too many tats but maybe some brain.
Ray's eyes are stone and coal. His physique looks like
it was once prime, fit and tight
before slipping into this looser form, a perpetual
slow leak of flesh. He studies a map on the floor,
points to the southeast section of the city.
"So maybe cruise around in there, ask around
working in ones or in twos. I don't care."
Bone wonders about this. Lark always had a plan, always cared.
Ray likes to improvise,
filling in the blanks
with little more than dense muscle.
But leaning there against the wall, Bone remembers something too,
an idea Lark was toying with,
something to do with the pound.
Bone never knew exactly what the idea was or even his part.
It hurts his head to think like this,
piecing a plan together from nothing,
his mind drowning in the folds of its own confusion.
He decides to simply begin putting what he knows into motion,
figuring that if he acts out the scenes,
the rest of the play will come to him.

Later that night Sasha comes to his bed
slipping in next to him as he lies curled up on his bunk.
"Move over," she says. Bone makes room.
They curl up like wisps of smoke
wrapped around each other.
This is the first time. Bone wonders
what it means. A promotion?
A level up in the pack? The end of the indoctrination?
"Rub my back," she says, ever so softly exposing
something feminine in her voice.
Bone hasn't been with a woman for a long time.
Lark took them to Vegas a while ago. But that was

somewhere beyond the distant past.
He rubs her shoulders, pushing back her hair
to touch the bare whiteness of her skin.
His breath feels shallow in his lungs.
She is silent, but her neck bends to his touch.
Her body has as many scars as a choppy sea.
Somehow she wears it well. Then, she presses her hips
against him.
Before they even begin he knows
it will be over quickly.
Bone grabs, tugs, pushes. She yelps. They keep it muffled.
No sense in waking the dogs.
His hand on her naked stomach, his teeth
on her neck, so close together he's hearing
echoes of his breath on her flesh.
His eyes are blinded by the blackness of her hair.
He inhales deeply, trying to hold on to something from this.
Fast rhythms and heaving chests pass
and when it's over she lies there breathing deep
for a few moments. Then, pulling her clothes on
she tells him
"Ray wants you in the first van tomorrow,"
and rolls off into the darkness.
Then there's nothing.
No lights, just the sighs of sleeping men.
Some tossing. Some turning.
Bone almost wishes she hadn't been there.
It's like she only came into his world
to show him how empty it would be
without her.

XIX

In the dogcatcher's house,
she's beginning to worry.
When she's in Anthony's arms it's not so bad.

It's safe and quiet and warm there.
It's the rest of the world that has her on edge.
But where is Lark?
What happened to the pack?
What happens if someone shows up?
What will she say?
She wrings her hands,
pulling at the length of her finger bones
as if hoping to draw answers from her body.

The worst secrets are the ones
that sit like spiders
waiting to bite.

Anthony is aware of her in the other room.
Sometimes he wants to go in
wrap her in his arms, hold her
until her blue eyes turn their focus away
from whatever haunts her
to find him again there
kneeling beside her, patiently removing the thorns.
Strong love can hold on to anything fairly given,
he knows this.
He has held her in Pacific waves
standing against the tide that pulled firmly at their sides,
"See," he said. "We're stronger than this."
She looked in his eyes.
She was almost there
but not yet.

That morning, sitting in the kitchen, she smiled.
"Why you smiling?"
She said the sweet scent of the jasmine in the garden makes her
    smile
and the toasted smell of the bread makes her smile
and the roasting of the coffee makes her smile.

"You've got a good nose," he said, kissing her.
And like that her face froze, and she
left the room.

The same way it went down when she was reading that day
and he said, "Hey, instead of a dog,
maybe we could get a cat?"
And she said, without looking up, "No."
"What, are you allergic to cats?"
She looked up, eyes cold. "No. I just don't like them.
and they don't like me."

He worries that this
is beginning to feel like
driving in a car through the mountains,
finding a great song on the radio
and then as you pass out of its range
hearing it flicker and fade.
Snap, pop, and
then it's gone.

XX

Lark waits in the cage.
The other dogs are worked up.
He has his own kennel but still
he has to watch his step.
Dogs will fight first, think later.
And he's got to conserve his energy.
So he's avoiding them.
He eats his food, tries to savor it,
but the luxury of the Pasadena Animal Shelter
turns out largely to be a myth.
It's okay enough.
He can stick to the plan.
He eats his food,

disappointed at every bite.
In the end, he thinks, a prison
is always a prison.
The vet was thorough with the checkup and
Lark was a little nervous
though the differences between what a dog is and what he is
are not the sort of thing anyone can easily notice,
even among experts, it takes a highly trained eye.
The vet prodded him, pressed on his glands, pulled down his
    eyelids
and counted his teeth.
This is where the city kennel would have spayed him,
but instead he gets a needleful of antibiotics
and a pat on the ass.
Afterward he rests, listening to the vet
on the phone carrying the weak end of a fight that slowly
    escalates.
"No, I can't pick that up. It's your prescription."
Lark thinks, people have a tougher time working as a group than
    dogs do.
People make for messy packs and awkward teams.
"And I picked up the laundry last week and the week before
    that."
Perhaps because people don't resort to the decisiveness
of violence quite as quickly as dogs do.
"Listen, I have a full-time job too."
Perhaps because they don't submit to their leader
as completely.
"That's not what I mean. You don't understand."
Perhaps being free of a language is a blessing for dogs.
"Why do you say that, why do you always have to hurt me."
Since dogs aren't continually surprised when
those soft and easily broken tools called words
fail them time and again.
"I love you."

Words, those simple clumsy clay blocks
that one hopes will support such enormous walls.
"I do, I love you."
Words, the small weak things
that come tumbling out of men.

"But I love you."

Lark lies on the table sighing, blinking,
as the vet's fallen tears
dampen the aluminum, bending the light.

Back in the kennel, during visiting hours,
a sloppy-looking couple comes in.
Lark doesn't trust the man and doesn't like
the way his shirt is untucked.
It's these little things that matter.
An older lady comes in.
Her eyes are dark mean beans.
Lark hears her say her last dog ran away
and he's sure he knows why.
He growls as she walks by
so softly no one can notice
but something inside her hears and she stays away.
Finally, toward the end of the day, a woman walks in.
She has some elegance, perhaps a bit of money.
She's nervous in a nice way.
Lark likes the way her fingers dance about as she talks.
She's looking for a big dog she says.
Lark is sitting up straight.
She lives alone, she says.
She needs one who can protect her.
As she passes by his kennel
soft paw on the cage
looking into her eyes

cocking his head sideways,
Lark groans a little
like a lovelorn Elvis.

XXI

Peabody gets another call
from the lispy fellow.
"Detective, I am sorry to hear about Calley."
Peabody tries to take his time,
tease it out.
"No sorrier than I was. Did you know he was going to do that?"
"Not exactly," the voice purrs. "But he was a troubled man who
obviously made some poor decisions along the way."
Peabody signals to the guy at the next desk to start a trace.
"Yeah, yeah, we'll all miss him. Who are you anyway?"
"I am simply an interested party, an observer on the sidelines."
"Observing what?"
"A good question, Detective, an excellent
if slightly obvious question. But what about you?
Did you observe anything?"
"When?"
"At Calley's house. Did you see anything unusual? Any strange
    people or animals?"
Why's he saying animals?
Peabody thinks about the dog.
Why would this guy know about that?
"Not really, no."
"No animals, really."
The guy at the next desk says it's coming from a lobby phone
out at a hotel in Pasadena.
Peabody nods his thanks.
No use chasing that down.
"Nope, I'm telling you, it was just Calley
with a mouthful of bullet."
"What a shame. I was really hoping our friends would show

   their hands a bit."
Peabody waits to hear more.
"Excuse me, sir, look, I'm just a cop
      and so I think like a cop and as far as I can tell,
there's not much worth looking into here."
"What about Mason and Turner?"
Peabody sits up. "As far as we know, Turner just disappeared."
"Well, if that's what you're thinking, I can only say
I underestimated you, Mr. Peabody. Good day."
The phone clicks dead.
Irritated, Peabody pulls out his notebook
and calls in the plate he saw at Calley's house.
It's not much, but fuck it, it's something.
That dog he saw is alive, it's warm,
so it's got a trail he can follow.

XXII

Things are getting cold in Anthony's house.
She makes strange noises when she's sleeping,
and beneath the sheets she moves her legs
like she's running,
chasing something.

"What's the matter?"
"Nothing."
He's got to leave for work soon,
and though he doesn't want to leave her like this,
he doesn't have the time to sort through the brooding.
She's got some books open on
the kitchen table, businesses she says
she's thinking of opening.
"Why don't you take your work out to a café today,"
he says. "Maybe you'll make some new friends."
She sips her coffee. "I had some friends,

they all disappeared."
He kisses her forehead
"I'm sorry but, hey, you got me."
She squeezes his hand, just enough.
It's these small physical touches
that hold them in the moment,
keeping the goodness from slipping away.

He drives to work
wondering, what is it inside her?
He would read her diary if she kept one
read her mail if she got any.
It's tugging at him like an undertow
toward the deep black sea.

Back in the kitchen, she's feeling stuck.
There's so much to move on from
so many swords hanging over her.
The future looms like a brooding cloud bank.
Step by step, she has to get free of it all.
She pours herself more coffee and thinks forward,
making a list, counting day after day
until she knows
what to do.
First things first.

In the car, the rap song has every other word beeped out
as if the small words themselves were a dangerous thing, and not
the ideas of violence and waste and ridiculous luxury
that the songs clutch in their rough embrace.
Everyone is always looking in the wrong direction,
we worry about our lovers while losing our jobs
we stress out about cancer while our children run away
we ponder the stars while burning the earth.
Lark used to say the bullet we're running from
is almost never the one that hits us.

* * *

She is looking, every day, slowly tracing a pattern,
hunting, seeking the scent,
beginning her search from the last known point
where the old pack's house used to be
over to the old office space downtown
then to just outside Anthony's kennel
where Lark's plan first led her.
Cruising slow, eyes open, till the early afternoon
when she chooses a spot,
parks, drinks an herbal tea,
and quietly waits.

XXIII

The little man is back in his hotel suite.
It's late, but it could be any hour as
he moves about, talking in his endless fashion,
this time about the planet Mars
which sparkled behind the sunset tonight
and set his mind buzzing.
The big man sits across the room watching
the little man, whose name is Mr. Venable.
Mr. Venable smokes a cigarette and drinks a glass of rye on ice.
He is small, nearly a third the weight of the big man, and he is
      wearing
a white full-length nightgown,
almost Victorian, quite elegant. It would be amusing
if he were not so serious.
The big man, still wearing his suit, listens to Mr. Venable's ramble
waiting for him to arrive at something resembling a point.
"Remember, this is a planet we have known about for centuries,
      with its sister Venus
appearing just after sunrise or just after sunset, but they do
      avoid each other
like children playing

some sort of game,
hiding behind the horizon in the folds of their mother's skirts."
The big man blinks, bored, waiting for more.
It comes. It always comes.
"Do you know why they named these two lights Venus and Mars?"
The big man shakes his head no.
"Because, like love and war, they never arrive together and yet
they are always there
on the edge of the sky,
so close to us.
They never go away."
The big man waits for more.
"We need to embrace the love and the war.
Not one, not the other," says Mr. Venable,
gingerly closing the shade,
"We must hide from neither and master both.
If we can master both, my friend, we will
master so very much.
For that is all there is, in various shades, within us each,
behind every gesture, every nod,
A little love, a little war."
The room is silent for the first time in a long while.
The air conditioner seethes behind the drapes.
The big man sighs
digesting all these words.
He's heard better
but still he mulls it over,
searching out the nut, the kernel,
and finally, brow creased, he nods. "I see."
Mr. Venable takes a last sip of his drink, crushes his smoke,
and crawls into the hotel room's large bed.
The big man watches with studied patience, then
rising, takes off his suit, and slides naked into the bed as well.
He wraps himself gently around Mr. Venable,
a dark oyster surrounding an ivory pearl.
They rest beneath the sea of the night.

XXIV

Lark sleeps in front of the TV
Bonnie strokes his hair,
rubbing the scruff of his neck, right, there.

He had planned to lay low for a week,
figure out her story, her schedule.
Then move it into gear.
But
the good life has its numbing consequences.
Like lotus-drugged sailors in a distant land,
failing to raise their oars and return home.
Lark feels little compulsion to do
anything.

Bonnie rubs that spot behind his ears.
He spends nights of
narcotic comfort splayed out
on a sheepskin rug
at the foot of her bed.
She scratches his belly just so
as he softly kicks his leg.

The past rises like vapor to surround him,
clouds of memory float through the living room,
his first job, a law firm where
he was the too bright boy, accomplished
far beyond his age. He exalted in the firm's appreciation,
as drunken spiraling nights out with his colleagues spilled
one into the other. The emptiness of the mornings
were soon buried beneath the successes of the day, the hollowness
of those accomplishments filled full again

with the liquid of another liquored night.
Then, early one dark morning, just after closing time,
while driving to meet up with Lark at some raucous bar,
his closest friend wrapped himself
around the streetlight and had to be rushed to the E.R.
In the waiting room, a drunken Lark passed out only to
awaken and find a strange man sitting beside him.
Lark didn't know where he came from, but
there in the limbo of the waiting room, they began to talk.
The stranger was still sitting beside him
when Lark got the bad news.
Lark wept and, for the first time in years, felt something deeper.
The man listened, talked, helped him, guided him
and then, a few sleepless nights later, folded Lark
into his first pack.
Years passed, groups of dogs
ran this way and that
as Lark mapped his course with a sure precision,
finding his way, building his philosophy,
content, finally, to be living a true discipline,
a perfect balance,
until it all crashed down
like the timbers in a burning barn.
Bonnie massages the tuft of fur beneath his chin.
It feels good, just like that.

Lark lies in front of the TV
it's an easy place to stay,
she watches good shows and he
actually hasn't seen anything for years.
Running the pack didn't leave much time for cable
but now, goodness, even the soaps are engaging
and the nightly news blows his mind,
it's like watching the earth being skinned raw
every night at eleven.
He closes his eyes.

She scratches his hind.
Mmmn.
Sleep.

The days unfold, repeat and rerun.
Bonnie laughs at the TV. Lark gets playful,
jumps around the room
makes her laugh some more.
She brings home scraps for him from her office lunch.
She rubs his high haunches.
She picks up his shit.
Who knew
life could be this good.

It was supposed to be a week. It's been six.
No rush, really,
the packs will still be there.
The war is waiting.
Just a little nap.
The war is always waiting for us.

XXV

Peabody the cop drives, thinking about the dogs.
An old conversation from years past drifts back to him.
On a stakeout that tested their sanity and bore no fruit,
his partner, the wise man who taught him the clockwork of the
    world,
said to Peabody, "You know why we domesticated dogs and
    cats?"
"Why?" asked Peabody.
"Well, see, some people think it's because they're carnivores,
and they'll chase down rats and mice and other vermin for us,
keeping the campsite clean, so to speak.
But my particular theory is that we keep them around because,
    well,

they're funny."
Peabody remembers the tired smile they shared at this thought.
"Funny?" Peabody asked.
"Yeah," his partner said. "Cats chase their shadows,
hang on the curtain,
and dogs, well, they chase their tails
stick their nose in your crotch
and hump your mother-in-law's leg.
They're just funny.
Bunnies are cute, but they're not funny,
so we left them in the wild.
But parrots talk funny, so we took some of them home too."
Peabody had thought about this for a minute before offering up
what he thought was the perfect challenge.
"Monkeys."
"What?" his partner said.
"Monkeys are funny," said Peabody, "so, why didn't we pick
    monkeys?"
His partner sighed and shook his head with sad dismay.
"Monkeys? Jesus.
Monkeys' idea of fun
is throwing their shit at you.
Monkeys always take the joke
a step too far."

Peabody misses his partner.

XXVI

Ray is listening. Bone knows he hasn't got much time
Five minutes, tops.
Bone's been low on the totem for too long
and after one night with Sasha
he's got an appetite for more.
It's all about pecking order in this pack
here where the hungers of the favored are fed.

So far, Ray has barely acknowledged Bone's
      existence
but when he was asked for five minutes
he gave it to Bone without question.

"What's on your mind?" asks Ray.
Bone answers provocatively; he knows it's his moment.
"We're stupid. Lark had plans, I know them."
"Oh yeah?" says Ray, raising an eyebrow. "Why should we fol-
      low Lark's plans?"
Bone's not a lawyer like Lark or Baron, but he feels this is right.
"Lark wasn't an idiot," says Bone, "and if we don't know his
      plan,
it doesn't mean it won't come to us.
Let's just put the wheels in motion. Let's kick it forward.
We've been sniffing for Lark for months now
and we've got nothing. So before we walk away
and leave him to his own dead-end path,
maybe we should take a look
at what I'm talking about here."
Ray doesn't say anything, he stares ahead.
It seems like he's studying the cracks
in the wall, searching for some kind of a map.
But then he simply nods
and heads off to find Baron and Sasha.
Watching him go, Bone thinks of how
he hasn't talked to Baron since the pack was overthrown.
He doesn't care, water under the bridge and all that.
But if Baron was Judas to the last pack, thinks Bone,
Ray had better watch out.
'Cause who's to think Baron's going to be any different
now.

Word comes down, Bone is transferred off the pack search.
Word comes down, he's supposed to look into the kennel.
Bone runs across the lot to the car,

moving out alone, hungry for credit, for merit,
for more of that dark, wet
Sasha.

He drives downtown,
death metal screams its radio love song to LA.
A maze of exits and municipal signage and then he pulls in
to the pound. Walking into the mason building
it seems to Bone like centuries have passed
since he came here that day with her, looking for a job.
He barely said a word then, says little more now.
At the front desk a tired soul tells him that Anthony is out
won't be back for most likely a few hours.
Bone's got a head full of nervous energy, can't stop twitching.
He heads back out the parking lot and then, whoa,
what the hell, there she is,
Lark's girl, the pack's girl, but here now.
Bone tries to think through it, figuring it makes some sense.
The last time he spent any time with her
was when she brought him down to meet Anthony.
Now she's standing with an impatient posture
like Bone's late or something.
She's leaning on his car a little pissed.
He approaches slowly, warily.
Her mouth is tight and angry.
"Where the fuck have you been?"
"I wasn't expecting to see you here," he manages.
"I been following you since you passed me way back on
    Wilshire,
honking my horn the whole way,
you didn't fucking hear it?" She rolls her eyes, exasperated.
"Sorry, I had the radio playing."
At this she softens a bit. She looks great to him.
He thinks, "She was always so untouchable."
His nerves still feel shaky, but whatever,
he wants it now, he'll take it.

"Where's Lark?" he asks.

"I dunno, Bone, he's dead to me," she says.

"Things sure change fast."

She shrugs. "Look, we should get outta here, we should talk.
    Really,
I want to hear what's going on with you."

"Sure," Bone says, wondering how to play this, "maybe we
    should go somewhere, you
want to follow me or—"

"Why don't you drive us. One car's simpler. Then you can bring
    me back, okay?"

"Sure," Bone says.

She steps close to Bone, almost whispers.

"We could go out to the hills, we could go for a run tonight."

Back in the pack, Lark kept her apart,
she was the dry match
and they were the fumes of gasoline.
Bone never got near her.
But now,
now she leans against Bone.

They drive east. Making small talk,
Bone is tense about the clock.
He digs a little for news.
"So, where are you living?"
"Chinatown," she says. "I've hooked up with a guy
in the garment business."
"Free clothes."
"He prefers me without them."
Ha, ha.
She puts her hand on his wrist, sending his pulse soaring.
"Lark would never let me be with you."
Her fingers rest between Bone's.
His pulse moving so fast, it's breaking land speed records.
He aches from heart to gut to groin and looks for off-ramps.

"Lark had his rules," Bone says.
Her hands keep roaming across his legs,
her lips move to his ear and she whispers,
"Lark's not here."
Bone accelerates.
She asks about the end of the old pack
he fills her in, he keeps his cool,
desperate now for an exit.
Her hands keep roaming
the old distance and
the old rules seem skies away to him now and—
—yes, there's a West Covina exit.
"Gas," Bone says.
"Uh-huh," she says, moving her hand
to his crotch.
They roll into the Shell station. Pull in the back.
Then, faster than time,
she's leapt over,
her tongue is down his throat.
She straddles his lap, grinds against his thigh.

There's always the question, like man or dog?
Here and now, the pleasure of a dog's love
is more intense, but the appreciation of a human's
more delicate, more sublime. Bone decides they'll stay human.
She unbuttons
his shirt, runs her hands on his chest.
Licks his neck.
A pause, deep breath.
"Jesus Christ," she says, "not here. Not in the car. In there."
She points to the station's restroom.
Bone nods.
"I'll get the key. Give me a minute."
Bone watches as the Indian gives her the key. Nodding. Smiling.
She runs to the john door.
She holds up her hand, one sec. He smiles quick

bangs his hand on the steering wheel and waves back.
He suddenly feels he's waited five years for this.
Yeah. He bangs the driving wheel again with his fist and then
gets out of the car. The light feels too bright,
the day is as raw as he is.
He heads to the restroom,
turns the greasy door handle, walks in.
Two stalls.
"Hey baby—" he says.
She comes out of the stall, a dog.
"Aw, hey, baby. Don't cha think—"
She jumps for him. Angry. Teeth bared.
"Oh my god no."
As a dog, he could take her, but she's too far ahead
she'd kill him quick if he tried to change now.
"Fuck!" She gets his arm and doesn't hold back. Bites through.
And the blood comes fast.
He shouts out in agony. Praying for the Indian attendant.
He kicks but she takes the kick without losing her bite
and dodges the next.
His arm is sopping red as he kicks again and
loses his balance, slipping on his own blood
to the wet concrete floor, landing hard on his side
holding his arms over his head.
She knows how to fight, she knows how to make this fast.
She bites his stomach from the side, cutting so deep
her teeth are scraping against his rib.
"Oh, oh Jesus Christ."
She tears into his calf—muscles, tendons.
His arms instinctively react, reaching down,
but then she goes for his face.
He tries to punch, but an artery in his leg
is open, he can see his stomach
slipping out of his gut,
and then the arm is useless.

* * *

Her teeth hit his neck.
The last thing he sees are her eyes.
The last thing he feels is the heat of her breath on his neck.
The only thing he hears
is the might of the surging blackness
as it softly growls
for him.

XXVII

Twenty minutes later
she quietly washes her hands
and pulls on her underwear.
She looks around, double-checking.
The bones are gone,
tucked beneath his shredded
clothes in the trash
and the floor is licked Ajax clean.
Maybe someone will notice later,
but probably not. Minimum wage
tends to elicit minimum attention.
She grabs Bone's wallet and his cell and his keys.
As she runs across the parking lot,
she waves through the window
to the turbaned cashier.
Smiling, the Indian waves back.

The blood is warm in her belly.

On the car ride into the city
she wipes the red traces
stuck like ketchup to the corner
of her dark lips.
The song on the radio sings
Hey baby, hey baby, hey.

XXVIII

Anthony comes home
and she seems relaxed in a way
he hasn't seen since early on.
She folds up in his arms.
Without many words
within minutes
they're making love on the couch.
Her smile is wide,
her passion exhausting.

Afterward, she cooks dinner and listens
as he talks about the dogs
and the day's long runs in the truck.
She comes up behind him while he washes the dishes
stroking his hair, her head resting on his back.
She sighs contentment
without making a sound.

He doesn't know
what made her unwind
but as they make love again that night
her eyes locked with his, his with hers,
he only hopes it will last.

XXIX

Peabody pulls into the neighborhood.
He had run the number off
the plates from the mystery dog's truck.
They belonged to an Emilio Ruiz,
age sixty-five, retired, living here in San Pedro.
Small bungalow blocks from the water.

If the neighborhood was nice
people would say it had character,
as it is, the place is just plain poor.
Peabody works these patrols alone,
explaining little back at the station.
After all, in order to describe the case
he'd have to understand it himself.
One dogcatcher disappears, looks like murder,
turns out two guys have gone missing.
A third eats a gun, maybe out of guilt, but maybe
out of fear,
either way, it's ifs and maybes and too odd
to explain to anyone downtown.
It's tough and lonely
working on your own,
at the last of your own straws,
where questions only breed more questions.
But here he is now
knocking on Emilio's door.
A young guy with the looks of a surfer comes to the door.
"Hi," says Peabody. "I'm looking to meet a Mr. Ruiz."
"Oh, hi. No, he's not here now.
He left this morning."
The kid is confident, strong and so blond he's almost albino.
A beach kid doesn't add up here.
"Um, okay. When do you expect Mr. Ruiz back?"
The surfer pauses and then smiles.
"He'll be back later, why don't you give me your number.
We'll have him call."
"I'd rather see him, if that's okay."
"Sure, sure. We'll let you know when he's here." The kid seems
    unfazed.
Maybe it's all nothing.
Maybe Peabody's just trying to build a story
where there's really nothing.
"Okay, thanks, see you later."

The screen door slams.

Peabody walks away from the stoop, watching
out of the corner of his eye as the kid recedes
into the house.
He runs through all the answers, something
didn't sound right.
He walks around the block, mulling it over while
looking for a human face,
for instance over there,
on the corner, an older woman tearing all the plants
out of her tangled garden.
"Morning."
She looks up and grimaces, not too happy
about giving up the time.
"Do you, by any chance, know a Mr. Ruiz?"
She doesn't react, she's either thinking of a response
or waiting for him to move on, or maybe she just doesn't
comprende and
Peabody isn't in the mood to test his rusty Spanglish
so he nods
and begins to walk away.
"Ruiz is a son of a bitch," she says.
Peabody swivels around and she looks at him.
She's got a southwestern rhythm to her speech,
a high Hispanic accent that hints at the desert.
"I haven't seen him for months though.
Don't think he's around, just the two guys and a girl
living at his house and
driving his truck."
"Months? Really? Do you have any idea who these guys are?" he
    says.
She shrugs. "*No se*, I don't know, but they only seem to leave the
    house at night."
"Really?" says Peabody again.
"Listen," she says. "Ruiz used to fight dogs, he was a *puta de*

    hijo,
seriously, ask anyone on this street and they'll tell you,
he was a bastard. Crazy and mean. He might still be around,
but I haven't seen him. And I don't know who those kids are
living there in his place. But I'll tell you what,
they're not family."
"When did you first notice them?" Peabody asks,
admiring this tough old girl.
"I don't know," she winds down,
returning her attention to the torn-up yard.
"You'd have to let me think about that . . ."
then she hits the weeds again,
pulling up their root systems, fist after fist,
oblivious to Peabody waiting there.
A minute or two passes.
Peabody waits.
When she finally looks up, all shades
of pleasantry are gone.
"Aw, hell, just mind your own damn business," she says.

He goes back to his car, still parked across
from Ruiz's little house,
where he adds up what little he knows.

She said Ruiz had been gone awhile,
the kid said he left that morning,
but she also said Ruiz might still be around,
so nothing solid to go on there.
Though the kid had said one thing,
"We'll have him call."
and something is funny in that phrase,
something he can't put his finger on.

He pulls out of the spot, drives to the Ralph's
gets a large coffee and a bag of carrots
drives back to Ruiz's neighborhood

parks a block down behind the house.
And waits.

A call home.
Peabody listens to his son make noises into the phone,
tells his wife a little about his day,
all the while he studies
a light in Ruiz's bungalow.
Finally, out of the alley,
a small figure emerges.
"Honey, I got to go."
The shadow comes closer and he sees it's
a girl, blonde too.
She walks right to the car and taps the window.
Some cover.
Peabody rolls down the window,
"Yeah?"
"Hi, I'm Annie."
"Hi."
"Are you the guy looking for Mr. Ruiz?"
She is cute, sixteen going on twenty-two,
Her style is sweet and a little
spacey, no surprise in these longitudes.
"Yes, I was hoping to talk to Mr. Ruiz."
She eyes the inside of the car. "Are you like a cop or something?"
Peabody smiles. Yeah, some cover.
"I'm a cop, sure, and I have some questions."
"Mmmn," she says, studying a split end for a few seconds.
"He's not coming back tonight,
he got stuck making a delivery down in San Diego."
It's not that she's a bad liar,
she just doesn't care enough to try.
"Well," says Peabody. "I guess
I'd better come back another time."
Annie nods, grins sweet, almost like she's
being patient with him.

Being patient with the whole world too
while she's at it.
"Okay," she says. "'Cause if you're going to wait
I could get you a sandwich."
He chuckles at the funny, awkward path
this case is taking.
"No thanks." He smiles. "Anyway, how did you
know I was here?"
"Oh, we smelled you," Annie says,
then walks away.

XXX

She sits in the car and pulls a bag
from under the passenger seat,
a ziplock bag holding a bloody cell phone
and a bloody wallet.
A universe of information can be held
in two fists.
The wallet has some receipts: gas, takeout, etc.
All located around Long Beach,
so she figures
that's where they're based.

Before she took him under
Bone had told her a bit of what was what these days.
Six of the old pack were with the new pack,
Zack was dead.
Nobody had a clue where Lark was
or Cutter and Blue for that matter.
Baron was the one
who had made some bad deal
selling them all out.
She nods to herself.
Baron was smart like that, always thinking.
Whatever move he had made, it wasn't a stupid one.

But it didn't matter a bit.
What mattered was this:
there were five dogs who knew her.
Five she has to sort out.
She'll take the rest too
while she's at it.
Fucking vermin.
Fucking world.

She pauses and thinks about her old boyfriend
Pete, of the sweet eyes and mean hands.
Perhaps now, while her blood is up
she should address that too.
She remembers him holding her down,
shouting in her face.
His belligerent mouth inches
from her squinting, terrified expression.
That was so many versions of her ago
but the bruises that hung to her flesh for weeks then
became shadows that still linger inside her
no matter how bright and sunny the days become.
Lying like arsenic seed buried
beneath so much sweet fruit.
Pete, she thinks, twisting the bloody
ziplock, I'm coming soon.
Lark isn't here to protect you anymore.
He's not here to calm me down.
It's a big town
but she's ready
to clean it up.

Programmed into this cell phone are numbers.
The blood sticks to her hands
but she doesn't notice.
She texts the first number in the memory.
"Spent the night watching dog kennel. Dead end.

Nothing there. Heading now to Echo Park."
She hits send and waits ten minutes,
watching children running
across a school yard, fearless, energetic
and unstoppably random.
Children, the word catches inside her,
children. She remembers
babysitting in ranch homes,
combing doll hair, playing house.
She closes her eyes.
Those games become dreams
that still dream on
in softer worlds.
She opens her eyes again, looks down
and sends the text to the next number.
Children. She shivers.
Think of something, she tells herself,
stop remembering and think of something else,
think of what a lovely term "memory" is
when applied to a machine.
Yes, that's it, we name everything we can a "memory"
We hand our lives—
our addresses, our letters, our numbers, our photos, our dreams—
to these dumb throbbing machines
as we become emptier, remembering less and less
of what matters while these circuits
deftly struggle under the load of our own confusion.
Of course, at some point, we are no longer concerned,
we're buried or worse, while the electronic world
holds on to our lives, waiting for us to return
and give it the meaning for which it starves.

Fifteen minutes later with no answer
she sends the same message to the next number.
She breathes deep and looks up
at faces of young girls and boys running laughing round the

park.
Everything hurts at moments like these.
The buzzing of the phone surprises her.
"Meet you there" the message reads.
She puts the phone back in the Glad bag,
wipes the dried blood from her
fingertips, and quickly drives away
from all the children.

XXXI

Perhaps it is a change in the wind
Santa Anas or worse
but as Lark lies in the house
with Bonnie sleeping soundly,
his muscles tighten
as his mind races ahead,
like a pack
chasing the scent
of something that must die.

XXXII

The phone in Cutter and Blue's hotel room rings.
Cutter answers.
"It's Lark."
"Man!" Cutter jumps on the bed. "We're in the finals!
Can you fucking believe it?"
"Really?" Lark barely sounds interested.
"Yeah, Pacific Regional, Section I Division. I'm telling you Lark,
    if we win this—"
"It was never about the winning. Cutter, have you noticed
    anything strange?"
"What are you talking about?" Cutter stops jumping, sits on the
    bed's edge.
His eyeballs dart around the room

as if he's spinning on some drug
but it is merely the cabin fever setting his rhythm off.
They've been waiting between matches and tournaments
working on their game, studying books, playing the computer,
bouncing off the walls.
"Remember, you were sent up there to look for something."
"Yeah," says Cutter. "But you said
focus on the game. I mean, the pack is gone,
we have no idea what to do,
and where the hell are you?"
"A friend's house."
"Okay. Well, I'll tell you what, Lark,
we'll keep our eyes and ears peeled for something,
      anything.
but what if we win this tournament?"
"I'll take you to the International House of Pancakes."
Cutter smiles. "Sweet. That's all I needed to hear."
There is a pause,
then Lark speaks up. "When's the final?"
"Two days, we're up against some guy named Venable and his
      partner—"
"Okay," Lark interrupts. "Good luck, just keep me informed. I'll
      call."
"Yeah. No problem." Cutter is about to hang up
but then, "Lark?"
"Yeah, Cutter?"
"Is there a plan?"
"There's always a plan."
The click
comes just as
Blue swings into the room,
four cheesesteaks in his mitts and two six-packs of Diet Coke.
"Wuddup C. Who was on the phone?"

XXXIII

Down in San Pedro
Annie takes two cigarettes
out to the back stoop.
She sniffs for the cop,
the one who's been watching.
No sign, she unwinds
and lights up.

Nobody else in the house smokes,
and she's been trying to get down to just one a day.
She's almost there.

The trick, she's found, is to use that time
to sort through the difficult things,
so that a cigarette becomes like a therapist,
keeping her company while she gets it together.
With every session she feels a little better,
exhaling it all,
releasing the bad stuff with every breath,
at least the parts
that will let go.

Annie watches the cigarette smoke
slip off into the night.
She listens to the crickets
and remembers the jungle.

Annie's pack was larger then, twenty in all,
Surfers and brothers and she loved each
with a butterfly gentleness that brought sweet smiles
to their faces. All of them bobbing there in the surf,
waiting for the waves.

They had traveled south together, deep down into Central
    America
looking for good breaks they could ride
and thick forests where they could run.
They parked their long boards off the Osa Peninsula,
on a beach they dubbed Ciudad del Perros.
Dashing and darting through the rain forest at night,
they carved out a hidden paradise free from any visitors' or
    strangers' gazes,
only the twitching eyes of rainbowed lizards watching them
as they hunted and ran and rolled in the lush ferns and tall
    grasses.

Beneath that dappled canopy, three of her dogs once
trapped and killed an alligator,
marinating its tough meat with papaya juice.
Come sunset, they grilled it on the campfire with fish tacos
and a pot of caliente chile and black beans.
Guitars came out with warbling song and
laughter rose up to the stars.

Almost a year into this tranquil time
some local poachers hidden in the undergrowth
hunting for iguana
spied two of her brothers
jerking through the throes of their transformation.
Racing into the sunset's pink light, the poachers
brought to their sleepy village a true tale
of gringo demons and blonde devils
and so with righteous anger the locals came storming back
through the thick, moonless night,
descending with lit torches and loud fury
on the resting pack.
Trapping the sleeping boys on the beach
the villagers unleashed their gunfire,
while the red-faced priest screamed instructions.

Trees were soaked and lit with kerosene.
Those who escaped ran through
the blackness of the night into the unknown
their speed fueled by fear
their fear fueled by the screams
of those who didn't escape.
The screams were like the wolves of old,
the martyrs of legend,
whose agony taught the black crow to cry.

Ten dogs were left and they ran for days.
She ran in the middle of the pack,
the other dogs wanted her there,
to keep her safe.
Moving over dry mountains and across plateaus
shaking in the darkness with an ever-present
fear and bewildering anger until
sleep would finally come.
Then up again,
licking faces awake to run farther.
They had no money, no clothes
so stayed dog
and picked their way up north.
Nicaragua, Honduras, Guatemala,
moving slow enough to find what would feed them,
moving fast enough so the *camposinos* they robbed
never saw enough to know.
On into Mexico.
Edging forward, tongues hanging loose,
paws cracked and bleeding, but onward they ran,
until they fell into a different stripe
of bad luck, one that took them down
to a lower level of hell.

The second cigarette is crushed out.
As the therapists like to say,

"Looks like our time is up."
Annie closes her eyes
and sniffs at the night. She knows the cop
will come back, sit in his car,
wait for something.
Oh yeah, she thinks, we'll give him something.
She gets up from the stoop,
and stretches her bones before heading in
thinking how amazing it is
that she still can find a way
to smile.

XXXIV

Anthony loves how the days unfold,
everything seems more tame and quiet,
dogs sense his confidence and practically run right to him.
And she has some new strength.
He doesn't ask about it,
the less said, the better.
Maybe it is the exercise,
she runs now and is working
with weights in the garage.

It's a habit of late
when he washes the dishes
she comes up from behind,
her arms wrapping around him
resting her cheek on his back and
quiet, still, he inhales the moment,
feeling the depth of her invisible smile
in every breath.
He strokes her hands beneath the warm water
time becomes something different
the steel of its progression softens
as in the mist before you wake

when you can move the furniture
in your dreams.

If not a skip, then a definite lightness to her step
as she makes beds, folds laundry
circles want ads.
He's been there, he kisses her cheek
and brews another pot of tea.
A spirit has been cast out
a curse lifted.
Everything is working
for a change.
Her appetite has become tremendous in every way
they make love in the kitchen, the living room,
and she eats huge plates of pasta.
The only hint of any trouble comes as
she's finishing a big bowl of Bolognese,
dressed only in a thong and a tee.
"I think," she says, her words slightly garbled,
her mouth full, chewing as she gestures with her fork.
"I think maybe we should get some guns."

book three

You can't own something unless
   you can swallow it.

CHINESE PROVERB

Oh the werewolf, oh the werewolf
comes travelin' along.
He don't even break the branches
where he's been gone.

MICHAEL HURLEY

I

"Yo bro," Jorge says to Frio, "I skip school
because at this point
appearing would just freak them out.
I would be an apparition.
a bad dream spirit, rising up
in the middle of my math class like a goblin.
Teachers would stare, mouths would drop,
    you know?
It would be as strange
as Aliyah showing up or Tupac
or, damn, my Uncle Leon's hand coming back
from Vietnam.
That's how gone I am
from school anyway."

Frio's cousin lets them work for him
down by the docks, which is fine
but it's nothing like serious pay.
They run goods around, the extras that slide
off the cargos and into the open pockets
of Frio's cousin. Jorge gets a little
or less. But he likes it better than school,
he doesn't get hassled and nobody asks questions
like, for instance, who won the Battle of
damn man
we're all fighting the Battle of whatever
aren't we?
Every day.
It never ends.

Midday, middelivery,
Jorge's drinking with Frio in the car

parked outside the package store.
The mercury and the sun are both high,
as Frio talks about solar power
something he saw on the Discovery Channel
how the light will save us all.
Jorge says shit man, people talk about Jesus like that.
Frio whistles low, looking up
as a shadow blocks the light.
Jorge looks up and catches it too,
she's nothing but silhouette.
But what a line, thinks Jorge. What a fine line.
"What are you dudes doing? You want some work?"
She's got a voice. A little low, a slight rasp
somewhere between the soft growl of an engine
and the purring of a dark cat.
"Aw, honest, lady, we're a little juiced up,
we can't do much
and actually," Jorge takes a swig. "We're technically
in the middle
of a job right now."
Frio takes a sip of his beer.
"You look like you could be handy," she says.
She stops blocking the sun
and now Jorge can take her all in.
Tough as steel she is, tips of tats sticking out of her sleeves,
she's kerosene and sugar.
Barbed wire bent to make an angel. Yeah.
"My partner and I need some help," she purrs.
The boys shrug, this delivery can wait.
Nobody needs them for much today.
Not for a while.

She sits in the back.
They roll some weed,
weigh their chances with her
and ask about this work.

She says it's easy. But, she says,
men have been disappearing from the job.
"Then the work can't be that easy, man." They laugh,
giggling on tokes.
"No, it's easy," she repeats. "And the dividends are nice."
The boys aren't sure what she means,
but yeah, they've got a guess.
She has them pull behind a warehouse.
"Wait here for a minute."
Jorge watches her enter the building,
wondering if the weed is making him this high
or if it's just her doing it to him.
But then his afternoon dreams vanish like a puff of smoke
as a stocky short man strolls out
built like some old fighter, but little.
The man pauses
looks the boys over through the windshield.
Frio weakly waves.
Jorge giggles.
The man sighs a beat and walks toward them.
"You look like weak sons of bitches."
"Hey bro." Jorge shrugs. "We're just here to help."
The two of them, the guy and the girl, stand watching.
The boys move sacks of grain around,
one pile is moved ten feet to make another pile.
There's no truck, no loader.
"Shit bro," Jorge says. "This feels a little less
than pointless."
"You'll get paid," the man says. "That's the point."
Jorge and Frio are soaked through with sweat
by the time they finally kick off.
"Hey," says the man. "You guys are all right,
lemme buy you a beer."
They lead the boys on a fast drive
through a maze of warehouses
and dry cinder block. Left and right, right, right fast.

Rust metal and piles of circuit boards
abandoned to rust, loading flats, smashed lumber.
Left and right, left and left fast
Left then left. Jorge's about to hurl.
The girl is grinning, she likes this ride.
They pull to a stop at another blank warehouse.
One door, no windows,
inside, though, it's cozier, some couches
with the stuffing and springs loose,
an old bar lined with Patron and Tuaca.
Postcards of naked girls on a ranch
litter the dusty mirror
tequila tequila tequila yeah.
The girl doesn't drink but talks
she's a runner she says
she takes care of her body.
The boys size her up again
it all feels good again for a while but
her laugh is a little cockeyed
her eyes dart sideways
and she keeps looking at the guy, her friend,
with something in her eye Jorge can't follow.
He's flooded by booze by then
trying to think, then he's trying
remembering to try
to think.
Space starts wavering and melting even
spinning a bit
Jorge doesn't like it here at all.
He tries to stand but feels woozy.
"I didn't catch your names," says Jorge.
"I'm Ray, that's Sasha."
"Is she your girl?" asks Frio.
Ray doesn't answer, changes the subject.
"I lost three men last week from my crew."
"So I hear," says Jorge, "tough times."

Ray snaps his fingers, "One left, then the next,
then the last. It's got to stop."
"Our crew," she says, looking intently at Ray.
"What?" Ray stops and squints at her,
trying to fathom where she's pushing him, but already pissed.
"You said 'my crew.' It's not your crew. It's our crew."
"Just shut up, you fucking bitch," he says.
"Fuck you. You tiny-cocked motherfucker."
"So, it's like that is it?" he snaps,
quickly pulling out a knife,
the sight of which stirs the boys out of their stupor.
Ray's been drinking as much as any of them and
he comes at her with the blade, swerving.
"I'll take your eye bitch."
She spits at him, then kicks the knife out of his hands.
Ray hold his wrist, "Ow, you cu—"
She punches him in the jaw.
Shit bro, thinks Jorge, these are some dark creatures.
He starts slipping toward the door.
Sleepy-eyed Frio follows behind him.
They've seen enough to know
it's time to leave.
Inching to the exit, eyes glued
as Sasha and Ray
hit and kick and fight each other
with a drunk and exhausting mix of
physical passion and drunken bitterness.
She's giving as good as she's getting,
blow by blow, till one slap spins her vicious face
toward the boys and—like that—she switches, shouting,
"Fuck Ray, they're getting away!"
Ray looks up too and then moves
faster than Jorge can.
Ray's arm is against Jorge's throat,
pressing his head hard against the wall,
so that Jorge can feel the grit of the concrete

grinding against his skull.
Sasha's on Frio, knee on his back, fist full of his hair
pinning him down on the ground.
"What the fuck bro—"
Ray's fist coils back
then black.

Jorge wakes up tied to a board.
His nose is killing him and
there's a bandage on his arm.
He hears Frio weeping over in the shadows.
She comes. Stands over Jorge. Says nothing. Walks away.
So that's what an angel of mercy looks like.
Jorge lies there thinking of school.
How the light comes in through the windows
over the biology class's little plants
and the masking tape with everybody's name on it.
He had a teacher once. Miss Peña.
When he was young and innocent
he wanted her.
That is what he's thinking about
tied to a two-by-four,
trapped in a warehouse
on a Wednesday afternoon.
Boy, he thinks,
I'm going to hell.

III

Peabody's desk phone rings.
Picking it up he thinks
there's a point in your life
when the youthful promise of
every phone call
devolves to a point where
each phone ringing

only inspires an "uh-oh"
or "oh shit" or "what now."
Could be a minor irritation
or it could be something worse,
but odds are that ringing phone
is up to no good.
"Hello?"
"Well, what have you learned?"
Uh-oh.
It's that freaky velvet voice.
"Um, sir, before we go any further,
I have to tell you
there is information you have
that I need
so please identify yourself."
There is a pause, what is that sound?
Coquettish laughter?
"You must watch them, Peabody,
there is something there."
"To be honest, sir, I'm not watching anything.
I'm just not that interested," Peabody quips.
"Why is that? No intrigue? No mystery?"
"I need a reason. I've got other cases."
"I'm sure you've been there."
Peabody's a little miffed. "How are you so sure?"
"Friends in high places. Just go back
and watch them, Peabody. I swear,
you will discover amazing things."
He looks at the clock, sighs. "Honestly,
I'm more interested in you than in them, sir."
"Well, watch them, and once you have learned
what you need to know
then we can talk."
"In person?" Peabody asks, skeptical.
"Oh, I will gladly buy you dinner."
Then, a gentle click.

*   *   *

Peabody makes his rounds the next day.
He wasn't lying to the man, the work is piling up,
Files waiting to be filled, depositions,
old cases to be finished,
and new situations are evolving. Life is like that
it doesn't wait, flows on, buries the living with the dead
unless you somehow stay ahead of it.
He's on the phone questioning an old lady who has a
      story
about her neighbor.
The neighbor was being beaten regularly
then she finally struck back, but in the worst way
taking a curling iron to her boy's flesh.
Hurting the son to injure the father.
A city service person is sent over. It's all true.
The mother is put in lockup. More paperwork.
That's all he sees.
He sits at his desk, his stomach a stewing mix of coffee
and frustration. He calls home, the kid is asleep.
He listens to his wife talk. There's something automatic
about the steps they take together. He teases her a little,
enough to keep it human, not so much as to be romantic.
Because love isn't going to get him home any earlier.
And they can't afford another kid.
Kiss, kiss, I'll be in after you're asleep.
There's something I've got to do first.

He signs out for the night,
he's not telling the station about his next patrol,
after all, the lisp has people watching.
Okay, well, watch this, he thinks,
disappearing into the darkness.

Pulling back into the stakeout block, Peabody parks
farther down than he was before.

Figures he'll sit here for an hour
see if anything "amazing" turns up.
He's unsure how he's going to handle this.
Maybe he'll check in once a week.
Maybe every day.
Maybe it's just a chance to get away from it all,
to quietly pull in somewhere and watch the world go quiet.
He waits. He's got the radio on low
there's a game being played somewhere in the world.
Scanning the stations, there's a man on the radio whose hate
is almost bewildering. The man is complaining about Mexicans.
Mexicans? Why? Really,
in this in-between world, what is a Mexican?
Knock.
Fuck, he didn't see her coming.
Knock knock.
He rolls down the window.
"Hi." Annie smiles. "Are you still looking for Ruiz?"
"Yeah," he says. "I was just coming by to ask."
"But you've been parked here for an hour."
Sometimes, caught in a lie, all you can do is smile.
She smiles back.
"He's not here. He's off in Mexico looking for dogs."
"I thought you said he was in San Diego," Peabody pushes.
"I guess he kept driving. He's unpredictable like that."
Again the big smile. "Why don't you give me your card
and I'll call you when he comes home."
Peabody doesn't really know what to do,
so he sticks to a rule of thumb:
when in doubt, go forward.
He hands her his card as he plays his hand.
"Here you go, ma'am, but to tell you the truth,
I get the feeling he's not coming home."
The smile is still there. Now it is irritating,
the young smile of a girl
who knows the truth

but keeps it tucked in her back pocket.
"Now, why would you think that?" she says,
already stepping away from the car
as Peabody answers, "I dunno, ma'am,
like I said, it's just a feeling.
But, all the same,
I'm going to keep watching you,
and your friends,
for a little while at least."
Stepping into the night she says,
"That's funny, because it seems like
you're the one who's being watched."

Peabody peers into the night
that she has slipped back into.
Looks around at the brightly lit houses
grimaces to himself
and fires up his engine.

This girl
is irritating.

III

Bonnie is beginning to think she's nuts.
It's not a good feeling. Her therapist
is trying to help but
it's the little things, you know,
that can send you around the bend
and you're never sure why.
It's just, well,
something seems off-kilter.
As if someone has moved pictures around
or rearranged the furniture
and everyone is acting like it was always the same.
Good thing she has a dog.

* * *

She named him Buddy and that's what he is,
sitting obediently when she comes home.
He never chews things, never barks, and
brings her the leash when he has to go out.
If it wasn't for him, she really would be nuts.
Her therapist prescribes an antianxiety drug,
which doesn't seem to help, in fact,
she feels even more disoriented.
Now, where did that notebook go?
She thought there was a pencil in that drawer.
She talks to herself going through the house.
Or, to reassure herself that she's not going too batty,
she talks to the dog.
"Oh, Buddy, are we out of yogurt already?"
"A half tank? I just filled it up yesterday."
"Oh Buddy, I thought we had some more ice cream."

Sometimes she thinks reality is only imaginary
and these little lapses are the moments when we see
behind the curtain.
Her therapist changes the prescription and adds
a sleeping aid.
She fills it.

"Oh Buddy." She sighs. "If I only had a boyfriend,
he could tell me I wasn't crazy.
Then again,
I'd probably misplace him too."

She works out, her schedule is fierce,
running in the hills with Buddy on weekends
and early mornings.
Getting rid of that extra tension
hoping to feel grounded again.
But it doesn't work. She wondered if it was Buddy,

though her allergist says not to worry.
Finally, when the disorientation becomes too much—
when she starts hearing echoes of a man's voice
murmuring through the house,
voices her spiritualist says are an old ship captain's
and her Chinese herbalist says are demons of chi—
she finally gives up and
checks herself into a healing ranch
down near Palm Springs.
It's run by raw food enthusiasts who say that
it should only take
two weeks
and five thousand dollars
to put the pieces back together.

She drops Buddy off at her sister's.
Her sister's boys love Buddy.
Ethan, the soccer star, young and
bright as tomorrow
is petting Buddy's coat
as Bonnie pulls out of the driveway.
Wiping a tear out of her eye
she heads off down the road
to something that feels safer.

IV

1 a.m.
a cloud enshrouds
a good idea as
Ethan blows a bong hit
into Lark's face.
"Stupid dog."
Ethan's friend Andrew
uses his fat fingers to fill the bong again,
lights up and sucks in.

"It's two hundred bucks for that bud," says Ethan.
"Deal me in," answers Andrew
looking, as he exhales,
like some strange reptile.

Lark tries to focus
Who am I?
Lark.
Where am I?
I am in Bonnie's nephew's room.
Why am I here?
His thoughts wander.
He knows what the problem is.
He knows it's his own fault.
Shouldn't have finished the yogurt.
Should have put the pencil back.
But there are a million details to manage
and all things considered,
Dragon's shepherd broken shoe gum
Wait, Who am I?
Lark.
Where am I?
I am in Bonnie's nephew's room.
Dr. Dre is playing.
Bonnie will be back in two weeks.
So much work to do,
can't stay here, where
two teenagers rumble in and out
and Dad works late
coming home with the scent
of whiskey and another woman on him.
Lark is the only one who notices.
Then again, the Mrs. cries when she's alone,
listening to Christian radio and
making the mess complete in this
broken empire.

It's not like it was at Bonnie's.
Her sleeping pills gave Lark
the whole night to himself.
And while she was at work
he worked too.
Only sleeping after she came home
lying at her feet
snoring deeply just as we expect
a good dog to do.

Here comes another cloud.
Buzzrot worms candy pillows sea whiskey.
Who Am I?
Lark.
Where am I?
Yellow button rooster traitor

"Stupid dog,"
they chortle.

2 a.m. and Lark is up
still foggy as he slips out the door
wearing Ethan's clothes
and Ethan's cash.
He waits, waits, waits for the bus.
LA public transportation tries the patience.
He winds up sitting with three sleepies
and a black woman who looks angry as hell,
riding the bus at this hour, no doubt she has her reasons.
Lark gets off downtown, rounds some dark blocks
stops at a warehouse building and buzzes.
"Shit man, who is it?"
"Lark, open up."
"Hmmmn." The voice is heavy as a dead man,
but the door is buzzed and Lark rolls in, taking the elevator up
then opening up the doors and turning on lights

in a loft littered with yards of cloth and half-done stitching.
A man comes out of a dark corner room,
squinting at him, "What are you doing here at this hour, bro?"
The guy is heavy, in boxers, no shirt.
The gold chain around his neck says "Tati."
A scar follows a crooked path
from his navel to his left shoulder.
But the way he carries himself,
even sleepy, he's a bear you wouldn't poke at.
"Long time, Tati."
"Yeah, long time." Tati, waking up, smiles
as he watches Lark help himself to the fridge.
"Tati, I'm going to need your car for a while."
"How long?"
"Does it matter?"
Tati's smile wavers. "My car?"
Lark nods as he drinks the water.
Tati was once someone in certain circles
ten years and twenty pounds ago,
but things happened back then
leaving deep scars and comeback debts
that are thicker than blood.
It's all dancing fast across the inside
of Tati's mind right now.
His smile grows again, big and true.
"Sure, man, take the car.
Far as I'm concerned,
it's yours."

Driving out of the city center
Lark sees the sun rising up in the east.
He thinks of her, he thinks of Baron, he thinks of the boys
the fallen and the ones who are still out there
reaching onward toward
the fingers of the coming light.

He pulls up in front of Bonnie's.
He knows the key is in the cactus pot
He knows the security code is 323
He has the computer on.
He has a week till she comes back.
And now he has a car.

One thing that's nice about this town,
just like seeded soil on sunshine days,
LA will blossom for you.
All you need is intelligence, time,
and a solid automobile.

In moments he's found six churches
worth a visit, each one a new age variety
where the lost ones land like dandelion seeds.
He's found a methadone clinic
near the beach, sure to be populated
with souls as empty
as cracked swimming pools,
and he's posted a notice
on an extreme sports site
offering "Self-Reformation,"
a radical technique
for anyone seeking
"discipline, adventure,
and dynamic physical
transformation."
Out of these three paths
he might be able to sew together something
resembling
a somewhat decent pack.

V

Game day.
Cutter and Blue are up, showered fresh
as springtime ducklings, they've even got
ties and church shoes on.
Hair parted like choirboys.
These are the regional finals
goddamn it.
Let's get serious.

The smooth carpet
feels like luxury, the staff
nod and smile as they pass.
It's been a month of generous tipping and
now everyone working here treats them
like champagne kings.

Hitting the tournament room,
Cutter greets Sara Dudley
from the oversight committee.
Blue pours them each a glass
of orange juice from the buffet table
which is overflowing with pineapple, melon,
pastry, and cream. It's all as abundant
as any civilization
could ever hope to be.

They've seen these fellows around here before.
Cutter sizes up Mr. Venable.
The man looks sharp and cagey,
he smells like bay rum and lavender.
The big fellow, Mr. Goyo, wears the same scent.
Cutter wonders what else they share.

Blue looks at them too.
He notices the way Venable's eyes
don't match his smile, eyes warm,
smile cold, eyes alive,
smile dead. Blue doesn't know what this means
and he can't read Goyo any more than
he can read a stone.
But he figures the play of the cards
will say a lot, it always does.

Cutter and Blue have their own conventions.
Their play has mystified
everyone from San Luis Obispo to Laguna Beach.
Their bidding leaps like electricity arcing.
Venable and Goyo have a quieter style.
Cutter can tell that Goyo is the machine.
Venable lets him lead them, Blue can almost smell
the numbers burning in Goyo's mind.

Prim Sara Dudley announces the end of the first session.
It is now eleven thirty.
Cutter and Blue are up, two rubbers to one.
But it's been tough, a battle won by small degrees.
At the coffee station they're huddling, reviewing their hands,
when Venable comes over and interrupts
with some simple words that
throw the entire day
completely upside down.
"I'm sorry," he says,
"to hear about your friends."

Cutter's and Blue's eyes lock, everything stops as
they survey the quiet room.
In other times, the blood would start flowing
but now, there's Sara Dudley checking the cards

as a waiter methodically refills the water pitchers
and Mr. Venable saunters back to his table
to whisper in Goyo's ear.
Cutter's hand goes to Blue's shoulder.
"Let's finish the game," he says.
"The guy could just be fucking with us."
Fires devouring mountains inside him
need to be quenched. Soon.
But first, there are cards
to be played.

Predictably the next rubber goes poorly.
For the good part of the early afternoon,
their rhythm is off.
It's as if Cutter and Blue are trying to communicate
through rusty, broken radios.
Cards fall uselessly on the table,
as hand after hand fall dead beneath
the engine of the big fellow's mind.
It churns on as Venable hums concertos,
his game gaining
the sort of momentum
that has always helped the assured
crush the confused.
Blue can't hear anything but his heartbeat
while Cutter has flashes of the past, the pack
Lark, Baron, Con, the girl, Bone, Zack, the rest.
Aces are seizing the tricks,
and tricks are slipping away like time.
Cutter just wants to change now and run out
all the strength in his bones.
Run past the concierge.
Run down the street.
Run into the hills.
Run to the lakes and rivers where the pack
would find the peace that comes away from the city.

Where these animals all once ran,
where they belonged,
together.
His concentration is shattered, his eyes filling with tears.
And then he goes for the one strategy that might just
buy him some time.
He falls hard to the floor and closes his eyes.

In the banquet room's bathroom
Blue throws water on his own face
while Cutter breathes deep.
"I haven't thought about them," he says.
Blue crouches down to where Cutter is sitting
on the gray tile floor, beneath the fluorescent
     lights.
"I know. But now, we just need to win."
"Why?" asks Cutter.
"Because Lark told us to."
Then they do something they have never done.
They reach out and hold one another, embracing
like brothers.

Five minutes later, they emerge
and engage.
They grit their teeth and
gnaw through the rest of the day
feinting and thrusting while
defeat ebbs away
like the end of a red tide.
"We are wolves," Cutter chants
in his mind.
"We don't find the weak. We
don't prey on the slow.
We simply eat absolutely
fucking everything."
The answer is literally there

in the cards.
If you were watching
you would see four men
playing classical music
with nothing but cards for an orchestra
and, in the end,
Cutter and Blue's song
is just a little bit sweeter.

Sara Dudley and the other associates
present the boys with their check.
There is a picture taken for *Bridge Monthly*.
As Venable and Goyo rise, Venable extends his hand.
"We should play again," he says, smiling.
"Yes. Soon," Cutter replies, shaking
the man's small, soft hand. "Let's do that very soon."
"Why don't you come to my suite tonight?" Venable grins
with all the confidence of a sure winner,
leaving Cutter to wonder exactly what he's won.
"Yeah, okay." Cutter is
exhausted, curious, and hungry.
"We'll see you there."

VI

Frio and Jorge have been beaten bloody
every day. Waking up
sometimes in rooms filled with men
other times they rise in rooms
filled with barking, snarling dogs,
teeth bared with growling wet spit
spraying out onto
the boys' cowering bodies.
Ray feeds them meat stew
and offers cryptic advice:
"The change is in you, boys."

"The power comes from within."
"There is your destiny, take it."
Then the men come from behind.
The boys raise their arms but the
blows persist, raining down again and
again till the blackness returns.

One morning, the beatings are coming down,
as they always do—like cruel, unrelenting storms—
Frio and Jorge have their backs to the concrete wall, they are
struggling, shouting, begging, crying
when there is a new sound, a strange one.
Jorge turns to see Frio's
eyes squeezed shut. A gurgling, growling noise is
coming out of his guts as he bows over.
Jorge thinks, that's it, he's dead.
But Frio's body trembles and then
in a wild spasm, his flesh starts to
swell, bulging pink and raw.
Frio's eyes flare with panic as his bones shift
beneath the changing skin, he reaches for his friend's hand
but finds his fingers curving in, as bone yields to claw.
Jorge screams now too, high pitched and unrestrained
he shakes with fear as
furred needles puncture Frio's face and arms.
Angry teeth and pointed snout mouth and eyes that hold
nothing familiar.
His clothing is torn as his body, in thrusts and jerks,
reshapes itself down to all fours.
Jorge screams louder. Frio barks back.

The men step back now
and bend down,
beginning their own dark change.
Within moments Jorge is surrounded by
a room full of angry dogs.

* * *

As Jorge leans against the wall,
the sound of his heart beating in fear
almost drowns out the barking of the dogs
who stare up at him with knowing eyes.
Frio is no different from the rest of them.
Jorge breathes deep and tastes vomit in his throat.
The door is unbolted and Ray enters.
He's holding a .44 and the barrel
quickly finds its way
to the side of Jorge's head.
"You've seen the change," Ray growls.
"You've seen the destiny.
Either find it within, man,
or accept the end."
The steel is so real
as Jorge inhales his fear
and screams a new sound
that can only be called
a howl.

VII

Reading the paper, she scans an article
while hummingbirds outside drink with their
insatiable, jittery thirst
compulsively sucking the nectar
from the violet curling petals.
Anthony turns the pages of the sports section.
She smiles because she loves his every motion.
She's never felt it quite like this,
where the love runs so deep
and plays out as simple
as any child's game.
She turns back to her paper,
reading in the lifestyle pages about

how some psychologists believe
a few hidden secrets
can actually help the average relationship.
Yes, it's true, they say, surprisingly
the stupid drunken office kiss, a love sonnet from a neighbor,
an in-law's sloppy groping
during dinner's dish clearing,
these can all be buried happily beneath
the small and constant waves
of studious devotion until eventually
it is all simply
carried out to sea.
Yes, it turns out,
the open, completely honest relationship
may be as much of a myth
as unconditional love itself.
Even one good-size secret, these scientists say,
even an affair that rises and then falls within a few seasons
even this won't rock the foundation
if the foundation is granite strong.
As she reads, her foot plays with her bag beneath the chair.
She has three cell phones in there
each wiped clean of the blood.
The owners have left the world,
their pain ended,
screams silenced
and much of what they ever were
is now buried within her.
The pack is drying up like a puddle in the heat
and she is as unforgiving and uncaring as the sun.

She is merely killing the spiders
as she always does
whenever she sweeps out the house.

She drives to the ocean with Anthony once a week

they swim and kick high against the waves,
his boyish smile ear to ear as
she hears laughter that's so loud and full
she doesn't even recognize it
as her own.
This is love.
And now here in this morning,
this is love.

She looks up at Anthony,
thinking how, if he knew,
if he had any idea,
then the soil of her Eden
would be ripped away
leaving her alone
on this unforgiving rock.
The secret must stay
and—according to the scientists—
the love will live.
The heart is quite comfortable with secrets.
After all, its home is a dark wet place
tucked in among all the other organs
who aren't talking either.

She smiles, touches his toe
with hers.

The idle morning trickles on, pages of the paper turn
until a crime scene photo
leaves her thinking about her own recent acts.
They were all so stupid,
these weren't victims, they were fools.
Why do they go out solo?
Who's running that damn pack?
Lark would never let his men go out alone
unless it was undercover

but each one she has called has appeared
as lone as a lost lamb.
They think they are strong, after all
they have guns in their pockets,
but bare teeth to an arm slow
a gun's progress considerably.
Cocky men's eyes grow bald with fear
when their flesh is torn open
and they face
their weakness.

Tomorrow she knows
the tactics will have to change
her luck has held three times
and as Lark has always said,
luck is stupid as a cow
and as blind as a bat.

What would you do
to protect the love you have?
Would you kill?
Would you hunt to kill?
Would you kill without mercy?
And if you wouldn't
then how precious is your love?

She comes around the table
and straddles Anthony's lap,
he laughs, still trying to read his paper as
she smiles and lifts her shirt.
Within a few simple, fevered beats
his lips are tasting the salt of her skin
while she grabs a handful of his hair
and holds him tight.
Later, think later,
for now there is only this moment

his hands, his body
and limbs stretch, muscles expand
as his breathing reaches
deep within her.

The heart is a bloody thing.

VIII

Peabody turns onto the block
ready for another night of the endless stakeout.
Watching the nothing unfold, as his partner used to say.
Twelve slow nights.
He's about to switch off the ignition when he sees the dog
trotting down the street
cock of the walk, so self-assured.
It looks like the one back at Calley's.
Peabody coasts just behind,
ready to throw the beast in the back of the car
drive it to animal control
and wait to see who shows up.
Suddenly the dog stops
looks back over its shoulder
and stares into Peabody's eyes
with an absolute directness.
Peabody slows the car even further,
pulling over to the curb
stepping out slowly, leaving the motor
running. No sudden moves but then
bam, the dog is off and running
tearing across the twilight green lawn
and leaping nimbly over a low fence.
"Fuck." Peabody jumping into a run,
chasing a damned dog, trespassing
and digging up turf with every step
sure that some irate citizen is looking out

and calling 911 right now.
He vaults the fence with less grace than the dog
and races between the dry stucco walls of houses
pushing through colored sheets of clotheslines
and rushing out onto the next street
just in time to
meet the full speed
of an oncoming car.

Barely conscious, Peabody lies splayed on the pavement.
The dog sits beside him.
The driver of the car gets out, the passenger too,
they carefully lift him into the back of the station wagon.
The driver whistles, the dog licks the driver's face twice and
jumps in the back.
Off they go.

When Peabody opens his eyes it is night and
they are driving up the interstate.
To his tumbled mind
it seems the stars have spilled out of the sky
to roll across the highway.

Waking again, he first sees the girl
leaning in through the open hatch of the wagon.
"Don't get up, you've been hurt."
He begins to move but a sharp
searing pain reminds him she's right.
"Where am I?" he asks.
"Zuma Beach. We just wanted to get some waves in."
"Why didn't you take me to a hospital?"
"Oh silly." She leans over and kisses his cheek.
Her breath smells sweet and honeyed.
She leaps up, pulls a board from the roof of the car
and runs across the darkened beach.

Peabody sits up to watch her slip into the sleek waters
and makes out, glinting across the surface,
two other figures sliding between the waves and the night.
Then he leans back, closes his eyes,
sucks in all his curiosity
and rests.

When he wakes up again he is in the small room of a cabin,
where a woodstove is kicking out heat.
In front of him sits a glass of water and
across from him a one-eyed Hispanic man.
"You looking for Emilio Ruiz?" the man says.
Peabody doesn't even register the name at first.
"Who?" he asks.
"Emilio Ruiz? Annie says you're looking for me."
"Oh yeah." He sips the water and tries to clear his thoughts.
"Who sent you to look for me?" The man's bright eye gleams.
"I don't know. A lead," says Peabody.
"A lead? What is this? What bullshit are you talking man.
I'm busy, I haven't got time for this shit. Hey!" Ruiz bangs the
    wall with a stick.
"Hey, get this guy outta here!"
"Relax, relax." Peabody tries his best to do the same. "I'm looking
into some things down at the pound."
"The dog pound?" Ruiz's good eye has a strange glint to it.
"Look," says Peabody, as the pain shoots across his spine
and down his leg, "I think I need a doctor."
"Shit," mumbles Ruiz, banging on the wall. "He needs a doctor!"
No response.
"You know a guy who sounds like a princess?" Peabody asks.
The one-eyed man says nothing,
stares at the wall he's been beating.
"You know anyone down at the pound?" Peabody asks.
"Nope. But I bought some dogs from the pound once."
"Really? Do you remember who you bought them from?"

The man smiles ruefully to himself. "I don't know. It doesn't
     matter.
I bought the dogs and the dogs became my redemption."
This man is talking crazy, thinks Peabody,
which sparks a question.
"How do I know you're Ruiz?"
Ruiz stares at him. "You really a cop?" he asks.
"Yes," says Peabody, finishing the water.
"Then why don't you just ask for some fucking ID," says Ruiz,
throwing a wallet across to him. With that motion disclosing
the fact that he has only one arm.
The license is legit, with a younger and brighter Ruiz
staring into the DMV's camera. Even then though
he looked like a man daring the world
to tear into him.
Apparently he got his wish.
Peabody throws the wallet back, asking
"Why haven't you been home?"
Ruiz counts the three dollars in the billfold before
putting it away. "I've been traveling,
working with some other dogs."
"Someone said you raise them to fight."
Ruiz looks up quickly. "Oh no, no." He shakes his head.
"No, I used to, I used to, fought 'em into the dirt,
but the last fight dogs I bought were those ones
I got from the pound. I'll tell you,
those guys sold me some beasts."
Ruiz studies the ground before going on.
"So now, I just take care of the dogs.
Any dogs that come here, I baby."
He pounds on the wall again, yelling
"I Baby Them!"
Peabody is tired of being stuck in this muddle of riddles.
He's having trouble with his eyesight to boot.
And, it seems,
his mouth and his mind

have stopped working together.
"Who are the girl?" he asks,
trying to shake off the fogginess. Thinking,
has he been drugged or was it the accident?
"Who is the girl?" Ruiz corrects, looking at the fading cop.
"Yes, who is the girl?" The room keeps shifting and
changing angles on Peabody. He squints to focus.
"Oh, Annie," says Ruiz, smiling,
happy to keep feeding him puzzle pieces as he falls.
"She used to work for me
but now I work for her."
Every star explodes bright in Peabody's brain
before the darkness returns.

When he wakes
he's looking at an albino nurse
in the city hospital.
There's a blue uniformed cop standing next to her.
The two of them look to Peabody
like the earth and the sky
in a snapshot.
"Your friends dropped you off, Peabody."
"What friends?"
"ER said it was a girl and two of her buddies."
"How long have I been out for?"
"Three days. But you were missing before that."
"How long was I missing for?"
"Two days."
"Jesus. Where's my wife?"
"She just went to get some coffee and a snack for your boy.
Don't worry, she'll be back soon."
There is a pause, the nurse adjusts the pillow,
the cop struggles to keep eye contact with Peabody.
But Peabody's head is spinning again,
seems like the gyroscope won't ever wind down.
"What can you tell me about your friends?" asks the cop.

Peabody looks at the man, tight in his uniform
Peabody thinks about the girl on the beach.
He thinks about odd Ruiz in that locked room,
handicapped and cocky with an almost wild pride.
And the surfers riding waves in the night.
Back to the lisping man on the phone.
Back to Calley eating the gun.
Back to the dog on the road.
"Friends," the cop had said.
The word reminds Peabody of the times when
he's trying to make up the guest bed for visiting friends
staying late after dinner and too drunk to drive,
how he turns the sheets this way and that,
upward and backward,
trying to get the ends aligned, searching for the right corners.
That's where he is with this case now.
"They're not my friends."
"Well, what happened, Peabody. Was it a kidnapping?"
Peabody keeps his mouth shut,
holding on to the leads and clues
like a child clutching his marbles.
He doesn't know why he holds back.
Maybe fear of a leak in the office
finding its way to the lisping man's ear.
Maybe because he thinks no one else has the bones
to work this case but him.
But, honestly, thinks Peabody, it's probably
just pride.
Talking about it now would only unravel
this strange ball of string
while holding on could bring him a good case,
a case that's his and his alone.
If his gut is right, this is something big.
So maybe he just doesn't want to share.
He didn't think his ego was like that.
He thought he was honest. The good cop.

But then again, he thinks,
even Jesus caught his own reflection
now and then.
He tilts his head back, "I don't know anything."
"Really?" The cop cocks his head like some curious rooster.
"Yeah. That's what I'm saying. Last thing I remember
I was sitting in my car eating a bag of Fritos.
Now could you go find my wife?"
Peabody exhales, avoids the cop's unswerving gaze.
The room's already empty as far as he's concerned.
"Oh yeah . . . ," says the cop
somehow still there, still blue, bringing him back
into the bleak light of the hospital room
and dosing him full of reality
with one last piece of news.
" . . . thought you should know,
somebody torched your car."
And all Peabody can think is,
"Okay, what next?"

IX

Lark is driving.
He's got one day before Bonnie gets back.
He looks across at his passenger.
The kid looks like he's about three weeks past
being a good kid.

Lark found him hustling.
This kid, Jason, has A.D.D. which makes the hypnotic
drawl Lark has used so effectively in the past
difficult to say the least.

"Jason, let me ask you something. Do you
want a taste of real power?
The kind of power no man is ever truly prepared for?

The sort of power that rearranges the whole world just for you?"
"Yes," says the kid, "Power, yeah, power, and, um, Starburst.
You got some Starburst?"
Trying again, a few blocks later,
"Have you ever longed for a place that was all your own?
Have you ever wanted friends who would die for you, Jason?
Do you know what it's like to live by your own rules,
not the rest of the world's, do you know what that's like?"
"Yeah," says Jason. "And you know what kind of popcorn I
    like?"
In the end, the kid seemed both relieved and disbelieving
when Lark told him he wasn't paying him for sex.
"I just want to talk."
"Boy, I gotta tell you,
therapy's not really my game," said the kid.
But he came along just the same, hoping
for the things we all hope for,
Snickers, Starburst, M&M's.

Lark's last pack was easier to build
hanging out near the VA
watching for young GIs, fresh out,
unemployed and jonesing for discipline.
But he can't go back there
wherever his old pack is now
there's a fine chance they're
pulling in their fresh troops
exactly the same way, assembling a new army,
watching and waiting
for Lark to show.

So Lark's playing a new game
working with material like
Jason, the hustler
Marco, the recovered addict
Eric, the failed real estate agent

Arturo, the evangelist
and a young man named Bunny
who seems fit enough
but is given to dancing beneath streetlights
to the rhythm of
burning man flashbacks and smooth entrancing beats.

Lark and Jason pull up to the house,
a Silver Lake ramble where
rooms spill into rooms
and the slant of the floors
hint at the unsettled faults below.
"Come on in, let's talk." says Lark.
"Do you have any orange soda?" the kid asks.
"Maybe, Jason, let me check the fridge."

The others are all sleeping,
Lark's been running them through the paces at night
which leads to sleepy days, only rising for carbs
and the rigor of more training.
As they pass by one room
Jason's young eyes dart in
to find Bunny lying next to Maria, the new girl,
her bare breasts spilling out from beneath the covers.
Jason forgets about the orange soda for a moment.
His attention snaps back when Lark says,
"You want to play a game?"
Now Jason's ready, he's played these games before
with bankers and movie people and men whose odd tastes
and sometimes cruel needs
befuddled even Jason's simple philosophy.
Three months on the street and not a single game was fun.
"Yeah, sure," he says dejectedly, starts taking off his shoes
preparing for the pain and worse, the loneliness.
"No, no, sit down, grab that console," Lark says sternly.
Jason, confused, lifts a prehistoric plastic device from the couch

while Lark turns on an old Panasonic TV.
"Ever heard of Pong, Jason?"

The theory is simple.
Every boy, every man, is really
a bit of a golden retriever
or a big chocolate lab.
Watch any man's eyes
at the bounce of a ball.
His head tilts slightly sideways, just a hair,
as a primitive focus
comes to life.

Follow the ball.

The basketball, the tennis ball, the baseball,
the golf ball, the lacrosse ball, or in this case
the mere symbol of a ball, a plain white dot,
floating across a dull, black screen.
And just like that, the pupils sharpen their gaze.
The game begins.

Stay with the ball, follow the ball.

The mind opens there, a psychological soft spot,
where reason's stubborn persistence fades
and some underbelly is exposed.

Just follow the ball, stay with the ball.

"Jason . . . ," Lark says carefully,
sending the electronic dot sliding across
the electronic net, " . . . have you ever felt
like you were somehow
different?"

X

Let's go back to that bedroom.
Lying there, naked, sleeping
resting as fully as a ship sunk in the sand,
there lies Maria.

This girl is the third Lark has had
in a pack of his own.
There was the first girl, who died in a story
so sad no one speaks of it.

Then there is the second girl
gone now from the pack
but very alive in their minds.
Only Lark knows where she can be found,
at home with the dogcatcher
sleeping by her side.

And then there's the new girl.

Some people say Maria
is the most beautiful word in the world.
That's what her mother would say
braiding her hair before church.
And that's what her father would say
as he crawled between her sheets.
The world, as a result, turned backward
where blossoms buried themselves while
roots reached like starving fingers
to the gray and fruitless sky.
And love was hate and the touch
of what she ever wanted poisoned.

* * *

The first time a boy her own age tried to kiss her,
a boy she adored,
she scratched and wept and ran.
Her father had grown bored or felt guilty but in any case
had stopped but by then it was far too late,
her body was anger, her blood laced with glass
shredding at every vein and ventricle as it ran through
in the years of haunted silence.
Nobody knew.
Nobody saw.
Welcome to Gesso Copy Mart.
Open 6 a.m. to 9 p.m.

She's the one laughing just enough,
she's the one not giving anything away with her eyes.
Her every gesture is a perfect cold lie.
Lark had come in for some leaflets he was putting up
in church cellars and community halls.
He saw her face.
Read her expression.
So he came back, Xeroxing things he'll never need.
Talking. Small questions, launched softly into the air.
Talking.
Waiting.

Maria was different from the last girl.
That girl was hurt and wide open
when he found her
hiding behind her tears on Abbott Kinney.
But Maria was more guarded.
He could sense her quietly looking
for the tender spot,
the place where she could reach in
and tear the heart
out of the world.

* * *

He walked with Maria,
across a town that hates walking.
He spoke carefully,
assembling the words that always worked,
describing a new way of life,
one that gives the powerless power
and lets them leave the past behind.
The simple desires.
As they walked by strip malls and gun shops,
low-cost dentists and gentlemen's clubs,
and the cough of traffic whirled around them,
petal by petal, he peeled away the locked bud
of her anger. She said nothing
but her eyes flashed and her moods boiled
then passed, hints of storms that never broke.
She mumbled, "I don't understand what you're saying."
But her eyes suggested she wanted something to be there.
He said, "You know, whoever hurt you
dies every time they look in the mirror.
That is how they pay."
She crossed her arms.
"And one day, Maria, you will die too,
but there's no reason for you to die
every day."

He needed a girl, plain and simple.
Nothing else will hold a pack together.
But he wasn't sure what he was unleashing
into the wilds with this one.
It all burned so deep for her.
At dusk, sitting on a bus stop bench,
he said, "Tell me when you're ready to change."
She watched the sun drown in
a cauldron of clouds.
For the first time, she took his hand
and, leaning over,

whispered in his ear,
"I'm ready now."

That is the new girl.
Lark has let her define the discipline.
He prefers the Ukan way,
a path they say
traces back to the Native Americans
of the north. The Ukan rule is simple,
abstain, and ride the tension.
But he can't be there to guide the new pack,
he can't write all the rules,
he can only provide a rough map.
She prefers leading by enticement,
rewarding the dog who serves the pack best.
It gives her the power and she likes calling the shots.
Curling up with Marco, sweating nights with Bunny,
making them work for her, to Lark's ends,
making the pack work her way to Lark's destination,
sealing her flesh
to the chosen one of the moment.
It's not a path Lark knows.
But, as he watches Bunny juggling four eggs
on the front lawn,
Lark thinks to himself there are no rules anymore
there's only the ever constant
law of evolution
become what is or you will be
what is not.
And while you're at it
keep on living true to
the lines of the old children's story,
that still echo in your memory.
Go dog go.

* * *

He checks his watch,
it's time to head back to Bonnie's.
And he drives away
Bunny is still juggling.

XI

This day for Anthony
begins just fine as he
kisses her sleeping, naked back then
shower coffee radio news drive.

It's his turn to be in early
and he's the first one to hit the cages,
humming with a fine attitude.
He turns on the lights
only to find something
he sure doesn't see every day:

a naked man
lying amid the dogs.
Anthony observes him resting there,
beat to hell and fast asleep.
He looks so peaceful.

Anthony dials 911, they say
is the guy breathing?
His breathing is fine. So 911 says
it was a busy night
chill out, take a number, we'll be there.
Anthony gets a first aid kit.
Smelling salts wake the stranger
whose eyes flit around the room.
The man starts to get up but the motion
of the earth pulls him down, he takes a queasy stumble.

"Relax, the paramedics are on their way."
With that, the man is up hard
and it takes a bolt of strength from Anthony
to hold him down.
"Sit there, buddy, I have some questions."
The stocky little man pushes back, straining,
even craning his neck
trying to bite at the dogcatcher.
Anthony shoves him down
almost yelling now,
"You'd better fucking cut that out."
The man goes slack.
"How did you get in here?"
The little man sighs. "I dunno. I drank a lot
must have been the butt of
some kind of dumb-ass prank."
"Okay well, tell it to the cops,"
the thought of which sets the man's eyes darting
like lost minnows in a fierce current,
he's vibrating desperation,
but Anthony holds him tight.
"What's your name, buddy?"
The little guy makes one more jolt for freedom,
twisting loose and starting to run
before Anthony performs a simple leg sweep
taking the guy down again.
Anthony leans over, puts his knee into the stranger's back,
and—grabbing a handful of hair—
he pushes the man's face
against the cold concrete floor.
"Look, I should probably mention,
I'm trained in martial arts,
so there's not much point in even trying to run.
Just answer my question.
What's your name?"
The little man lies there,

wincing, bitter,
and tonguing a loose tooth.
"Ray," he says. "My name is Ray."

XII

Back in the bunker, curled up next to Frio,
Jorge thinks about the last two days.
His tail slaps steadily against the floor
beating out the rhythm
of what went down.

They told him it was supposed to be cut-and-dried,
a milk run for him and Frio.

First the Econoline loaded up.
Ray drove, hunched over like
a man with nothing good on his mind.
Sasha rode shotgun, her black hair pulled back,
her mood as dark as ever.
The rest of the crew jammed into the rear seats.
Jorge thought the van was like a dark pistol
and they were the bullets inside.
The other dogs had told Jorge about these runs.
They'd hit forcefully. Clean out the speed labs. Cause some pain.
The only ones in the pack who knew why they did this
were Sasha and Baron and Ray.

Sometimes, it was said, survivors were left,
badly maimed
but with just enough of a mouth
to tell.

Jorge had said good-bye to his mom
the night before.
Calling on the pay phone,

he said he'd shipped out,
"Good money in Iraq, Mom.
Relax, relax, don't cry . . .
Frio and me, we hooked up solid."
But she cried on and on until
Ray reached past Jorge
and clicked the phone dead just like
the executioner flicking the switch.
The receiver was passed to Frio.
He dialed. His mother cried too.
Walking away from the phone
Jorge sucked it up. "Fuck it," he thought.
"I'm a superhero now."

The van was on the road for a while,
coming up from the docks.
The sinking sun shone through
the windshield,
bathing them
in a sea of raw gold.
A row up from Jorge,
sitting ramrod straight, with a newborn confidence,
Frio wore the sunset like a shimmering warrior
all painted for battle.
They passed one familiar exit after another
and Jorge thought
of the hours of his life spent on these freeways
zooming with a smile on his face
off to theme parks and cousins' houses,
barbecues and french fries and other ice cream destinations.
It felt like all that had happened
somewhere else to someone else,
someone as far away now
as the vanishing sun.

They exited the freeway and pulled

into a neighborhood
just east of Huntington Park.
Ray slung the van up a drive and shut off the engine.
He pointed to Frio and Penn and said,
"After you change, hit the back of the house,
and be ready to rush."
Two others were chosen to watch the side.
Sasha and Jorge were to go with Ray,
while the one named Otto was left guarding the car.
Ray and Otto waited while the rest stripped out of their clothes,
T-shirts and jeans stashed beneath the van's seats
as the change began. Midway through his own change,
Jorge was hit with that scent again,
the one that was growing familiar,
the odor of smoldering wood and wet mold.
They'd told him it only bothered him
'cause he was young, a pup still.
Of all the dogs, he finished his change last,
yowled quietly,
stretched his legs
in the narrow space between the seats.
The whole van was a pent-up kennel, ready to burst.
Finally when things felt quiet enough,
Ray hopped out and opened the back.
Everyone darted to their spots,
adrenaline high and footfalls silent.
The house was cheap stucco.
Ray went up the steps and rang the bell,
Sasha and Jorge at attention by his knees.
Everyone had seen the diagrams, this was clockwork.
"Follow my lead," Sasha had told Jorge the night before,
pointing to chalk marks sketched out on the wall
that loosely resembled football plays.
So now there they were, the big game, and even when
the house's one light went out,
Jorge wasn't worried.

The door opened just
a crack. "Yeah?" the crack whispered
like a puff of smoke.
"Lucifer sent me," said Ray.
"You know Lucifer?" The voice was almost a hum.
"Yeah, lemme in," said Ray, rocking himself
ready for action. He was like that, one of those pop-pop
    firecrackers
you throw against the pavement.
Sasha sat back, suddenly relaxed
and cool in the moment, so cool
that Jorge relaxed too and sat down on the porch,
casually following her lead.
Perched there, ears forward, they followed the exchange.
Ray's voice was tense, buzzing with nervousness, "Come on
    man."
"You wanna come in?" the crack asked.
"Yeah, that's what I said, fuck!" shouted Ray.
Then he kneed the door, hard, so it burst open
revealing nothing but the pitch-blackness inside.
This was the moment they were supposed to rush forward
but Jorge was watching Sasha,
and she hadn't moved.
Ray was expecting Sasha to jump in too, that was the plan,
and as he looked down at her in confusion,
the voice inside said,
"So come on in."
Four hands reached out from the house,
grabbed Ray by his shirtsleeves
and sucked him into the dark, slamming the door behind.
All the while Sasha sat there motionless.

Ray's shouts and cries and yelps
bled through the cracks in the stucco,
Sasha turned and trotted back to the van.
Jorge followed her lead.

*　*　*

They sat in the van with Otto,
looking into the dark house.
The other dogs soon
trotted back from their stations,
all of them
except Penn.
They waited.
Jorge sniffed at the cool air through the open window.
He couldn't hear Ray moaning anymore.
But even at that distance,
he could smell Ray's pain.

Rules are rules and plans are plans.
So at the prearranged time, with Penn still missing,
and Ray still in the house,
Otto put the van into drive
and off they drove.

Jorge lay in the back bench wondering
why Sasha didn't make a move.
Why did she let them take Ray like that?
Mysteries were never his thing
the end of Scooby-Doo was always a surprise.
So whatever, they came here as six men and a woman
they left as one man driving three dogs and a bitch.
Who is Jorge to say why?
He licked his balls and waited for orders.

Back at the warehouse, not a word was said,
Sasha didn't even make the change
just slipped in through the door.
Jorge hit the bunk for a nap.
Exhaling like only a dog can do.
He had about ten minutes curled up before
all the lights popped on bright

pans were banged, yelling, a dog nipped his tendon.
They were all rousted to the main hall,
an old storage space that reminded Jorge of
a cargo hold on some TV spaceship.
Half the crowd was dog,
the other half men,
all looking up
at Sasha who now stood next to Baron.
Jorge waited for Sasha to speak and explain,
but it was Baron who stepped forward.
"Listen. Listen!" yelled Baron. "You want to listen!"
Jorge had never heard him speak
and was struck by the gravity in his tone.

"Listen. Ray is gone. I'm here to tell you this.
Ray is gone and he's not coming back."
There was little reaction in the room.
They all sat and waited for the future to arrive, as it tends to.
"I am taking over this pack. Right now.
If anyone chooses to challenge, as is his right
by the rules of the clan
you have three days. Announce your challenge
and I will fight you fair, one on one. But attack me
as I move through these halls
and my old clan will take you."
Baron paused to let this threat sink in.
"If I am still leader
after those three days, if you let me stand,
we will talk and we will plan
our path, our strategy,
our way against our uncertain enemies and our
certain victory.
And, yes, do not doubt me, do not doubt this,
our victory will be a sure one.
More sure and more certain than the seasons of the year."
He paused again and put his arm gently around Sasha.

The rest of what he said was lost on Jorge
for at that moment Jorge was watching
Penn, the man they had left
at the dark house who now
stood just behind Baron, eyeing the crowd.
And then Jorge knew,
Sasha. Penn. Baron.
They had hatched and
they had schemed and
most importantly of all,
they had won.

Meeting adjourned. Back to the bunk.
Everyone slept fine.
Some coup d'états
are kinda like that.
Exhale, unwind, and sleep Jorge
'cause here comes the dream
of the bunny rabbit.

XIII

Peabody is at his desk.
Thoughts of a honeyed blonde in San Pedro
and an angry one-armed man in a shack
keep tugging at his mind.
He looks at the picture of his wife and boy,
thinks of how good it feels every day to come home
and have that wave of love
cascade over him,
how that goodness lifts him up.
But the blonde slips into his thoughts again
like some sugar sap dripping from a tree far above.
He hasn't returned to San Pedro since he got out of the hospital.
He's thinking maybe life's too short
for a case that wasn't a case at all

just some strange dogs and a lisping whisper
over a distant phone line.
He reaches to pull the picture of his wife closer.
"Hey, I found Ruiz," he thinks. "That's all I wanted to do."
He remembers Ruiz banging and yelling out the door.
Who was out there?
Where was he?
In any case, he doesn't need any more questions.
He's got a pin in his leg
and, mulling over Ruiz's arm,
or the lack thereof,
Peabody finds himself thinking
that maybe he got off easy.

"Hey, Peabody!" Moxie calls across the room
the guy has a Kojak lollipop in his mouth
and an ear to the phone.
"Weren't you looking into something at the pound?
I got someone on the line says they got a John Doe there."
Peabody itches his back.
"Living or dead?"
"Well, they took him to lockup for assault and trespassing,
so I'm figuring the guy's got at least a little life in him.
Though they're saying the dogcatcher,
um, an Anthony Silvo,
had to kick the living shit out of the fellow
just to keep him down."

You either trust or you distrust coincidence.
It's either small doses of magic pulling
you to your appointed destiny
or the devil trying to lead you
down to the thorns.
Peabody has no way to know this,
but there is an old lycanthrope legend that got it all right.
The story goes that the universe is run by two simple things,

a prime mover and a coyote.
This coyote is a wily dog born
from ancient trickster bones,
Loki, Hermes, the northwestern Raven of lore,
all glimmer in his aluminum eyes.
And while
the prime mover makes
the world simply by
dreaming of its own dreaming
spanning all, shaping all,
the coyote mostly sleeps,
his chin to the ground, one ear perked up,
his body resting in the shade of the prime mover's infinity.
Coyote awakens at something like the smell of bacon
and trots across the kingdom of heaven
hopping down into the world,
sniffing for mischief.
And as the prime mover contemplates
the contemplation that therefore spawns existence,
and time passes without passing,
the coyote sprightly follows the dusty trail back home,
where he dances around the prime mover
eagerly barking and yipping and telling tales
of coincidence wrought, good luck won,
bad luck earned, loose ends that were somehow connected,
all thanks to this little mischief mutt:
the longed-for lover shows up at the bus stop,
the ex-roommate appears with the missing keys,
the thought of a distant friend sails across the mind
just as she strolls by the café window.
"Hey, what are you doing here?" a happy voice sings.
The winning lottos made of birthday numbers,
postcards sent to the dead letter office
that still somehow deliver meaning,
wrong number callers who somehow fall in love,
and the ragged luck of pulling an inside straight

on a last chip on a last bet on a last day.
Coyote wags his tail and brags:
of the taxicab pulling up at the first raindrop,
the wrong turn leading to a better place,
the guilty soul arrested for a different crime,
the critical ally sighted through the ancient hotel's
revolving doors in some faraway destination.
"Hey, what are you doing here?" a voice happily sings.

All this vibrates and shimmers
around coyote as he makes his way
connecting the wonder moments,
for good or for ill
and coming home to tell his story,
wagging, grinning, barking.

But the prime mover simply
revolves on in silence
deaf to everything
moving like a whale
swimming through the
endless blue seas of
its own deep and infinite dream.

Peabody knows nothing of this fable,
and if he heard it, would shake it off and return
to the last words that resembled anything like sense to him.
Though, really, the last words made no sense at all,
" . . . they're saying the dogcatcher,
um, an Anthony Silvo,
had to kick the living shit out of the fellow . . ."
And Peabody wonders what the heck is going on
down there at the city pound.

Putting on his jacket
he checks his pocket for his keys,

relieved to know that where he's going
holds just enough mystery
to keep the sugar blonde
out of his mind.
At least
for a little while.

XIV

"This is a violent city
and I don't mean rapes and bloodshed.
I mean the existence of every ounce of it.
This entire vast urbanity was bludgeoned from the earth,
torn and wrought,
piece by piece. A thousand bricks.
A thousand tiles.
The concrete and the steel girders
all bitten out of the soil and the rock.
Then, of course, it's brought here,
to the desert, to death itself.
Not to mention the water, oh yes, the water
pilfered from hundreds of miles away,
where birds and tree roots awoke one bleak day
reaching for moisture once easily known
and now finding only empty dust,
because that moisture's all been pulled here, to be with us
shimmering in the sweat of porn stars
cleaning the endless stream of dirty cars
washing the hands of plastic surgeons
after they've performed
yet another critically important implant."
Venable falls silent and gazes out
the limousine's window.
Goyo says nothing.
Cutter and Blue say nothing.
They've been riding with Venable for a few weeks now

playing cards and watching his back,
long enough to know
these odd sermons just flow out of him.
Venable is quiet now too. Thinking.
"Officer Peabody has been disturbingly quiet of late," he
    observes,
sighing a little. His eyes take in the passing traffic.
Everyone waits for what's next.
But before it can arrive,
the cell phone rings.
"Hello?"
Cutter and Blue can hear only one half of the conversation.
"I'm not entirely sure I understand." Venable's face is serene.
"Well we will certainly try."
Hanging up the phone he says simply,
"It appears we must take
a small detour from our appointed course.
Goyo, ask our driver to find
the Los Angeles County Jail."

As they pull into the parking lot
Venable reaches for the door, then stops.
He looks at Cutter and Blue and speaks
with a pastor's gentle tone.
"When I told you two that I would help you find
some satisfaction for what you had lost,
I had originally meant it symbolically.
I would give you a new sense of belonging.
New friends, a new 'gang' if you will,
along with a prosperity that,
despite what people say about such things,
can always fill the emptiness inside.
But"—Venable nods toward the building,
smiling ever so slightly—
"things have changed.
Within those walls is the man who led the attack

against your friends. He expects me to free him
and for business reasons, I will.
But that is as far as my loyalty to him extends.
Once he is outside those walls, my protection
vanishes like so much cooled steam.
If you believe vengeance breeds any kind of satisfaction
then I can only say I have delivered on my original promise
in a manner so timely
it even amazes me."
He looks at Cutter and Blue.
They understand.

When Ray walks out into the white light,
crossing between the parked cars,
Venable is by his side, patting his shoulder paternally,
while Goyo follows silently.
Stepping into the limo, Ray sees Cutter and Blue.
They are unknown to him and he eyes the scene warily.
But there are words of reassurance. Handshakes. Smiles.
Still, Ray looks uncomfortable, sitting with his hands in his
    jacket pockets
smelling the burnt rubber of his own bad luck. Venable talks on,
speaking of a ranch out of town
where Ray can hole up, a lawyer will be found,
the maid will cook him a hearty dinner,
then, of course, feathery pillows.
They drive up into the canyons
the road twists and turns for miles.
The sun is just beginning to set as the car stops
at the head of a long red dirt drive.
Venable says, "You three go ahead,
this is the point where I lose my reception."
He holds up his phone. "Goyo and I have two quick calls to
    make.
Just walk up to the house, we'll be right behind."
There is a pause,

Ray's jaw muscles clench. "Why don't I wait with you?"
"It's private business, Ray. Now honestly, I helped you today,
so please don't make yourself a nuisance. Goyo and I
won't be but five minutes."
Ray gets out.
Cutter and Blue follow.
The three walk up into the twilight.

Within a few moments one man
screams. And screams. And screams.
Then silence.
Venable shakes his head,
"Violent world indeed."

He searches for Peabody's number,
and waits for the boys to return.

XV

Miles away, Baron lies awake
caressing the small of Sasha's sleeping back
thinking about the three lost from the pack.
Ray just let them fall away, but Baron's thinking
in his new world
every loose screw will be tightened.

XVI

Across town, her eyes open in the night,
she watches Anthony sleep.
He smiles in his slumber
as her lips touch his cheek, the nape of his neck,
kissing down his chest,
between every rib, and the room
begins to whisper with the moonlight.

* * *

XVII

Bonnie is awake, scratching behind Buddy's ear.
She had smacked her soccer brat nephew
when she discovered the dog was missing.
And drove off tersely with her sister still yelling.
But then as she pulled into her drive,
there was Buddy. Wagging his tail,
truer than anyone, any man certainly, had ever been.
She fed him a steak that night.
And let him sleep on the bed.

XVIII

Bonnie is awake, scratching behind Lark's ear.
Why he came back is almost a mystery to him.
He could have stayed with Maria
to watch over his newborn pack
but he can concentrate here, he can relax.
He needs to think about more than just those dogs,
and here, with half-closed eyes, he can survey the
    larger scene.
He wonders what happened to Cutter and Blue
who seem to have checked out of their hotel.
And what happened to Baron?
Lark's chin rests on the bed's comforter
as his mind chews through it all.
But that first question still itches,
why is he really back here?
Why did he come back to Bonnie?
Lark's heart is a cold and empty chamber, dusted clean,
and locked up tight.
But the thought of Bonnie coming home
to emptiness, to desertion,

made him feel
something.
Compassion? Devotion?
He wouldn't know the words,
but now, yeah, he's happy
curled up at her feet. Thinking. Ever thinking.
And she scratches behind his ear
Yeah, there, that's just right.

XIX

Maria lies between Jason and Bunny.
None of them had anything before
and now they have the everything of
one another.
They wrestle with passion
sweating through the sheets in the afternoons,
resting to lick where it's sore,
then starting again, with laughter.
Now Maria listens to her house of boys
breathing deep through the night.
She wonders why Lark doesn't stay here too
but she doesn't need him, not now.
She smiles and closes her eyes
safe as any queen in the heart of her hive.

XX

Peabody sits in his living room.
The clock reads 3 a.m.
He toys with his pain medication and sips
some scotch. He checked on the boy,
watched guns and badges on TV
and now sits with something in his stomach
that feels like fear.
Where's that coming from?

* * *

When the lispy fellow called
Peabody had told him he was done
watching for the blonde.
The lispy fellow had waited a bit before replying,
"Well actually no, no you're not."
Peabody asked if that was a threat but the phone
was already dead.
Damn.

He tried a trace on the call again
and this time got back "Renee Industries."
The Internet says it's based in Barbados.
A few more clicks yielded some answers:
a midsize firm, offshore, blue chip,
legal consulting, clientele unknown.
Leaving more questions:
Why would a lawyer in Barbados bother with a blonde
living out some surfer free-love fantasy down in San Pedro?
Why would he care?

Peabody had put off his visit to the dogcatcher for another day,
he came home early, cooked dinner with his wife
read his son three books and then poured three scotches.
This is his fourth. It's three thirty in the morning.
He raises his glass
and toasts the night,
go to hell.

XXI

Annie steps out onto the stoop and looks around
one cigarette is held between her thumb and forefinger.
The boys have been gone for too long
and being alone in the house leaves her feeling a bit vulnerable.
The trees' shadows spook her as if she were still a child.

But then she settles down,
remembering that, in fact, she
is what the world's afraid of.

Annie sits on the stairs and contemplates the single cigarette,
charmed that she's this close to giving it up.
One cigarette. Maybe this idea of using each smoke
as a little therapist is a good one.
Maybe she should patent it,
write a book, go on TV.
She smiles to herself.
It shouldn't be this hard, in fact
she only recently began smoking again.
Her system had been clean for years,
but coming back to LA had ignited a yearning for it
that she hadn't felt since she was a teenager
hanging around in 7–Eleven parking lots with friends,
always pretending to be older than she was.
Maybe that's why she hungered for it,
it was, in some backward way, a symbol of innocence,
a small piece of the time before.
Physically, she knows, she shouldn't need it.
Dogs are supposed to beat addiction,
there's something in the change,
that cleans the blood.
But the stress, the city, the memories,
her lighter flares up.
Another session,
one of the last.

Her mind wanders along with her pack,
down in Mexico, fleeing north,
just a few miles over the Sonora border
they swam together, chins above the water
crossing over the river
to rest in the shade of the trees.

For three days they lay there
healing cracked paws and tired bodies,
stealing off now and again to the local dump
foraging for carcasses and scraps.
Someone must have spotted them in their comings and goings,
for just a day off that spot, heading north again,
they heard the roar of off-road engines and suddenly
they were being chased full bore across the desert
not as devils this time, simply as dogs,
by three pickup trucks and rifles
whose carefully placed shots
(just over shoulder, just beyond heel)
herded them to a dense circle.
Annie's boys huddled round her defensively,
Snarling wild, snapping at the men
who fired their guns into the air,
driving the dogs
into the bed of the truck.

The big factory was to the north,
on the rough side of the border city called Nogales.
The workers came and went
while the fenced yard of wild dogs provided security.
Choler and venom bristled there
as the raw summer heat fired the dogs' anger.
Annie and the rest were thrown in with them
finding dirt and dust and bad meat along with
an endless mean war against the other dogs.
Snapping, biting, her pack was naturally stronger but tired
and then more tired as the battles wore on.
One of her pack went down after a week
when a canine's teeth cut
through his throat, another days later
in a fight so ugly, so brutal, that
little was left of him in the end
but the stench of his blood.

Down to eight, they tightened the circle further still.
The men came out for their breaks to watch the fights,
hollering from the far side of the chain-link fence,
laughing together, one good time.
Another of her pack went down, felled by
a brindled son of a bitch who
wouldn't stop biting and chewing and tearing
even after the dog
had long stopped fighting.
And then there were only seven.
In the night, between fights, her pack lay there looking out
at the glowing eyes of their enemies. She thought,
We're going to die if we stay here much longer.
She thought, It is time for a sudden move.
It's time for a radical plan.
It is time for me to do something
for them.

Because there was no security but the dogs
nobody saw her change, no one saw her at all
till the late shift was leaving, one fellow glancing into the cage
saw a lady
lying there amid the dogs, naked, her eyes closed,
her blonde hair fanning out
like a halo of gold. The six others
surrounded her, facing the world.
There were shouts, a chivalrous rescue began,
as the men distracted the dogs with hoots and yells,
the one who first spotted her
rushed in to scoop her up in his arms.
Her pack watched through the fence as the man carried her off.
She wasn't escaping. She wasn't running away.
They knew this.
But in their distraction they didn't see
the coming attack

as the old, burnt curs,
smelling a weakness, struck quick.
She heard the distant chaos.
She heard the barking of her boys.
She heard the last yelp as one went down.
And as Annie was carried away
down the red dirt road
toward an uncertain destination
she thought to herself,
Now we are six.

In the breezy San Pedro night
the cigarette is crushed out.
This is the tough part for any therapist,
letting go in the heat of the moment.
She closes her eyes and
puts her memories on a shelf.
There is much to be done,
there is some serious judgment
coming down.

XXII

Just before the first light
a sea of restless dogs
rushes along the edge
of the chain-link fence
impatient and nosing forward for
the wet ground meat and dry meal
generously shoveled out
by a one-eyed one-armed man.

book four

Like dogs in Mexico,
furless, sore, misshapen,
arrives from laborious nowhere
Agony.

DENISE LEVERTOV

Be kind, for everyone you meet
    is fighting a hard battle.

PLATO

I

Baron's up and barking,
Sasha nips at heels, herding.
The bunker's rousted hounds slip out of sleeping
storerooms and run together to the open space.
Baron hasn't slept well for weeks,
the missing dogs
and weight of the future
churning through his mind.
Memories of Lark stalked him too
as he ran through lessons learned over years
spent watching scrappy souls
as they were forged together
into the tightest of packs.
But now is Baron's time,
thinks Baron. He's hoping the rest of them
are ready to follow this dream,
a plan born from long, insomniac nights
spent sifting through the remnants of Lark's old plan.
Why did Lark send the girl to the pound?
And then send Bone with her?
Finally Baron reached a place
where the pieces came together.
He saw civilization crumble before him,
and he smiled.

He leaps onto the crate and looks into their attentive eyes.
Sasha climbs up behind him,
her hand on his shoulder, bringing him strength.
When Baron first came here on his mission for Lark,
Ray suspected nothing,
he simply needed men like Baron.
So Baron slept and ran and sparred with the pack, taking

mental notes, looking for the chinks in the armor
that Lark and his pack could exploit.
Then, the night Ray
sent Sasha to him,
when she bit his chest and he slid inside her,
there was something in their violence together
that bled years of barbed anger from his bones.
When it was over he lay there
breathing,
wondering,
finally asking,
"Is it always like that?"
She turned to look at him, exhausted,
her eyes showing something close to fear.
"It's never like that."

In that moment, everything
was recalibrated.

Call him a Judas if you want
but he did it for reasons
much older than silver.

Baron raises his hands.
"This is the time, this is when we plant the seeds of the future.
We are evolving this pack, we are evolving the plan,
we have ambitions." He steps forward and raises his voice,
almost shouting now. "Ambitions beyond
what any pack has ever dreamed.
We are going to reshape the world."
He knows as the words leave his lips that it's working,
his passion is moving like a fever through the pack.
Baron changes gear, putting his shoulder
against his argument and pushing it forward as great leaders
    always do
sometimes to great ends,

other times simply to the end.
"We will own this city.
We will be its soul and it will work for us.
We will drink from it. We will savor it.
It is going to be profound,
it is going to be delicious."

Sasha steps forward and barks out orders,
they pass out pictures of Ray,
of Lark, of the girl.
Tighten the screws.
Rewards are mentioned,
greater goals stated,
men start heading out as instructed
their noses filled with the scent of the hunt.

Sasha will lead one team,
seeking jobs as delivery men for any service,
just get a truck, get a uniform, get a job.
Get to the front door, look at faces,
read the mail, know the town.
Find them, finish them off.

Baron is going
to meet a man named Potter
a lawyer in the city
who will provide some critical ground cover.

The rest Sasha sends down
to the dog pound,
in one form or another.

II

Asher runs after a golden ball, smiling.
The green of the lawn is his universe.

A man passing by leans over
and picks up the loose ball.
Alice jumps up from her bench.
"Hey, that's my son's."
"Yes, sorry," says Venable, smiling
with exquisite politeness. "I must say,
he is a lovely, lovely boy."

Peabody comes home from work
driving his new car which is something of a misnomer
since the car's actually just as used
as he's been feeling of late.
The house is surprisingly dark as he limps in.
"Honey?" Nothing.
His heart stops.
"Alice!" he yells again.
Nothing.
A vast fear yawns in his belly.
But then he hears Asher's cry, "Daddy!"
Such relief.
"We're here!"
They're in back, they're in the back,
he reassures himself as he heads through the kitchen
thinking "we never hang out back here—"
then, stepping through the sliding door into the backyard,
he stops short to find
he has guests.
Sitting on a fat man's lap, Asher is smiling,
holding his golden ball.
A short man in a dandy suit sits across from his wife
as two other men, handsome and fit,
lean back in the patio chairs.
Alice is up. "Honey, this is Mr. Venable.
We met in the park today."
And Peabody suddenly feels a sense of bewildering clarity
hitting him like a cannonball

as the dandy opens his mouth.
"Yes, I was surprised when I heard Alice
was married to the same Detective Peabody
I had been doing some work with," he lisps, then
rises to offer his hand.
In the moment of reaching out
Peabody intuitively pushes his anger and fear aside
figuring for the moment the best thing to do
is roll along, keep it low.
He shakes Venable's hand warmly.
"Yes, of course. Mr. Venable, it's nice to finally meet you."

III

Maria works the bar, tight shirt, impatient eyes,
always looking
for the ones who are strong and lost.
She keeps them there, late, talking.
She calls Lark and leaves messages on his cell.
He comes in if she's kept a lost one
there past closing, drinking, talking.
"You gotta meet my friend," she says.
It's been working, the pack is growing,
steady and strong,
the plan is a plan.

Lark comes in early tonight,
no reason to be there except
back home Bonnie had gone down just after eight
lulled by pills and wine,
asleep on a pile of magazines,
so he headed out to check on things.
Now Lark's sitting at the bar listening to
a band playing covers of old Chicago tunes
in Spanish. Sheecago.
Songs from his FM youth

weave in and out of translation,
Spanish to English and back again,
like when he was a kid and his father drove him
across acres of avocado farms
and Lark would fiddle with the radio,
up and down the dial,
mariachi to rock, Sinatra to salsa, two cultures
swimming together in the airwaves,
"Twenty Cinco o Seis" to
Four.

Maria, wiping her hands on the towel, says,
"A guy came in earlier tonight, wanted to pay
with the coin he got from A.A.,
his anniversary award."
"Sounds like he needed a drink."
"Yeah." She smiles, holding up the coin. "I gave him one."
Lark shakes his head, there are so many ways
to get lost in this town.
"I'm going for a smoke," she says. "Come out with me."

The evening is cool for LA. There's been talk of rain.
Maria breathes in deep, flicks her smoke,
looks him in the eye. "So, Bunny says you want a new van?"
"Yeah, we're going to need a bigger one. Maybe two."
"Jesus, Lark, how big are you gonna make this thing?"
"I dunno, Maria. Big enough to fight another pack."
She smokes,
nodding, impatient, a little surprised,
a little pissed.
"A whole 'nother pack?" she says, adding, "there's another fuck-
    ing pack?"
Lark nods. "Honestly, Maria, there are probably dozens.
Who knows? I don't. But the good news is
we only want to fight one of them."

"So, how big is this one we're going to fight?" she asks.
"I have no idea."
Maria picks a piece of stray tobacco from her tongue,
"Well fuck the van then, get us a bus."
Lark smiles.

Inside the bar, it's "Sabado
en la Plaza" being sung earnestly
by the giant lead singer. Sangria flows,
margaritas flow, beer flows.
Lark dryly surveys the scene
but everyone seems secure here, no one
to chip off the wall and drop into the mix.
He's almost ready to go but Maria
puts her hand on his and says,
"Come back to the house with me,
I want to show you something."
Bunny cleans glasses
bops his head along to the music.
Lark agrees to wait and orders
another ginger ale.

Closing time, his car
follows hers, left on Beverly, all the way out.
They pull up at the house
where everyone is asleep.
She whispers something in Bunny's ear
and he scurries up and out of sight.
"What did you tell him?" asks Lark,
following as she wanders through the foyer
up into the master bedroom.
"I told him to get some sleep," says Maria,
lighting a candle on the mantel.
"So, what did you want to show me?" asks Lark,
sitting on the corner of her bed.

She turns and stands
less than an inch from his face.
She pulls her dress off over her head.
He looks into her eyes
as she runs her fingers
through his dark hair.
The room resonates with heartbeats.
He takes her hand.
"I'd love to. But, Maria, if I was with you here," he says,
    "right now,"
he collects his thoughts, chooses his words carefully.
"If I took this," he runs his hand along her bare back,
"believe me, we'd lose everything. It would all slip away."
"How do you know?" Her voice carries a slight ache.
"Maria, right now that's about all I do know."
Lark gets up, touches her chin and meets
her gaze. It's dark and tough in there.
"You are so strong. So wise.
So different than the girl I met in the store."
He kisses her forehead. "And I've already given you more than
anybody ever could."
He watches as the look in her eyes changes,
the darkness passing to something slightly more bemused.
He sees that Maria's prodding the world, looking for
what will bite and what will tear.
She's putting them all through their paces,
flexing her muscles,
testing her strength.
Lark sees it all and feels the relief,
at least it's not love.

Putting on his jacket, he
steps out the screen door to the
fresh air of freedom, then
drives off to a woman across town

who feeds him kibbles and bits.
Satisfaction is a strange thing,
found in odd corners.

The last thing he hears
as he leaves the house that night
is Maria barking
for Bunny love.

IV

Anthony wakes to find her arms are wrapped around him
he's thinking that there's just a little more
tension in her hold
than one would expect
from simple affection.
She's holding him the way
one holds a trunk full of love letters
when your ship has been sunk
and the current is pulling you out.
He rests his lips
on her cheek
on her eyebrow and on the softness
beneath her neck.
It is another day.

In the kitchen he notices
a line of ants crossing over to the sink
He remembers a story his judo teacher once told him
about how the roots of man began long ago
with us lying on our sides, in our stupid prehistoric way,
watching with a dawning concentration
as the ants swarmed in song line threads
across the bleached desert earth
while, across seas and valleys,

other men stood looking up
their attentive eyes following the bees that murmured
around the honeycomb.
We mimicked their organization,
we copied their discipline
we got up from the ground, dusted ourselves off,
and made our own wars
so that our greatest battles are
only shadows
looming up over time's expanse,
all born from the tiniest of ancient conflicts:
Ant versus ant.
Bee versus bee.
And now
a dogcatcher
late for work.

There have been more new guys,
it's a tough and lean and silent crew.
They train fast and take off on their own runs,
returning with their kennel trucks brimming over
and humming with the panting
of quiet and contented canines.
Anthony's one of the few now
who's been around long enough
to sense something's not quite right.
But he can't put a nose to it.
And nobody else seems to notice.
He still feeds tacos to his three dogs.
He has moved them over to the adoption pens now.
But nobody takes them, people love the new mutts too much.
These new ones all play like dancers in a chorus line,
bouncing with bubbly skips
whenever prospective owners come strolling through
then slumping back down once their visitors depart.

One of the new guys is named Frio.
Anthony trains him for two days.
The kid won't answer any questions, not even
"You ever been to Yucca's? For Mexican food?
Habla Espanol?" Nothing. Blank.
"Aw forget it, we don't have time."
Coming back from the firing range,
Anthony swings by the house to pick up a bag lunch
she made for him.
She doesn't notice and
Anthony doesn't catch it either as
the kid stares at her walking down the path,
watching her like he's known her
his whole damned life.

The Frio kid hits his marks, finishes his training
and moves on into the ranks.
Anthony looks in the mirror and
wonders if these new guys hate him
like he hated Calley.
He remembers the kerosene
of Calley's breath, and as he mulls it over
his mind jumps track, slipping to the easy river
where his woman's love for him resides
and just like that, he feels her kisses
warming the inside of everything
and smiles.
Yeah, Calley was an asshole.
His insecurity dissolves like smoke in the wind,
because if a woman that good can love him that right
well then. . .

That's what love does.
It chases the dragons away
before their claws can sink in.

V

Peabody the cop drives toward the city kennel,
his gut unsettled and his mind unable to sort this out.
Venable, the fat Polynesian, and the two other goons
popping up at his place the other night
still doesn't sit right.
Nothing was said, no threat, nothing but charm
which made his wife even hard to deal with later.
But when she went inside for more iced tea, Venable pushed the
    point.
Peabody shrugged, kept it vague as to
whether he would keep watching
the blondes' house.
He told Venable a little of what he'd learned,
but not too much.
Acting without any real calculation,
just keeping it all close.
"We're interested in everything," said Venable,
"the girl, the dogs,
even this one-eyed man you describe. Everything.
But most of all, whom they all might be working for."
Peabody didn't say anything, waited for whatever came next.
"I'll gladly pay you for as long as it takes."
Peabody sighed, said, wow, well, you know, maybe.
Money is money and "Why do you want them, anyway?"
"Would it surprise you to learn that they are criminals?"
"I can't say it would surprise me, no."
"Would it surprise you to know that they are killers?"
"Really, who did they kill?"
Venable thought for a moment before answering,
"I'm afraid that falls outside your jurisdiction."
"Well." Peabody smiled. "At least we don't have any secrets."

* * *

Peabody's been meaning to go back to the pound
to see the dogcatcher for weeks now.
Ever since they heard about the guy showing up in the cages.
That guy skipped bail and disappeared.
So no rush there.
But Peabody still wants to see the dogcatcher,
since this all started the day they met
at the house where a dog's footprints
crossed the floor of a bloody room.
Everything in some way
seems to lead back to that day.
Worth some time,
worth some questions.

He pulls into the lot, turns off the ignition,
walks through the entrance and sees Anthony.
Anthony recognizes him,
gives him the "one sec" as he walks toward a phone
that lies off the hook.
Then Peabody the cop watches
as it all begins
to go
seriously
wrong.

VI

She had been thinking of Seattle again
or Spokane or just someplace north
of LA, maybe up past San Francisco
where she could travel with him
through redwood and the fog
listening to old Al Green, her fingers
intertwined with Anthony's
as they took the curves and vanished softly
into the white haze of the coastline.

On the rare clear evenings
they could watch the sun retire
tucking itself down behind the sea.
And there on the beach,
lying with their bodies together
they would warm each other through the night
until those first fingers of dawn
came to tap them awake from their sleepy embrace.
These futures surge through her mind, then hit a wall,
as the questions rise to slow her dreaming down.
What if she did go?
She wonders about Lark.
Could she trust him? Would he follow her?
Would she be safe?
Probably? Maybe? Is that enough?
These beasts track not just with the scent, but with the law too.
She would need to make a new identity, but so what?
Is she even safe now? From the pack? From Lark?
That thought trips her up.
She's trusted him since before she made the first change.
But now she's something else.
And as much as she hates to admit it
every time the phone rings she fears
it's her past calling her back again.
She wants to hide her blood and the beast within.
She wants all the demons to sleep.
And Lark is the greatest monster of them all.
The father and the guide, the priest and the hunter.
Love him as she does, she knows
Lark stands on the road between her and the future.
He bares his teeth in her dreams.

All she wants is Anthony.
She tells herself
just talk to Lark.
She tells herself

it will all be okay.
Lark will understand,
she tells herself.
Just talk to Lark, talk to him.
And she wonders
if Lark would be safe
in a room
with her now.
All she wants is Anthony.

"Yeah, hi, Lark, I don't know
if you're picking up messages
but it is important. I need to see you
this afternoon. If it's possible.
Let me know.
please." She pauses,
impatiently wiping a tear.
". . . . Thank you."

She moves through the day,
the plan is a good one, a smart one.
Her ideas spin as the day unwinds
thinking of what she'll tell Anthony.
She's sure he'll go with her.
So sure. He's easy and true,
just like he promised.
It's all she needs.

She thinks of the first time they kissed.
How she met him that afternoon again
at the bar and he talked on, rambling over a beer
about three dogs he wouldn't put down.
He said he didn't know why.
He mentioned a dog he had when he was a kid.
He talked nervously, like a man who didn't want
to notice everything he was giving away.

His voice kept going
and she was looking into his eyes thinking about
his unspoken bond with those three dogs.
When he walked outside, they paused by the car.
She let him stand a little close
and smiled at a small joke, taking his jacket between
her thumb and finger. A small gesture
that opened the door.
Just like that.
As she stared at the ceiling that first night
her body softly falling back into itself,
she thought of how we dream of journeying
on spaceships to other universes, other worlds,
but really, for the forever,
we're stuck here on the dirt and
the only time we will travel anywhere truly unknowable
is when we slip into the skin of another,
venturing into their mysteries,
always hoping for
a safe landing.

The doorbell rings.

She swings by the bureau on the way to the door,
a small precaution she tends to follow these days.
Slipping the gun Anthony bought for her
out of the top drawer
she tucks it into her waistband.
The cold of the metal
chills the small of her back.
She looks through the eyehole
and sees a UPS delivery girl.

"Who is it?" she asks.
"Delivery," answers the voice.

"For who?"
"Anthony Silvo."
"You can just leave it there, thanks." Her pulse is up.
"I gotta get a signature," says the delivery girl through the door.
How do you measure something like this?
It could be the truth, it could be a lie.

The moment would be so small and almost believable
if she didn't smell the dog.

Closing her eyes and breathing deep, concentrating,
she can now hear
the dog's soft breath just outside the door.
She measures this moment, weighing the fear and
the quickening sense of desperation,
knowing that no matter what happens next,
so much is ending.
She times her moves fast, sliding the gun out,
squinting deep for the moment that is ripe to explode
one, two, three—
she pulls open the door full and fast
falling back as sure enough
the dog lunges in fierce and snarling.
So first
she fires one very loud bullet directly
into the dog's skull
sending him down empty and sudden.
Then, as the delivery girl leaps
over, screaming shrill,
she jams the pistol
into that open shout of a mouth
and pulls the trigger again.

Even before that echo ends
she's closed the front door with her foot and now sits

bloodied on the floor, sobbing.
That was just seven seconds.
So fast in fact that the dead things beside her
still twitch and rasp
in the thick expanding pool
of warm dark liquid.

She drags the dog into the garage.
Then the delivery girl.
She kneels by their sides.
She looks at the clock.
It's early. But there's so much to do.
Her racing pulse won't slow down.
She looks around for garbage bags and a butcher knife
before deciding that
devouring it all is probably the best way.
But first she'd better wash up the mess.

An hour later and the halls are scrubbed clean.
The ruined rug is stashed in the trunk of the car.
In the garage, she gets on her haunches next to the
    corpse
preparing to change into the kind of beast
that can do this sort of thing.
But then a dark voice cuts in
from behind her
"Hi," he says. "The door was unlocked."
She freezes, still on her hands and knees,
hearing only
Lark.

Exhaustion and desperation are
released with every sob.
Lark whispers in her ear.
She clenches his shirt in her fist,
wipes the tears from her face, and nods.
                    * * *

They get a box of matches down from over the stove
and light the papers in the recycling bin
along with the rose print curtains.
As the fire catches and smoke
begins to slip out the windows
they leave the house, walking
across the green lawn
of the quiet neighborhood.
They drive away,
turning the corner
just as the flames meet the fumes
of the open gas cans
in the garage.

VII

Baron leaves Potter's law offices.
It's been a small risk seeing Potter again.
They had worked together
back in Lark's pack.
But Potter had shown no signs of concern
at any of the changes. All Potter saw
was a big check after a long drought.
"Missed you boys," said Potter.
"We're back," said Baron.
Potter eyed his notes. "This is a funny sort of cause for you."
"It's not like I'm asking you to do it pro bono."
"No," said the lawyer, "but that's normally what something like
    this would be."
"Just stop the killing."

Baron's been finding his way, pushing his dogs
to fit his vision. It's not Ray's method, no more
moving the pack from bunker to bunker,
they can stay in one place.

Things can be simpler, less brutal.
It's not Lark's path either, there's no office for the pack,
no tailored shirts or pressed suits.
Baron's way is something faster, less calculating.
And he likes to think it's working.

On his way to the car, Baron calls Sasha.
She was sent to find the girl.
Should have been simple. No sweat. But still,
Sasha's not answering her phone.

Baron stops by the advertising agency on the way.
It's a quick meeting.
They think he's a philanthropist soft on mutts.
They show him the "Adopt Today" posters.
They show him the "Bring Benji Home" print.
They show him the "Better Than a Boyfriend" TV script.
He kills "Benji" and approves the rest,
signs a check to spill the work all over LA.
This town is about to go
absolutely crazy for canines.

Back in the car, he calls Sasha again.
No answer.

VIII

Ignoring every stoplight and fast as the car will carry them,
Peabody drives a shaking sweating Anthony
to what was his home.
Before Peabody even brings the car to a stop
Anthony is out of the passenger seat,
weeping,
running,
cops grab him at the line, holding him back
as he stares down at the blackened body

they're pulling out of the still smoldering house.
The face gone and the body still warm
but warm the wrong way and
far beyond recognition.
A woman, they say.
Lit fire to the house and shot herself, they say.
Anothony is shouting and on his knees.
Horrible tragedy, they say.
One of our grief counselors is coming.
He is on his side, already covered in cinders.
Nightmare for you.
She killed your dog too.
Stopping suddenly, Anthony looks up.
"What do you fucking mean 'dog'?"
Peabody looks up, catching it too,
just as sharp
but hearing it different.

IX

Baron paces the warehouse, impatient.
He's heard about the fire now, some of the pack
cruised by on his orders.
He doesn't like the sound of it.
If Sasha got the girl, she'd be back by now.
But he doesn't want to face that.
And if that girl got away, she's smart
so she'll run far.
If Sasha is lost, Baron's close to lost too
but he tightens his chest and stands up straight.
Love may have brought him here
but now power and the plan have their own demands.
Damn. He should have sent five, not two.
Even three would have been better.
He wasn't thinking straight.
He's been running dogs through the kennel

for two weeks, everyone is stretched thin.
He barks and sends four dogs out,
look for Sasha, look for the girl,
go, now.
Damn where is she?
Damn.

Knowing someone isn't coming back
doesn't mean you ever stop waiting.

X

Outside the station
Peabody dials his cell in the car,
while inside Anthony completes
the paperwork that always accompanies tragedy.
The lisp picks up.
"Hello, Detective Peabody."
"Listen," says Peabody. "I don't have time to fuck around.
There was a fire. Someone died today."
At the other end of the line
there is a sigh. "Oh, I'm sorry to hear that."
"Whatever." Peabody is impatient.
"It was at a dogcatcher's house,
his girlfriend died in the flames. With a dog.
And the fact is this was a dog nobody knew,
like there was a dog outside Calley's house,
like there was a dog I was chasing when I was hit,
and I get the feeling nobody knows who these dogs are
except maybe you.
So, yeah, honestly, straight up,
I need to know what you know about it all.
What exactly, what the hell
is going on?"
There is a long silence.

"I can assure you that even without knowing
the details, I had nothing to do with this event," says Venable.
"I can't be responsible for every stray in Los Angeles. Yes,
we have been following certain dogs, the dogs I sent you after
some time ago, but this strange event, this tragedy
doesn't fit into their style."
"What do you mean 'style?' Dogs don't have a style."
"Oh," says Venable, "these most assuredly do.
For these particular dogs, it seems to be based on revenge."
"Fuck this bullshit," says Peabody and hits "end."
He collects himself, and then calls back.
"Hello, Detective." The voice velvet with patience.
"Listen," says Peabody, "go near my family again
and I'll fucking kill you. Understand?"
Peabody feels the bottomless blackness
of this particular night.
"Yes, Detective, I understand. Now, please do me a favor."
"What's that?"
"Keep an eye on the girl. And the dogs.
Find out who they work for."
"Why should I do that?"
"Well"—Venable sighs—"because
I think you are smart enough to know
just how great my reach is
both in your department and in your life."
Peabody hangs up thinking
he's been feeling less and less like a cop
ever since this case began
and now
it's kind of like he's
no cop at all.

Anthony emerges from the brightly lit station
into the perfectly dark world.
He's numb and mum, completely carved out and shattered.

Peabody swallows his frustration
slaps a sympathetic smile on his face and leans his head out of
    the window.
"You want me to take you somewhere?"
Anthony shakes his head, stands there. Time passes.
"Look, I'm sorry, but I've got to get going."
Peabody looks at Anthony
who looks like a man who's lost
all his insides.
"I'm happy to drop you off somewhere."
Anthony looks around, finally speaking
"Maybe . . . the ocean, that might be nice."
"The ocean?"
"Yeah," says Anthony. "It might be a good night for that."

Peabody leaves him in Santa Monica
at the edge of the public parking lot
beneath the shadow of the Casa Del Mar Hotel.
Anthony walks away from the car
toward the ocean without
looking back.
There has to be something better than this,
thinks Peabody, watching this soul
disappear toward the sea.
But where is he going to go?
You've got to want help to get it,
and all Anthony wants tonight
is the ocean.

"Don't do anything stupid," Peabody says out loud,
unsure whether he's talking to Anthony
or himself.

XI

Sunny day, sunset night,
Bonnie comes home
and discovers Buddy sitting on the lawn.
Now how'd he get out?
And he's with a new friend
almost as big as Buddy, with
a beautiful coat.
The two dogs scamper around.
A little investigation shows
that it's a girl, my,
a girlfriend. Well, Buddy,
you're full of surprises.
And look how happy Buddy is.
No collar on the girl dog.
Betty, thinks Bonnie, I'll call her Betty.
I'll take her in for a bit, no need to call the pound.
Someone might come looking for her
and until then it'll be Bonnie and Betty and Buddy.
Quite a full house.

After Bonnie takes her medication
as she sleeps deeply
Lark and his old partner change back.
They sit in the dark kitchen, sipping from the same glass of
     water.
The hours pass as they fill each other in, stopping now and again
to listen as the house creaks or the wind gusts through the trees.
She tells him about the dog she's been hunting.
"Is that why you called me?" he asks.
"What?" She looks surprised, having forgotten why she called.
He looks her in the eyes. "Were you hunting me?"

She looks down at the counter. "I really don't know Lark,
but it doesn't matter now, does it?"
He puts his hand on top of hers. "No, it doesn't matter now."

"Do you know the story of the girl who came first,
the one who came before you?" asks Lark.
"Yeah, I've pieced it together," she says.
"So, you know what happens now."
"Yeah."
Any real pack has only one woman.
The delivery girl must have been theirs.
As long as there's a pack out there
searching for the one who killed their bitch
the one who took out their beacon, their center, their focus,
    their light
then their quest for vengeance will go on, unabated.
Their blood hunger will never wane.

She realizes she was a fool to think
she could seamlessly slip
back into the gentle world
into the simplicity of it all
into Anthony's arms.

"If he's with you,
they'll find you.
He doesn't know the ways,
you'll get caught, and then
you'll both die."
"I know," she says, "I know."
She empties the glass
and they agree to
lie low.
He'll show her the new pack
but she'll stay outside it for now.

It's Maria's, not hers,
So she'll stay here.

They change back,
and under the cover of fur
slip into Bonnie's room,
curling up at the foot of the bed.
Lying beside Lark's heavy slumber,
she winces in her sleep
all the way to the dawn.

XII

Jorge the man and Frio the dog
are curled up in the shade of the bunker.
Jorge is talking, reading Frio's response, the ear flick,
the tail thump, the snort.
"Yo man," says Jorge, "since Sasha's been gone
this pack is hurting. I tell you, it feels like the spine
just got clean ripped out."
Frio exhales. Jorge keeps talking.
"But we gotta stand. We gotta make it."
Frio is tired. Baron keeps them working, tracking,
scan the news, scan the streets, find the girl.
Last night, trying to buck up their spirits
he took them all out
down to the strip clubs near the airport
where they stayed till closing time.
They spent money on dancers and wasted the hours.
Today, everyone recovers and wonders
about the future. Even with the search for the girl,
and the greater task of putting the pieces of
Baron's dream into place, the pack still feels
aimless and drifting.
Jorge scratches Frio's haunches,

"We're gonna make it. It's gonna be good."
Frio sighs again. Because of the plan,
they're all working day jobs now,
Frio pulls long hours with the pound,
then comes home and changes into dog
because it just feels better that way.
A couple of late nights like the last one,
spent watching the silicon bounce
can wear a body down.

Jorge keeps talking, "You seen Baron? Baron's looking thin,
his eyes spark easy, like he's got kerosene in his head."
Frio looks across to the two empty bunks,
The dogs who slept there were moved into the pound.
A lawyer guy has stopped the city from putting any under the
     needle,
so these dogs just sit there, waiting for adoption.
Frio is only half listening to Jorge
mostly he's thinking about his new job.
The old-time dogcatchers down there talk about "the curse."
One guy disappeared, another shot himself,
then Anthony walked away when his girl burned down the
     house.
And the old-timers who talk about this curse
don't even know where the new workers who sit there listening
actually come from.
If they did know, thinks Frio, they'd really lose their shit.
He tunes in again and hears Jorge rambling on, "Yeah, well,
these may be tough times for the pack,
but from what I know of Baron's plan
the whole city is going to be feeling
a whole lot of pain
real soon."

XIII

Anthony's first night on the beach
he stares at the water, listens to the pull of the current
wonders where his tears are.
He senses the undertow pulling every wave back
sucking and tugging the world toward its darkness
he wishes he was ready to sink into it now.

Before her, everything seemed so loose and jerry-rigged
one day only barely duct-taped to the next,
but after she arrived, the ground grew firm beneath his feet,
the world aligned, the joints were tight
the beams sturdy.
And now all that fine work was
just as cindered and burned
as the body in the morgue.
There was not enough time with her
and now there's nothing to go back to.

Two days and a random fistfight later
Anthony is poking through a wire garbage can
looking for something to eat.
Hungry, with a fresh cut over his eye
he's digging deeper, his head burrowed in,
he's burying himself there
beneath it all.

XIV

Bonnie's tired,
she has her dinner at the table alone and
she's working her way through a half bottle of wine.
Her new dog Betty is lying on the rug, while

Buddy is asleep in the next room.
The local news is on just for sound,
just for company,
when suddenly up like a shot
Betty is on her feet barking
and barking, barking big
barking right at the TV screen.
Buddy comes bounding in and then
just like that both dogs are quiet again
sitting watching the TV like they understand everything.
Well that's just the craziest thing, Bonnie thinks.
She looks at the TV and it gets even crazier because
the thing is, you see, on the TV
they're talking about dogs.

Lark knows why she woke him.
There's Potter on the screen
talking about animals and ethics.
Lark remembers some of the work he had Potter do,
stuff that was too dirty for Lark's firm to get near,
and thinks that Potter talking about ethics
is like watching Satan sing about Jesus.
Potter is holding a news conference
announcing that the city's temporary ban
on putting dogs to sleep
has just become permanent.
A victory for dog lovers everywhere, says Potter.
Not to mention, thinks Lark,
a victory for dogs.
And yes,
Lark realizes that Baron must be behind this.
There's a trail blazing through his mind
as bright as the 101 at night.
Lark has almost every answer he needs.
Maybe his new pack isn't big enough
or physically ready to take on Baron's.

But Baron's just exposed his hand,
giving Lark the lead he's been waiting for.
And so, Lark thinks, looking across the room
at the kind woman picking at her defrosted diet entree,
maybe it's time to say good-bye to Bonnie.

He and the girl slip off that night.
Bonnie will always wonder
how they got out of the locked house.

XV

Maria lies awake again, breathing hard,
curled up next to Linus, a new recruit,
whose loving worship was another fresh blade of grass
growing over the black tomb of her past.
She stretches her toes and exhales
a happy sigh.

Hearing someone come into the house,
she slips out from beneath Linus's arm
and goes downstairs.
Lark's in the kitchen writing a note.
Behind him stands a woman with dark hair and
an expression of anger that makes even Maria cautious.
Lark looks at the two of them and then says to the woman,
"Go wait in the car." The girl heads out.
Maria gives Lark a sharp look.
"Who is she?"
"She's the past, Maria,
and"—Lark looks up—"that's all you need to know."
He goes back to writing while
Maria takes this in with her arms crossed.
"Okay," she finally says, "well, I got two more from the bar.
Turned them myself." A small smile of pride slips across her lips.
"Excellent," says Lark, still writing. "Did you change them yet?"

"They're changed and rewarded for it," Maria says, shifting her
    hips,
still feeling the soreness.
Lark stands up and hands her the piece of paper,
"Have everyone on that come first light."
She looks at the paper, a regimen, a schedule.
"Everything is accelerated, the game starts now," says Lark,
his voice as serious as ever but with
a hint of excitement in his eyes.
It's something she's never seen in him before.
Kissing her once on the cheek Lark says,
"You can call me anytime."
And he's gone.

XVI

Anthony's been living on the beach
for nine weeks now.
He's got all the crazies down,
knows who to talk to and has his own flight path
for weak soup and free sodas.
Unkempt, unwashed,
with a beard that makes him look
like a pathological Jesus, he's been
listening to nothing
but the clatter of shellfish falling
from the gull's beaks
and breaking on the rocks of the piers.
"That's my heart, babe," he murmurs,
watching the birds flocking down to feast.
Passersby think he's talking to himself but
he's not, he just talks to her from time to time.
At night he lies down on the benches and contemplates
the deception of starlight, long dead suns making small lights
almost bright enough to guide the way.
He sits at the tide's edge

letting the sound of the surf
chase the echoing song of her voice
clear out of his mind.

There was another fight with some lunatic
about whatever it is crazy people fight about.
The man came at him so fast that it took Anthony
a second to remember his moves. But he did.
He flipped the guy down on the boardwalk with such force,
splinters filled the man's cheek.
After that everyone steered clear,
which was fine with Anthony.

One night sitting there
he hears the humming of a new voice.
"You want some peanut butter and jelly?"
No one has approached him this gently
they should all know better.
He looks up sharply at the blonde girl.
With the streetlamp burning behind her, she has a nice glow.
So he scratches his ear, nods a little and, hungry,
accepts half a sandwich with some thanks.
"You surf?" she asks.
"No," he says and he gets up and walks away.

The next day she finds him again,
she starts out slow but nice
a bit more peanut butter, some carrots, and
a joke about the seagulls that makes him smile.
"Oh, you get it," she says, grinning.
"Yeah," he says and walks away.

The third day, as the sun
tumbles down from the sky
they begin to talk.
She tells him she lives with her brothers,

"But they're not really my brothers," she says,
"we've just lived so many places, done so many things."
Anthony chews some of the celery she brought.
"Have you ever had someone like that?" she asks.
"Sort of," says Anthony.
"But she's gone now?" she asks.
"Yeah, she's gone." He thinks about walking off now
but he stays,
taking another bite out of the celery.

"My brothers are up north, surfing,
and checking on things on our land, " she says.
"I get bored at the house.
I just quit smoking
and I get antsy
all cooped up inside."
The girl shares her past in
her singsong voice.
"I was crazy, you know?"
She says she used to be curious about everything,
always searching for the biggest high
the most delicious sugar moment,
the loudest music that would drown out her thoughts,
or the fastest ride that made the earth sweep aside.
Ultimately, she says, she was just a magician
trying to perform the greatest escape.
She tells of mushrooms and acid and dancing
and liquor and Brazilian herbal drinks that
reorganized the shape of the universe.
"And then you know what happened?" she said.
"What happened?" asks Anthony.
"I found something even better."
"Better?" he asks, "better than what?"
She smiles, gets up, and skips away,
"Come on!" she calls over her shoulder and he follows,
not from curiosity but

because there's nothing holding him to the beach.
She's the wind that's blowing
so he sails with it
because his sadness is feeling a little stale
here amid the speed junkie rhythm of the boardwalk.
Anthony gets into the car,
his grief
is still clinging to his bones
but he's heard enough from the hollow ocean
and now he's ready to go.

It's not that he's attracted to this girl,
she seems otherworldly,
a flower that belongs to no bouquet.
But she has a constant small smile
that has nothing to do with him,
which he likes.
Friendly but distant seems
just about right.

They drive thirty minutes south
pulling off the freeway into a Latino neighborhood
and parking in front of a small bungalow.
As they stroll up the walkway
she waves over her shoulder down the street.
"Who are you waving to?" asks Anthony.
"Oh, a cop I know."

XVII

It is only
a coincidence,
the path of Anthony's plan to disappear and dissolve
intersecting with the line of her pack's simple plan,
the plan her brothers send her out on

while they drive north and check in on Ruiz.
Every morning she parks the little truck and pokes around.
38 percent of the country's homeless
live in LA, and a lot of them prefer the beach to the concrete.
Living on a million-dollar beachfront
how crazy are they, right?
But they could use a little guidance.

If you're scrounging for driftwood souls,
this isn't a bad place to look.

She and her brothers have been illuminating
another way for these fellows,
far from the old shopping carts and empty 40's.
With her sunflower dress and dancer's gait
she wanders along the beach,
sniffing for the weak but strong
trolling for the troubled,
and Anthony was just one more
falling into her net.

It's a simple coincidence,
while up in the canopy of heaven
Coyote the trickster
trots across the sky
to tell the prime mover
what he's done.
This is a good one, he thinks.
This one's really going to wow him.
And just like every other time,
the prime mover really
doesn't
give a damn.

XVIII

Annie lights candles for Anthony
as some women are apt to do.
Anthony reaches beneath a dog-eared Orwell novel
and pulls out an old copy of *Thrasher*.
He unwinds on the couch, leafing through the magazine and
suddenly feeling tired in the plush warmth
of the pillowy room.
She puts a pot of herbs on the stove
letting them boil so that the wooly wet smoke
and the jasmine scent weave together into
a light, aromatic fog.
"Tell me what happened."
He pauses, puts the magazine down and stares at the ceiling.
He measures the trust of the moment
and then, choosing to believe in it, he simply says,
"She died, in a fire."
Annie turns down the heat, tucks her hair behind her ear.
"I had some brothers who died in a fire too."
The room is quiet.
She watches his eyes fade down
as the herbs and the embrace of the couch
lure him into his first real sleep in weeks.
She kneels beside the couch
and looks into his sun-worn face.
Sleeping men are so open.
Her finger traces the front of his shirt
stopping at his heart.
"So vulnerable," she thinks.
She lays her head on his chest
tears gleaming in her eyes
like small pieces of broken glass.

Some memories just rush over you,
like waters flooding down from distant mountains
long after the rain has passed.

She remembers being carried through Nogales.
In her mind, she is still there now,
naked in the arms
of the man who pulled her from the kennel's fray.

She had listened as the dogs' barks
faded away while the din of the town rose around her.
Feigning sleep, fearing the pace of her heartbeat
would give her away,
she kept her eyes closed and wondered
where each step was taking her.

Men gathered around them as they walked,
speaking quickly, apparently
unsure what to do with a blonde, naked girl
who had fallen asleep in the dirt of the town.
But born and raised in southern California, Annie knows
little Spanish save for taco, chimichanga, senorita.
And the factory workers have no English
but Nike and Coca-Cola and Ford.
So she didn't try to understand,
she didn't try to do anything but
keep her eyes closed
and pray.
The men
seemed hungry for the girl,
but the man carrying her shook them off, shouting,
and brought her to a boardinghouse.
A woman came out, there was more noise
more shouting.
Annie kept her eyes shut.
Finally, they took her inside.

Someone dialed a cell phone as
they laid her down on a couch in the front room.
They covered her nakedness with an old, stained sheet
and Annie waited wondering
where the river of events would eventually spill out,
when the moment of opportunity would arise,
"It will come," she thought, "wait Annie wait."
An hour later, she awoke with a gentle smile,
blinking and rubbing her eyes as other men came in.
These weren't workers, they wore nicer shirts,
clean jeans.
One sat on the corner of the bed,
his English was clear.
"Hello."
"Hello?" She bobbed her head.
He smiled and his smile was almost warm but mostly wary.
"So, what were you doing in the cages?" he began.
"Boy," she exhaled, feigning confusion, "yeah, let's see. . .
I was at a club, like at two last night and . . ."
She rolled her eyes and shook her head
as if the rest of it escaped her.
"Where are you from?" he asked.
"Well, a lot of places. I just travel, have fun, you know?"
He leaned back,
relaxed a bit, her blonde routine was working well.
"Crazy," she said, "crazy night."
He smiled.
Nobody suspects a beach girl.
"What do you need?" he asked, getting up, ready to go.
"Well, I think I missed supper." She smiled
trying to be the easiest thing
he'd ever seen.
"Oh," she added with a chuckle, "and some clothes."
The man looked her over,
"Why don't you come with us."

As the driver steered their black Expedition out of town,
the man introduced himself, "I am Tomas."
"I'm Anastasia," she said, remembering an old cartoon
about a princess lost in a foreign land.
"Well, Anastasia, you are very lucky.
Those dogs at our factory are trained to kill."
She nodded. "I'm sooo good with animals."
She looked out the window, unsure of landmarks,
wishing for bread crumbs
to mark her way.
Up a hill, they came to a large house,
the gravity of its luxury
pressing it low onto the horizon.

Servants moved through the place,
preparing a quick meal of steak and rice,
delivering clothes, a white T-shirt,
flip-flops, underwear.
She hadn't touched clean cotton for months
and, as the maid handed it to her,
the fabric was still warm from the dryer.
In her guest room she lay down with a cold glass of iced tea,
again pretending to sleep.
She thought of her brothers trapped in the cages.
A maid came in and refilled her glass.

In the afternoon she rose and joined Tomas for a cocktail.
They were almost alone, a waiter loomed in the back,
as did a bodyguard.
"What do you do?" she asked.
"Many things," he said. "I own the factory with my brother."
"Oh. What do you make there?"
He smiled. "We make pharmaceuticals."
"For who?"
"For American consumers."
"Oh," she said, giggling. "I'm American. Can I have some?"

He grinned.
Out of his breast pocket came a plastic envelope
filled with pure whiteness.
"This is not what we make. This is something better," he said,
laying out a thin line on the polished teak surface.
She remembered the bloody story of one of her brothers
and how drugs sometimes didn't sit so well.
"Not much," she said, "I'm a bit of a lightweight."
She inhaled a little,
felt the urge to change
surge up within.
She clenched her stomach to hold it down,
hoping that Tomas didn't notice.
She felt
a few blades of fur poke out
from her lower back
but as she exhaled,
"Whooo!"
they discreetly receded.
She smiled wide
at Tomas.
He smiled too.
"Yeah, this is nice, really, thank you so much for everything."
    She scootched closer.
She had never played this game before; she didn't have a natural
    false face,
but he wasn't reading her very carefully either,
his mind had already descended to what would come next.
He tucked his arm around her, pulled her close.

Nobody is ever afraid of a beach girl.

Two nights later, she rose naked
from his bed.
Slipping across the room,
she quietly opened the bureau drawer.

Digging around, thinking
"Surely, surely . . ."
Annie's hand found something metal.
Looking up at the dresser mirror,
she saw his shadow blearily rising from the bed.
"What are you—" were his final words.
The gun's loud report
shook through the house.
Fucking idiot.
She heard footsteps and crouched down, still naked, waiting.
A man came into the room with a gun and
one blink died one blink
as she fired she thought,
what bodyguard ever ran toward
a bullet like that loser just did?
What a moron.
What a complete fucking moron.
She put on a T-shirt and underwear
as she listened for any more footsteps
but the house was strangely quiet,
no bodyguards and no servants.
With a half a mind to half a plan,
she collected the wallets from the dead men.
Tomas's wallet was light and empty.
She wondered if the rich
always travel like that through the world.
But the other dead man's wallet
was so thick it felt like a paperback novel.
There was surely enough cash there
to make it to the U.S.

She grabbed the new corpse's gun, took a lighter and
the car keys from the countertop and,
walking past the bar,
a bottle of tequila too.

Moments later
she was gunning the SUV down the road.

The city was easy to find,
its milky aura shone in the night
like some man-o'-war glowing
in the dark sea.
But finding the factory was a problem.
The only good news was that while the whole town
would soon be looking for Annie,
no one would expect her to go back to the dogs.
She turned right and left,
her head out the window
sniffing the air.

At the sound of a siren, she turned down a warehouse stretch.
Putting the van into park, she leaned out and screamed as loud
     as she could.
Then listened for the call back.
Nothing.

Driving again down the empty streets,
her head still out the window
there was nothing familiar in the air.
The factories would be up near the border.
She took a screeching left,
and aimed toward what felt like the north.
Parking on a bridge, she leaned out the window
and screamed again.

A bark echoed in the distance.
A quarter mile away. Over to the right.
She drove fast.

Two minutes later, she recognized the factory wall.
She could hear the dogs barking wildly on the other side.

She had only moments before someone would come out.
Running barefoot to the corner of the building,
she tore off her sleeve and stuffed it into the tequila bottle.
Her hands shook as she tried to light it but
it caught quickly,
flickering with an orange jack-o'-lantern flame.
The thick glass of the window broke easily
followed by the sound of something else smashing inside
followed by a brighter flame still.
You could call it blind luck except as she well knew
places like that are always loaded with something
itching to blow.
Another explosion, louder, and black smoke billowed out.
Back in the truck, she shoved it into drive
and bore down on the kennel fence.
She aimed for the left side, away from where she knew her dogs
    would be,
toward the curs, noses to the chain-link, barking.
Yes, well,
meet the metal, you fucking assholes.
The fence went down hard, some dogs along with it.
She leapt out and put a bullet straight away
into a head.
Opening the back of the truck,
it was almost like they had practiced this chaos.
One, two, three brothers jumped in.
Where was Nick? Batten? Shit no.
They were down to four.

She jumped into the cab again just
as the men started running out of the factory,
firing out the window till her gun was empty,
sending the men diving to the dirt where the dogs,
unleashed and angry
were biting at anything that moved.

* * *

As she drove away
the workers' screams filled the air
behind her.

Her brothers changed in the back.
Palo rode shotgun,
his hand on hers.
Her face was wet.
They drove west, with the dawn behind them,
bruised and scarred and knowing in their guts
the darkness was far from over.

Five days later
they'd finally made it over the border
broke and tired.
The truck was left burning
in the Zona Norte section of Tijuana.
The wallets she'd stolen
had, in the end, yielded no money,
but among the thick billfold's contents
were sheets of paper bearing rows of numbers,
some sort of code.
It occurred to Annie and Palo that perhaps they held
a treasure nonetheless.
There was no time to figure it out.
They buried the wallets in a barrio alley
and carefully marked the spot.

A half mile from the border
they left another brother
dead in the soil,
shot by a farmer
simply looking after
his chickens.

So then they were three,

scarred and tired
fighting off the world from a muddy drainage ditch.
The neighborhood widow called the city
and Turner and Mason arrived,
stepping onto the scene
with wary, bloodshot eyes,
and guns loaded with tranqs.

The dogcatchers took them back
patched them up good but rough,
then turned around and sold them
to a fuck named Ruiz.

Annie gets up and turns off the light
letting Anthony sleep
she knows
the herbs will let him drift
off to that place
where everyone you've ever loved
still plays in the surf
and rolls in the jungle grass.

XIX

Bonnie is so sad
she leaves work early
to put up signs reading
MISSING, LARGE BLACK DOG
all around the neighborhood.
She knew that other dog was no good.
And the house seems so empty
without her Buddy.

At home she turns on the TV.
The commercial shows a local starlet
surrounded by mutts who lick her face.

"Adopt a dog today," she coos,
silly breasts heaving, "these fellows
don't have any issues so they're waaaayyy
better than a boyfriend."
The actress winks like a sloppy whore.
Bonnie is wiping away her wet tears and her running nose,
her damp hands leaving fingerprints
on the sides of her wineglass.

XX

Lark drinks his one hundredth hot lemon water of the week
hanging in the Starbucks across from Potter's office
using the wireless access to stay in touch with the new pack.
Lark's just trolling, waiting, sniffing.

He remembers a tale he once heard
about the town of the three-legged dogs,
some place in New Mexico where the mongrels and strays
ran wild after any pickup truck that passed by,
biting at the fenders, somehow certain they could win.
Time and again, tires squealed,
until each dog had paid the price.
He imagines them now hopping around on the red dirt roads,
their ears alert
for the sound of a car drawing near,
the fight still in them.

That's the spirit he knows he needs.
The way warriors
who have already chosen death
are always stronger than those
fighting to live.
You don't fight for life,
you fight for victory,
two very different things.

* * *

The morning passes,
she comes to cover the rest of the day
and Lark heads out.
The plan is simple: keep your eyes open,
watch for any stray member of the pack, anyone they know,
crossing the plaza.
It will take some time
but they will come. Lark knows this,
he sees the game, he knows the play,
all he has to do is find
just one of them.
Looking at her before he leaves, he's worried,
seeing in the shadowed and empty
envelopes of her eyes
only sorrow
and a rock-faced coldness.
All he can do is kiss her gently
on the cheek as he goes,
she needs healing for something that can't be healed
and he has so much work to do, so ever
onwards and forward, go.

Pulling into the Silver Lake house he hears
eighties Madonna pulsing from the windows.
He walks in to find it's all sweat and discipline,
copies of *The Royal Canadian Air Force Exercise Manual*
are strewn about on the floor as Ivan and Loren do push-ups.
It's almost cute, he thinks, watching them go.
And Chad and Bunny are running stairs, the creaking so loud
Lark wonders if the house can take it.
Bunny and Company
are on endless reps and algae banana drinks,
running six miles a day as humans
then sixteen more as dogs,
returning home with bellies full of raccoon and possum

even a wild pig they cornered up in the park.
Every breath, every exertion
all for the love of Maria,
all for the respect of Lark.
These dogs are knotting together,
working as one.
Lark looks at his watch and thinks
even with all this
they're miles from where they should be
to take on another pack.
He grimaces to himself,
remembering something the old hounds would say
back when he was a pup,
"It's not always the pack with the most dogs
sometimes it's the pack with the sharpest teeth."
Meaning maybe with enough hunger
maybe then, maybe just. . .
all he has to do is follow their scent.
All he has to do is find
just one of them.

XXI

Back at the coffee shop
she drinks her tea and keeps a close watch on the plaza.
They've been doing this for a week.
No sign of Baron, no sign of the boys.
Lark's usually right but she's got to wonder.
She wakes mornings in their motel room
turns on the TV, flops around,
masturbates thinking about how once upon a time,
sunny afternoons ago,
Anthony would, kissing,
move gently, lovingly, down her belly
open her with delicate attention and then
taste her like an oyster.

She comes,
cries for an hour,
bathes, puts on some lipstick
and heads off to meet Lark.
In the silence of the car,
she wonders about the easiest
way to kill yourself. Quaaludes and red wine
seem to be topping the list these days.
But a quick hot shower of silver-tipped bullets
sounds pretty good too.
In the coffee shop,
she sips her tea and watches
each one of the people coming and going,
thinking, yes, my fury could eat all of you, it really could,
the barrista boy, the fat woman with the scone, all of you,
your warm blood would fill my throat
the flesh from your limbs would be chewed and gnawed
the snapping of my teeth would splinter your bones,
your pickled livers would be licked and swallowed,
and finally, the points of my incisors would cut down
into the steaming, warm meat of your hearts.
I would wolf you down
in big, chomping bites.
And you would be gone, all of you,
the planet emptier and quiet,
all your busy rushing silenced
while my unquenchable fury
screams on.

XXII

The first light of the day
Peabody wakes in his car.
After the appearance of the dogcatcher last week
Peabody's been glued to the inside of his vehicle.
His head is running through logical twists

composing and stitching and drawing up
meandering conspiracies that explain Anthony's presence.
The honey in his mind has turned
to something cloudy and sour, everything's sore.
He has called the station to check in.
He's called Venable and assured him that he's on the case.
All the while aware that no matter what others may believe
this is his puzzle whose unwinding tale will ultimately be
his own possession, not the lisp's or the force's or
anyone else's. Newborn delusions crawl from conspiracy
to gold as his delirium builds the case
that will lead to book deals and talk shows
and television appearances and radio interviews
and based-on-a-true-story movies,
lead to him sitting there, at the awards ceremony,
perhaps with his wife,
all of these visions are
floating along with him now
in that special way dreams
come to men
who sleep in their car.

Waiting, waiting, he watches, sipping coffee,
scanning the paper, almost missing it when
the two emerge,
the blonde leading the way
a sleepy and unwashed Anthony
following shabbily behind.
They get into the little truck and
the blonde drives them away,
Peabody in tow.
They stop at a medical supply store up on Lincoln
Anthony waits in the car while the blonde goes in.
Peabody studies the window filled with wheelchairs and
        crutches,
wondering what she's got on her mind.

She emerges with a large box, puts it in the back.
Then she's heading North on the Pacific Coast Highway,
turning suddenly into a meandering canyon road
whose twists and turns cover miles
through small towns
and landscapes that seem to encompass decades.
One turn, it's the early seventies of shanty love,
the next it's the bare western lifestyle circa 1910,
then it's nothing but the brown hills holding the promise of
a dry and deadly future.
Down past a hill they turn into a ranch drive.
Peabody pulls over, not ready to follow them by car.
He swigs down half a bottle of water that's too warm,
pulls his gun from the glove compartment and steps out.
He stretches his legs, wringing the creaks from his bones.
The air feels still and hot and Peabody is suddenly aware of his
    stickiness.
No shower, no shave, and sweat leaking down his shirt.
The fence on the property line is only three simple strands of
    barbed wire but still
he manages to tear his slacks as he struggles through.
Some grit and straw work their way into his shoe as he walks on,
following the driveway as it bends behind a knoll.
In about ten minutes he's up the hill and can see
that the drive continues down a small glen,
around another bend, then out of sight.
He thinks about going back for his car
but the gravity of his curiosity
propels him forward
moving him on down the road
into the twilight's
distant barking.

XXIII

In the coffee shop it's the end of the day
and Lark has come to pick her up.
As she gathers her things, he glances over her shoulder,
where, through the window, across the plaza,
Baron is exiting Potter's office.
"Jesus Christ."
She looks too, her focus as keen as his.
"Lark, I don't know how I missed him coming in."
"It doesn't matter," says Lark, "just get the car.
I'll stay with him. Call me on the cell
and I'll tell you where to pick me up."
Ten minutes later she and Lark are tailing a black van
down 101, crawling through slow traffic
until they turn into the warehouse district.
Baron pulls into a lot where three other vans sit parked.
Hanging back, they survey the scene,
watching as Baron crosses to the warehouse door.
He's looking haggard, his face is thinner, his expression tired.
"Oh, Baron," she murmurs, her anger slipping for a moment.
Lark doesn't hear her as he dials Maria.
He's going to need some help
with what comes next.

XXIV

Cutter and Blue are chuckling at the airport bar
while Venable plays twenty questions with them.
"There is something about you boys . . .," he says.
They nod. They chuckle some more.
They figured out, long ago, how little this wise man knows.
Nothing really, only that there are bands of men
who will do his bidding

with little mercy and a horrific eye for detail.
When they first met him back in the bridge match,
they assumed he knew it all.
But it turns out he was only thinking about gangs
of the Sharks and Jets variety
he knows nothing of the fur or the fang.
Blue chuckles down his Diet Coke,
"We're different all right. But so are you," says Blue.
Venable leans back, "Interesting in what way?"
"Who do you work for? What do you do?" asks Cutter,
happy to turn the tables. "We muscle for you,
but we don't know anything about your game."
There is something fundamentally corroded about this airport
    bar,
the music leaks out, recalling some plastic era,
while the memorabilia hanging on the walls is reminiscent
of nothing worth remembering.
"Ah, well, at the moment, I work for—"
Venable smiles, catching himself, stirring his tea, "You're right,
I have been closed off, I apologize. I will let you know some
    things,
I will, in time, it will all unfold.
We have to trust each other, don't we?
We're a team after all."

They've been riding with Venable for weeks now,
working a little, insofar as they stand behind Venable
at meetings in air-conditioned suites and poolside shade,
listening to him move through this town with a tongue that is
both forked and smooth, languages spilling out of him,
Spanish, Portuguese, Thai, like some exotically fragrant bouquet.
But the main reason they stay
are the hours of bridge they play.
Venable clearly has an addiction that can't be kicked,
perhaps the only weakness they've found in him so far.

Blue and Cutter share the fever, happily spending one hour and
    the next
cracking the code of Goyo's brain,
working against the churning computer inside his mind.

Tonight though it's just the three of them
in the bright glare of LAX, sipping sodas, snacking on fries
waiting for Goyo to return from a flight south.
"Look, we have no problem with whatever you do," says Blue,
"but be straight with us. We're straight with you.
We deserve to know."
"Straight? Really?" Venable shakes his head.
"You both smirk like mischievous children
whenever I ask the most innocent questions about
you and your friends."
"Yeah," says Cutter, reaching for a fry,.
"maybe it's just that your questions
never seem that innocent."
Smiling straight into Venable's eyes
Cutter chews up the last of the fries.

Goyo arrives and they step into their waiting car,
Cutter and Blue in the back, idle and listening
as Venable recites into Goyo's ear a seemingly endless series of
    numbers
and random acronyms.
Goyo nods, his brain working through it
like some great, lumbering waterwheel
"567802 from 02101145" nod
"86040 from 02112065" nod
etc. and on ad nauseam and
Cutter and Blue don't even try to follow.
Cutter just looks out the window and wonders
why he spends so much time in cars
instead of running out in the canyons and in the hills.

There's game out there to hunt.
Packs of brothers
trotting across bone-dry landscapes
through poplar, aspen and sage.
"230399 from 01315050, 209944 from 774859603"
Man's minds dream in concrete,
pouring us into these city streets,
thinks Cutter, watching the highway,
yearning only for the feel of soft soil
beneath his paws.

They stop in front of a church,
Goyo gets out and walks inside alone.
"Why are we here?" asks Blue.
They sit in silence for a minute or two, then
finally Venable answers. "His brother was killed
one year ago. Today. "
"Were they close?"
Venable looks out the window,
"Oh, they had their differences,
but they were business partners, so yes,
in that way, and others, they were close."
Venable's voice drifts, as if the memory
is making him forget where he is or who he's with.
"The servants of the house,
those who were there at the time,
described the assassin.
One maid said she moved
'as if fire had flesh.'
I honestly don't know what that means.
But all the other servants nodded, agreeing, as if
she was some kind of white angel
born from the shadows of their nightmares.
Perhaps that's why they didn't try to stop her.
Of course, like many servants,
perhaps they simply hated their master."

Again silence while Cutter and Blue wait
for the rest, schoolboys hungry for a story.
"We've found her, I think," adds Venable.
"It took some work, many questions, not surprisingly
it is quite easy for a blonde to disappear
into Southern California. But, yes, we found her.
We tracked her, and we tracked the dogs,
expensive work, but seemingly fruitful.
The only puzzle piece that remains is who she works for,
we don't know, they're far more elusive.
We will wait, we have a man watching now,
a good man I believe, the police officer whose home we visited,
you remember him.
So everything should become very clear
quite soon."

They sit again, silent as Quakers,
until Goyo finally returns,
weighing the car down
with his considerable presence.
Venable pats his friend's knee
as they drive off.

XXV

Right about now,
Peabody is worried
about his balls and his face.
Barking, snapping, surrounding him
in the bleak afternoon light are thirty or so
feverishly snarling dogs
as dark and angry as an insane man's mind.
Peabody's already pulled out his gun and
fired some warning shots into the air
but that only seemed to make the dogs angrier
and he's got the feeling shooting two or three of them

will completely piss off the rest.
They had rushed up,
encircling him as he came round the bend
and blocking any retreat from the rear.
Now he simply stands with his hands raised in surrender
while they keep him at bay, angry and frothing though
none lunge too close and none bite,
they seem to like him
like they have him
immobile and stupid.

Then there's another gun blast, not his,
followed by a long whistle
at the sound of which all the dogs quickly
and obediently sit.

Peabody looks up the road to find
a couple of familiar shapes walking in his direction.
"Hey!" calls Peabody, "can't you call these dogs off?"
One-armed Ruiz doesn't say anything.
Next to him walks the blond surfer holding
a .22 in his hand.
The blond nods toward Peabody,
"Do you have a warrant?"
Peabody grins, a little reassured to be recognized as a cop,
and shakes his head,
"No, I'm sorry. I didn't realize I'd crossed onto private property."
The blond shakes his head. "Right. You probably
didn't notice the gate or the fence or any of the signs
reading PRIVATE PROPERTY."
Peabody shrugs.
The blond says, "You armed?"
Peabody holds up his gun.
"Do you mind dropping it?"
Peabody looks up quizzically. "Why? I'm a police officer."

"And you're trespassing," says the blond.

"I could just leave you here."

Peabody looks down at the dogs

thinks for a second, and then tosses the gun outside the circle.

Ruiz steps toward the gun, but the blond shakes his head no

and comes over to pick it up himself.

"Why don't you throw me your cell phone too."

Peabody shakes his head sadly to himself.

No cop is supposed to be in a spot like this.

This is why you stay in touch, keep a partner, follow the rules,

and, above all, avoid cases as fucked as this one.

He tosses his phone to the blond who pockets it.

"Okay, let's go back to the house," the man says.

Just like that the dogs are up again,

and they all start walking,

the dogs staying close

like rings around his planet.

The blond is going slow while scanning

the phone book on Peabody's cell.

"I'm not looking for any trouble," says Peabody.

"Who ever does?" says the blond.

Peabody shrugs. "I was looking for a friend of mine, named
    Anthony."

Ruiz and the blond look at each other

and Ruiz mumbles something.

You can't work as a cop in LA for fifteen years

without learning un poco Spanish.

What Peabody hears is

"El nuevo perro."

The new dog.

The blond nods.

"Officer," he says, "I think we should talk about things

other than your friend Anthony."

"We're going to talk?" asks Peabody, relieved,

the promise of conversation implies a future, so perhaps

the moment of vulnerability, the point of menace,
has somehow passed.
"Sure," says the blond. "We have a lot to talk about."

XXVI

Baron's nervous, twitchy,
wondering many things,
the most pressing of which is
whether or not to kill the whore.
He wonders what Lark would do.

There's something else on his mind.
The pack needs money,
the jobs have been slow coming in.
There's still some good trade off the docks and, among others,
there's the little man who pays them to hit the meth labs.
But Baron's spent a mint on the plan so far,
and accounts once richly spilled over
are nearing bare bottom.

The pack's been run ragged of late,
some working the pound, some tracking the girl,
the rest managing the push for recruiting,
retrieving the lost-and-found souls,
following Lark's old method
of pulling in kids from the VA center,
but also branching out into church basements,
juvenile detention centers, prostitution strips,
plucking up the ones who are already pretty deep in the cracks.
Then it's just a few weeks of indoctrination,
"Feel the power kid, listen to the dream, run in the hills"
and then send them straight through to the pound
where, thanks to Potter,
none of them can be killed or even castrated
as they're watched over by Frio and the boys.

Thanks to the large marketing campaign
currently inundating the city,
the people stream in and
pick up these mutts, scratch them behind the ears,
name them Sid or Buster or Burt and take them on home.
Once there, these new dogs obediently slip into their new role
filling a wide range of neighborhoods
throughout the greater Los Angeles area
each dog behaving, sitting, fetching,
waiting for the day when the final signal is sent
and the real change begins.

But first the whore.

Without a bitch signed on to call their own,
Baron's been buying time by renting whores
to feed and calm the troops, to manage the tension.
He hasn't touched one (the ghost of Sasha would tear
him to bits if he did, he's sure of it) but the pack
needs the release. It's an expensive staple,
even though the pack is far from picky.
Baron remembers how the Ukan way let
Lark invest cash in art, restaurants, land,
instead of burning it away
on libidos whose engines run red and fully charged.
Baron sighs. Second guesses. But
it's far too late
to convert this pack.

This one, this particular whore, she accidentally saw something,
stumbling upon a change in progress in the warehouse,
one of the boys turning with
his flesh glistening moist, fur protruding from the swollen skin.
The shock sent her screaming.
Who can blame her, thinks Baron.
It's a sight that can drive men mad,

one only the initiated should ever witness.
She went running and
would have been torn to bits for seeing things she shouldn't
but had escaped by shutting herself in one of the meat lockers
and has been wailing loud and high in there ever since.
Her shrill cries move through the whole bunker
like the haunting of a ship.

Baron stands outside the meat locker door
knocks gently.
"Open up."
There is only soft sobbing.
"Listen," he says with authority,
as the other guys sit with arms crossed, watching.
They still believe in Baron.
Baron's the only one with real doubts about Baron.
"Listen," he says, "either you trust me when I say
that we won't hurt you. Or
you stay in there and you die
of hunger and of thirst."
He pauses. Studies his fingernails.
He wonders if they should kill her or let her live.
"It's really your choice," Baron continues. "Choose life
outside, running around with your friends, the good life.
Or face the truth of what death means
alone inside that cold hole."
He pauses again, the sobbing inside distant
like it's coming from the bottom of a deep well.
Maybe she's calming down.
He looks at his watch.
He had hoped to meet with Penn about the pound.
Almost all the dogs are focused there now,
all but the recruiters and the ones he keeps at large,
noses to the ground,
desperately seeking to root out Sasha's killer.

He senses that's a dead end but
keeps them searching.
The pack needs the hunt.
Still, there's no sign, no trail.
Better to just look ahead.
The plan is a good one. Solid.
Lark would respect it.
Baron checks his watch again.
The weeping seems to have died down.
"All right," he says. "We're going to leave now.
You can let yourself out. Okay?"
He listens patiently for the
muffled and meek "Okay" that finally
squeaks out from behind
the locker's thick door.
Baron turns to the guys.
"Let's get out of here."
Stoney asks, "We're going to let her go?"
"Yeah," says Baron, "fuck it,
who is going to believe her?"
So they go.
As they walk outside onto the lot,
Baron looks around
still nervous, still twitchy, scanning the sky,
detecting a thin scent of trouble.
The only thing he doesn't know
is what direction it's coming from.

An hour later back in the meat locker
the door gingerly opens.
A small mascara-streaked face peeks out.
Doe eyes dart and,
finding the place empty, she runs naked, squeaking her fear,
like a mouse that has somehow slipped out
from the falcon's claw.

For the next two years she will tell anyone who will listen,
bored bartenders, other tired girls, half naked and impatient
    johns
about how she once saw
boiling flesh churn into fur and muscle and
teeth that grew sharp and eyes that blazed like a furnace.
They all look at her like she's crazy.
Until she finally falls from a tall story,
quite high and
completely mad.

XXVII

Back at the pound
in a steel kennel off to the side
three dogs sit watching the busy days,
as strange beasts
that smell like danger and act
as innocent as pups
are brought into the kennel and then, almost as quickly,
taken away, adopted by loving couples and young families.
The three dogs watch with arched curiosity
as they sit waiting
for the friend to return
the one who brought them affection
and good tacos.

book five

So inevitable seems the coexistence of man and
dog that, according to an ancient North American
Indian myth, the Great Creator in the Sky was
already accompanied by a dog when he created
earth and man.

THE PEOPLE'S ALMANAC

I see the gutter,
feed on the foolish
outrun and kill the strong
at daybreak I roam
awake to who follows me
I roam, I roam.
I am the hungry wolf

JOHN DOE & EXENE CERVENKA

I

Anthony wakes up in the night
thinking he heard her call his name
but knowing now it is only dream's deception.
His pack sleeps around him,
cold noses curled into warm bellies.
He rests his chin and looks up at the moon.
She used to play a game with him,
looking out their window.
She would say "Bucket Moon."
he would answer "Ladle Moon."
Night after night sky revealed a
bitten moon, a butcher's moon,
an apple moon, a thief's moon,
a rabbit—
"Rabbit moon?"
"Don't you see it?"
"I used to chase rabbits," she had said,
her voice sweet and tired.
"When did you do that?"
She rolled over and sleepy-eyed him
with a mystery smile.
A mouth on a breast
a hand up a thigh,
the opening, the gentle slipping in.
Christ he misses her.
He'd howl at the moon
but it would only wake the other dogs.

He wonders if he's not back on the beach
and this is just some broken man's hallucination.
Maybe he's sick on something he pulled
out of the dumpster.

That would add up.
This doesn't.
But it doesn't matter, it's quiet here,
there is a peace that comes with the pack.
So he sighs and slips off into his dreams
only praying as he goes
that he'll find her there.

Far above,
the dull, dense moon looking down
with a stone for a heart
and a rock for a brain
can only think
that Anthony looks
like any other dog.

Stupid moon.

II

In her dream she's a little girl
sleeping in the grass outside an ancient walled city.
Around her she can hear the rustling
of the tall grass blades as a skulk of foxes
moves past. Then
the wolves approach, two by two
she nuzzles their necks,
comforted by the lush warmth of their fur.
The last one approaches and, as she reaches for him,
the beast rises, revealing instead a man dressed in wolf fur
as a Native American might for some ancient ritual dance.
"I see," he says, "I'm not the only one who lies with the wolves."
She wakes with a start.

She looks at the long shadows falling
across the cheap motel room's walls.

She was so strong, she thinks.
Her love made her believe
she could devour them all,
an entire city of wolves.
Her love was so strong,
she thought she could drink the blood of the past
and make it disappear.
She was such a fool and
now, she thinks, she's just small again,
like she was before Anthony, before the pack, back
when she would lie on the floor
and Pete would stand over her yelling.
She can still feel him slapping her, pushing her,
bruising her as she lies alone in the motel bed.

Like a broken hare shivering
at the hunter's sure approach,
her body shakes with every breath.

Maybe Lark is right,
perhaps his plan can work
but first
she must find her footing again.
Days grow hotter and life grows shorter.
Time is somehow running out.
She flips her pillow
so she won't have to sleep on her tears.

III

In the motel's parking lot
hours of logistics later
Lark and Tati stand just beyond the shadows
winding up their business.
"Hey, do you remember the big one, the albino?" Lark asks.
Tati laughs. "That fucker, he ate everything we had.

What was his name, anyway?"
"I don't know, we called him Cujo," says Lark, smiling.
"Right. Man, funny how young we were then."
"Yep. Well, time takes what it wants." Lark shrugs.

Tati lights up a smoke,
there's just too much to be done
to spend time heading backward.

"You know, you don't have to do this," says Tati.
"What would you suggest?"
"Do what I did. Walk away."
Lark shakes his head. "You know coyotes never last, Tati,
I'm surprised you're still standing."
"Well," says Tati. "There ain't no hard-and-fast rules.
So, yeah, coyotes generally don't make it, but that's
because they can't let go of the pack.
They get all torn up
in the in-between.
But that's a bond
you've just got to break." He shrugs.
"Anyway, that's how I did it.
I'm only back in at all because of you, Lark,
'cause I owe you and all that.
Otherwise, I really don't give a shit about any pack."
Lark looks at his friend. "Well, I can't let go. Not yet."
"You sure about that?"
Lark watches the smoke curling around Tati's head
and nods. "Yeah, not yet."
"You know, Lark, I remember you
when you were one crazy puppy.
You had us all running in circles
always saving your ass."
"That was a long time ago."
"Yeah, but you just disappeared into all this,
the pack, the power, the idea of being

the big-ass alpha dog,
I don't blame you, it's a lot to manage,
but come on,
I mean, where'd the rest of you go?"
"Like I said, Tati, time takes what it wants."
"Yeah, fuck, I guess it does."

There is a final pause
as the embers of Tati's smoke
illuminate a small piece of the night.

"You'll take care of the vehicle with Maria?"
"Sure," says Tati. "Looking forward to meeting the lady."
"Thanks," says Lark, shaking his hand.
"Always," answers Tati, smoke in his mouth. "Anything."

IV

Across town, sitting in a bowling alley off of Pico
Peabody watches some of the most beautiful
bowlers imaginable. Farrah Blondes,
Betty Page Brunettes, all looking
like movie stills who have floated to earth
from some far, far lovelier place
as they throw gutter ball
after gutter ball.
The bartender explains that Fred Segal is having
their annual summer party.
"That's the makeup department, I think," says the
    barkeep
who, coincidentally looks like something the dog ate.
Peabody's not listening,
he's fingering the label of his beer
and watching his next appointment
sashay in through the doors.
"When I offered to buy you dinner, I thought you would choose

a more elegant experience." Venable approaches Peabody
with an open hand.
"I like the fries. Let's take a booth, just us two," says Peabody
shaking the hand, with a glance toward Goyo, Cutter, and Blue.
"I can assure you, there's nothing I should know
that should be hidden from my associates."
Venable's smile is cold and polite.
"Indulge me."
Venable sizes Peabody up, reads his eyes.
"Excuse us for a moment, gentlemen."

"You look a little worn, Detective."
"Yeah, well," Peabody takes a sip from his beer. "I've had my
    worries lately."
"About what?" asks Venable.
"Boy, you name it."
The little man scratches his head, "Well, I'm sorry to hear that."
Peabody leans forward. "Listen, I don't want to waste your time,
I just thought you would want to know: I found them."
A light goes on in Venable's eyes, "Who?"
"Who you're looking for," Peabody shoots back.
The little man grins. "You have? My. Well. Nicely done."
"Yes, and I've learned a few things along the way."
Venable shifts slightly in his seat,
realizing that the tack of the conversation
has shifted as well.
"Mmmn, feel free to share, Detective."

"Well, for starters," Peabody nods toward Goyo,
"I always thought he was Samoan.
I don't know where I got that idea.
But it turns out he's not."
Venable smiles. "No, no, he's not. He's from northern Mexico,
it's those beautiful almond-shaped eyes
that tend to confuse people, well, that

and his somewhat sizable presence."
Peabody nods, "Okay, now,
about the work you both do."
"The work we do?" says Venable, "We do many things."
"They said you're a big manufacturer of meth. And a distributor."
Venable grimaces slightly. "What an interesting and
if I may say so, ridiculous statement. Really. They said this?"
"We talked."
"Well, I wish you had consulted with me before you did so.
You were only hired for surveillance, Detective."
"Can't turn the clock back on that.
Anyway they know you, they know all about you."
"Do they? That's interesting. I thought I was the hunter here."
"Yeah, well," says Peabody, thinking about his fumbled attempts
down at the San Pedro stakeout.
"They have a funny way of turning the game around."
Peabody watches the little man,
wondering how to step forward in this conversation.
"The point is, as I said, I've spoken with them."
"And?" Venable's twitching with impatience.
Peabody settles back in his chair and
prepares to deliver the message he was handed
back up there at the dry ranch, "Well, the surprising thing is
these guys, the ones you want so badly, it turns out
they want to meet with you too."
Peabody lets this sink in, watching as,
for the first time since he met him,
a look of surprise dawns across Venable's tiny face.
The little man almost spits out his next question.
"Why would I ever want to do that?"
Peabody tries to decipher Venable's expression,
but it's no use, all Peabody is there to do is read his lines,
to put the game in motion,
to pose that one critical question the blond kid told him to ask.
"Mr. Venable, do you remember a man

by the name of Juan Garcia?"
Peabody watches the name drift across the counter
into the little man's waiting ears.

V

Up in the hills, the blond brothers
walk out with Ruiz into the yard.
"What's up today?" Ruiz asks,
looking at them with eyes that are somehow both
bitter and bemused.
"Today is something, Ruiz. Really something."
Palo removes a case from the trunk of the car
and rests it on the hood,
pausing before he unlatches and opens it,
"Take a look."
Ruiz steps up and looks down, his eyes changing quickly to fear.
"Oh shit," he says, "you can't be serious."
Lying in the case is a large synthetic limb.
Ruiz is trembling. "Come on, you guys, I've paid."
"Look at it again, Ruiz, check it out.
It's a prosthetic leg. Top of the line.
Hundreds of thousands of people use them."
"Fuck you. Come on. I'm saying I've paid."
"Really?" says Palo, pulling a chain saw out of the trunk
while his brother sits in the front seat of the car,
carefully juicing a syringe.
"How many dogs did you kill in your games, Ruiz?"
"I told you, I don't know. I can't remember."
"Two hundred would you say, Ruiz? Did you kill two hundred
    dogs?"
"I can't remember, man, I don't know."
"We were there Ruiz, we remember."
"I was fucking different then. It was a long time—"
"And you fed the dead dogs—you chopped up
and you fed all the dead dogs—

to their brothers and sisters,
isn't that right? Didn't you?
Didn't you, Ruiz?"
"I don't know, man, those guys who worked for me,
they were pretty fucked up. They did stuff—"
Palo reaches into the belt behind his back
pulls out a gun and presses it hard
against Ruiz's temple. "Shut up, old man. Shut up and don't
    move."
Ruiz trembles with anger and fear as
the other brother plunges the syringe into his arm.
"We were there, Ruiz," Palo says again.
They stand with him till his eyes
flicker and he falls heavily
into their waiting arms.

Gently they lower him to the ground
where the brother carefully
ties a tourniquet
around Ruiz' right leg.

Annie goes inside
as Palo fires up the chain saw.

Anthony, lying with the pack, looks up to see
the spraying blood staining the driveway.
Not for the first time, it occurs to him
that white folks seem to
have a corner
on the cruel and unusual.

Later, he finds himself sitting apart
from the rest of the dogs
happy to skip dinner
while they enjoy the fresh, warm meat.

VI

Lark watches through binoculars
from the roof of a neighboring warehouse
as the limousine pulls up in front of Baron's bunker.
Out of the long dark car comes a small creature and a big fellow
and wow who would have expected that, because there they are,
ol' Cutter and Blue, brushing themselves off as they emerge.
Last heard from long ago as they prepped for the Regional Finals
in a Pasadena bridge tournament.
Then, yes, the binoculars spot Baron striding across the lot,
looking just as surprised to see Cutter and Blue as Lark is.
Lark watches the hugs and grins and shucking and boxing
and more hugs. The little guy and the fat man seem lost off to
    the side
until the little one pulls at the smiling Baron's sleeve,
and whispers into his ear.
Lark wishes he could hear what's going on,
but this is as close as he can risk getting.
Too many dogs down there know his scent,
even this distance might not be great enough.
So he stays on the roof, guessing.
Whatever the little fellow says, Baron nods and
leads them all inside.
Lark puts down the binoculars,
never feeling as in it and yet
never feeling as outside of it
as he feels
right now.

VII

Baron chews slowly,
watching Cutter and Blue sitting a bench away

wolfing down their food while
slapping the shoulders of old friends and
savoring their beautiful reunion.
Baron doesn't trust this,
but he can't figure out the trap.
Something hasn't smelled right for days
and their presence just makes things feel
worse.

Venable only ever asked for one thing,
just knock out the cook labs.
Venable's scale of operation is huge while
the garage labs they take down
are always less than nickel-and-dime.
But that makes sense to Baron, after all,
competition is competition.

This time, however, Venable wants something different.
Some crew asked for a meeting
and he wants Baron to provide backup.
The meeting is going to involve an exchange.
Once Venable has what he came for,
Baron is supposed to take out the other side.
Straightforward stuff.
Couldn't be simpler.
But a lingering suspicion
sticks to his ribs.

Venable and his big friend drove away hours ago,
leaving Cutter and Blue behind to play with the old gang.
Baron waits until the two are done eating and
then sits down for some casual questions.
A couple of guys lean against the wall,
watching. A few dogs lie around the floor, watching too,
just in case they're needed.
All it takes is a signal.

"Have you heard from Lark?" Baron tries to keep it relaxed,
but he knows Cutter sees the men
and the dogs
and knows why they're there.
"Haven't heard from Lark in ages."
"Do you know where he is?"
"Come on Baron, we know what's what.
Lark's dead to us. Just fucking relax, okay?"

Baron changes the subject, asking about
Venable and anything they might know there.
Especially concerning this meeting.
They know a little.
According to them, Venable had been searching
for this crew for a while.
A girl on the crew killed the fat man's brother,
could have been a contract hit,
could have been just cold-blooded murder,
but she got away with it.
And it turns out she took something with her,
something they want.
That's what the meeting is about.
To get that certain something back.

"Stay here," Baron says, getting up.
He moves down the hallway, out of earshot,
and dials Venable's number.
"Yes?" comes the smooth man's voice.
"You said this exchange involved bank records," says Baron.
"Yes."
"What kind of records."
"As I said, that's not your concern."
"It's our concern if we're going with you."
Venable is quiet for a moment, no doubt weighing
what he can disclose on a mobile,

how far he can trust Baron.
"Well." Venable sighs. "Here is all we know.
My friend Goyo's brother Tomas had been stealing from him,
using a friend, one Juan Garcia, to launder the money.
When Tomas was killed, Juan was killed too.
The killer found the information on his body,
bank statements, account numbers
she took it all with her."
Baron relaxes a bit, the story fits
what Cutter told him.
So Cutter gets to live. Blue too.
Lucky dogs.
"One more thing Venable."
"What's that?"
"I'm doubling the fee for this job."
"And why is that?" asks Venable.
"Because it's that important to you.
We'll bring the dogs,
and they'll take these guys down,
but it's going to cost you double."
Venable can't conceal his irritation,
his voice cracks as he answers,
"Fine then. Double it is."

Baron goes back into the open space,
and offers Cutter and Blue a wide smile.
"Welcome home, boys."

VIII

"Hey, gorgeous," says Pete Howard
to the little black schnauzer
he passes by
on his evening jog,
"Hey, gorgeous," he says again, this time

to the golden retriever being walked by the old lady.
Pete smiles to himself, three miles should be fine,
loop around Pico and then back down Neilson.
The fading light's nice, he feels all right.
Pete's been thinking about buying one of those baby joggers
Not so much for the kid as for himself, pushing something
would tone his upper body.
But for the kid too, yeah, it would be nice to spend time with
    the kid.
After all, his therapist says Pete needs more gentle time.
Pete can feel the jangling in his bones, that's old age creeping up.
He's been drinking powders to increase his bone mass.
He feels good.
He hasn't had a drink in ten months.
He stopped for a lot of reasons, he didn't like the lack of control,
he didn't like the way the blood vessels popped on his cheeks.
And the DUIs weren't pretty either.
There's a plastic surgeon he golfs with
says he can get rid of the blood vessels
in ten minutes. Nice.
Peter turns up Brooks St., figuring he'll cut over to Seventh.

What's up with that dog over there?

Whose dog is it—that big one?
That's what Pete hates about this town, no discipline.
Some homeless joe dies and his dog will wander for days
before animal control picks them up.
What a dirty, scummy town.
Half the people in Venice don't even pick up after their dogs.
Makes a runner's life hell.
And this damn dog seems like it's following Pete,
a mirror image jogging along at the same pace, across the street
each paw landing
with the same rhythm as his feet.

* * *

Pete turns up Seventh and the dog crosses over
turning up Seventh, but staying on the opposite side.
This is weird, and not good, thinks Pete.

He starts looking around
for a cop car or something, someone he can flag down.

He crosses Vernon,
the dog crosses Vernon with him,
still on the opposite side.

The sun has set,
filling the skies with a soft golden light
that catches in the dog's glinting eyes,
eyes that seem to be watching him.
Not good.

This isn't worth it, Pete thinks, and doubles back,
running toward Vernon and checking over his shoulder.
Sure enough, the dog has turned around too.

Adrenaline courses through Pete's body.
Now he's in a full run.

And so is the dog.

Where is everybody?
He would flag down a car but that would put him
into the street, which is the no man's land
between him and the dog
a boundary he somehow senses he shouldn't cross.

They keep running, and now a palpable fear
is driving every one of Pete's steps.
It would be okay,
almost like the dog was playing,

if the hair standing up on its back
didn't suggest some
deeper threat.

His heart is thumping hard.
His Nikes are moving fast now.
The dog keeps up, it's clear this pace
isn't much of an effort for the beast.
There's menace in every step of the dog's gait.
The corners of its mouth are pulled slightly back,
revealing white teeth and pink gums.

Sprinting now and breathing hard,
Pete sees a couple of teenage boys
sitting on the curb up ahead. Pete slows,
he looks over as he does and sees the dog slow too,
but still no sign that it will cross.
"Hey guys," says Pete.
The dumb boys look up, slightly thrown by this sweating
     stranger.
"Listen," continues Pete, surprised that the fear
comes so easily to his voice, "you guys have a cell phone?"
"Yeah," drones one of the kids.
"Okay, do me a favor. Please. Call the cops and tell them
there's a stray dog chasing joggers. Fucking chasing me."
The kids say,
"What dog?"

Looking around,
sure enough,
no dog.

When he reaches home
there's a note taped to his door.
"I sent the dog and
I will keep sending the dog

and the dog will be there every day
until the dog kills you."

The most terrifying part
is that he recognizes
the handwriting.

Six months later, he has put on fifteen pounds.
He and his wife are living in Colorado Springs.
He washes the dishes, watches TV
and never takes out the trash.
In fact,
Pete stays inside
pretty much
forever.

IX

Finally chasing Pete
seeing the panic as it hit him
block after block, wave after wave,
she could taste it and
it was like candy.
Driving now, inland,
she wishes she could chase him every day,
just run him down,
but she knows he'll stop running now
'cause that's Pete. Only strong, never brave.
Her small smile fades to nothing
she drives on thinking
yeah, revenge is sweet, like they say
only it leaves your stomach raw
and it will carve you out
just like any sinful dessert
it's the course that
always promises,

but never delivers
any true satisfaction.

It's all right, though, it's a step back
from the shadows she's been hiding in.
Maybe soon she'll be ready to find Anthony again.
Then the two of them
could fight off every demon together.
She would tell him her secrets, show him
the way of her world. She paid too great a price
for hiding what she was from him.
And now she is alone.
But she could be his again. And he hers.
Driving on 10, she almost keeps going.
Her heartbeat is up and a soft thrill moving in her blood,
Then a car passes, shaking her out of her fantasy,
the shadows fall back into place and she recalls
that home is nothing now but ash
and the only slight glimmer of hope she has
is ringing right now on the cell phone.

Lark's calling
from the lookout
"Something's up." he says.
"I need you now." His voice is cold, bloodless.
"I need everyone."
He hangs up.
She doesn't say a word,
just hits the blinker
and quickly swerves his way.

X

Looking out the window of the Drug Enforcement Agency,
Peabody notices how clean the city looks.
Last night's rain scrubbed the smog from the skies

restoring LA's shine again,
like it's been through a car wash.

He's been waiting in the lobby
of the Santa Monica office all morning.
He came down on his own,
avoiding the official channels
since Venable has as good as told him
that all those channels are fouled.

The Fed's name is Morrow.
He's got a clean haircut
and suit that's diligently pressed.
One of those valley Christians, thinks Peabody.
Mormon? Maybe.
After the introductions, Peabody asks
if the D.E.A.'s been looking
into anything on a Goyo Castillo.
Morrow nods. "Goyo Castillo is very big."
Peabody laughs. "Yeah, I know, he's really fat."
Morrow shakes his head. "No, I mean his business is big."
Morrow fills him in on how Goyo runs one of the larger operations
the D.E.A. knows of, bringing massive quantities of drugs,
mostly meth, in from across the border. At a certain point,
Morrow stops talking, obviously it's time for Peabody to share,
"Okay, here's what I know,
Castillo's been working with this guy Venable.
Who is a very queer little fellow."
Morrow pauses. His smile slips away.
"Queer?" says Morrow.
"Yeah, queer, you know, strange and kind of gay," says Peabody.
Morrow smiles, even colder now, nodding along.
"So what I'm hearing here is," he says, "gays are, um,
queer and strange?"
Peabody senses he's taken a serious wrong turn.
Morrow leans back in his chair. "You know, this isn't

the Soviet Union. If it doesn't hurt anyone,
and if it's consensual, people
can choose any sort of lifestyle they want
and love whoever they want,
that makes sense, doesn't it?
That's what freedom is,
that's what being Ameri—"
"—Look, I'm sorry," interrupts Peabody, "I didn't mean any-
    thing,
really, maybe you could look in your files for him."
Morrow slowly turns and taps on his keyboard for a few sec-
    onds.
There is a slight pause and then the files begin
popping up on the screen,
one after another.
A quiet Morrow studies the data.
A few minutes later
he looks up at Peabody and says
"You know, this is the kind of guy
who gives homosexuality
a bad name."

XI

The sun is settling low in the sky
while Annie works out back, washing out the linens.
Palo is kneeling down in the gravel drive
hitching a third trailer to a third truck.
Two dogs are off to the side, sniffing a patch of grass,
sensing some stain of life in the dust.
Anthony emerges from the cabin, walking like a sleepy man.
He bites into a red apple.
"So, how long have you all had this ranch?" he asks.
"It was Ruiz's," says Annie. "He gave it to us."
Anthony mulls this over, takes another bite of the apple,
"That was nice of him," he says, heading back inside.

Annie wrings the crimson stains from the sheets.
She looks over to Palo.
"I'm not going up tonight."
Palo shifts his focus from the truck hitch. "Why not?"
"You know why. You don't need me.
    And Ruiz isn't well. That leg is infected."
Palo is silent, turns back to his work.
"How much more are you going to put him through?" asks
    Annie.
Palo finishes with the hitch, pulls to make sure it's secure.
"Maybe we'll just take a kidney and leave it at that."
"That's not funny."
Palo walks toward the house, stopping at the steps to the porch,
not looking at her. "We could use you there tonight, Annie."
"Someone has to stay and help Ruiz."
"Okay, but come if you change your mind."
"No. We'll be here. Just come home to us."

Twenty minutes later Palo and his brother leave the house.
One opens the wooden gate, the other whistles loudly,
there's a rattle of cans and the earth softly rumbles as
the dusty pack of dogs spills out from behind the house
silently splitting into three groups
that gently jump up into the truck trailers.
Anthony walks out onto the porch, putting on his jacket.
Annie kisses him on the cheek and says,
with a voice nearly breaking,
"Just look out for Palo."

Palo secures the trailer doors.
The two blonds and Anthony each slip in
behind the wheel of a truck, firing up
and driving away.
Anthony looks at Annie getting smaller
in the rearview mirror.
He has only a vague idea of what's up the road, but

he doesn't really care. It's funny how,
when love is drained from your heart,
when only flesh and broken watch pieces lie left
    behind,
even something as wonderful as magic
fails to be interesting.
"Ah," we say, or
"That's something else," our eyes dead
to the strange light.
He drives on toward nothing.

Annie had never promised him anything more
than a change, which was honestly all he wanted,
a new skin.
He wanted to strip away the pain but not the sadness,
he wanted to breathe real life into every memory
but still somehow let go,
he wanted to become something else
while holding on to everything he had.
All he had, it turned out, was love.
She was gone, but her love was still alive inside him.
It was the only thing keeping him on this earth,
the only reason he could find to continue,
to protect that one part of her that
still remained, her love for him,
the small ray of light that lay
within the shadowed hollows of his heart.

But he couldn't live without her,
so he took on another kind of life.
It was that simple.
So now he is simply something more
and nothing less.

The dogs are silent in the back
as he trails Palo up Interstate 5, then follows east.

Heading into the steadily rising and endlessly broken hills.
It's about an hour before they've stopped,
pulling into an abandoned tire dump
where old Firestones
Goodyears, Dunlops, B. F. Goodriches, and the odd Pirelli
Are stacked across acres like charred fingers of death.
They leave the headlights of the trucks on as
Palo opens the trailers and the dogs tumble out,
quickly vanishing into the fractured landscape
like black water soaking into the soil.
Anthony and the brother remove their shoes and their socks
and, making the change,
rise to shake off their dusty coats
and walk with Palo.
The parked trucks' headlights,
illuminating a path
through the valley of used treads
toward a certain destination.

Beside him and around him,
across the damp earth,
amid the darkened curves,
the hundred shadows
move too.

XII

Baron hasn't been in a limo for some time.
It makes him smile, remembering the luxury of the old pack.
He looks at Cutter and Blue, nods with a smile.
Venable is tucked into the corner
picking his cuticles while
the big man called Goyo rests with his eyes closed.
"I've been wondering . . .," begins Baron.
"Yes?" replies Venable.
"Since they have the account numbers,

why doesn't this crew just take the money themselves?"
"Well, I'm sure they would if they could,
but luckily, they would need to be part of Tomas's family,
his close family, and Goyo is his only kin.
For anyone else, the information is useless."
Baron nods. "I see."
Venable shakes his head.
"Tomas was stupid
to steal from his brother.
We would have caught him.
He was such a child.
My god, they're all children down there.
Were it not for Goyo's formidable mind,
Tomas would have spent his life lacing sneakers
in the maquiladoras.
Of course, then he might still be alive.
If you call that living."
Venable falls silent.
Baron prefers the quiet.

The limo pulls into the meeting place
followed neatly by three Econolines,
each a little battered.
Blue opens the back doors
and dozens of dogs leap out
their silhouettes cross the headlights.
Venable and Goyo walk ahead,
Venable clutching the case of money.
Baron follows a few steps behind.
Nearing the crest of the hill, they see a man with two dogs
ascending the other side.
"Seems he's brought friends as well," says Venable.
Baron looks around suspiciously, the air is heavy
too many smells fog his thoughts.

XIII

A few thousand feet up and a few thousand feet away
a black helicopter silently whirrs
unnoticed in the night sky.
On loan from Homeland Security,
the S–70 Blackhawk is loaded with a pilot,
a parabolic sound system, state-of-the-art electronics,
two officers from special ops named Samuels and Ryan,
the Fed named Morrow,
and Detective Peabody
who for the first time in a long while,
is beginning to feel like a cop again.

They are simply there to observe, listen, and record.
Though Samuels and Ryan are there in case
an opportunity for action arises.
Samuels is chewing gum methodically
as he plays with a wall of electronics
trying to pinpoint sounds on the ground.
Peabody and Morrow follow
the glowing orange dots of radar.
"What are those?" Peabody points
as a group of the dots slink across the screen.
"Dunno," says Ryan. "Could be coyotes."

"I'm getting something," says Samuels, and Peabody puts on
    headphones.
Through the whispering static, he can make out a familiar lisp,
caught midmeander,
" . . . yes, I believe I have heard about those dogs."
"These dogs?" This from a voice Peabody doesn't recognize.
"Yes," says Venable. "I believe they killed two men awhile back."
"Just two?"

"Two that I know of."
"Well," says the unfamiliar voice.
"I see you brought your own dogs."
"Protection. From those," says Venable.
Through the crackling on the line,
this pair reminds Peabody of old radio voices
cast in some vaudeville performance.
"Are you Mr. Castillo?" says the man.
"Of course not," says Venable. "But I speak for him."
"Is that him behind you?" asks the man.
"I'm really not at liberty to say."
Peabody admires Venable's ability to sound
perfectly irritating
with every word he utters.
"Uh-huh," says the man. "We came to meet Castillo."
Silence. Peabody wonders who is looking at whom,
what decision is being made.
Finally Venable snaps, "In that case,
then, yes that is Castillo. Mr. Goyo Castillo.
Now, we have brought what you asked for. And we
would like to have the documents."
Morrow looks annoyed,
this rambling information is vague and more or less useless.
Peabody feels sorry that he included him,
probably wasting his time,
but then, hey, welcome to the show.
After all, for Peabody it's been nothing but
vagaries and half guesses all along.
"I'd like to ask Mr. Castillo a couple of questions,"
says the unknown voice.
Peabody can't hear Venable sigh, but he can feel it.
"Surely you can't be serious."
"Back in Mexico, Mr. Castillo, you used dogs as guards."
"I am growing so tired of this obsession with dogs? What the—"
The voices cut off.

Peabody turns toward the screen where
a long rectangular object
slides into the frame and stops.
What is it? A truck? A semi?
And what's happening there in the back?
On the screen, glowing orange lights
begin flowing from the rectangle
like luminescent sparks
erupting from a Roman candle.

Venable's hiss breaks the silence. "Friends of yours?"
"No, I thought they came with you."
There is an angry bark, and another,
four or five more answer and suddenly
in Peabody's headphones there is a cacophony of howls,
the chorus of unleashed fury
loud, fierce, and mean.
On the radar
the orange lights surge together,
like hornets attacking.

Peabody looks at Morrow,
"What are we supposed to do now?"
Samuels smacks his gum, nods at Ryan,
and reaches for a case beneath his feet.

XIV

She had come up with the new pack,
in an old yellow school bus Tati had dug up somewhere.
She changed before she met them,
hopping onto the bus without looking at the other dogs.
Maria sniffed her once,
and recognized her from the night they met,

but the rest of the pack left her alone.
She was with Lark, good enough.
They thought only of the coming battle.

Some guy named Bunny drove while
the rest of them changed
one after another, from front to back.
She watched the whole bus transform
row after row, man to dog, man to dog,
a deck of cards cascading over
to expose some devil's tarot underneath.
Lark sat behind Bunny, showing him
how to trail the cars, when to pull up
when to fall away.
And once the cars turned into the dump,
he had Bunny pull over and let the bus idle.
Lark moved to the back, clearly and loudly
reviewing the instructions once more.
Once more, they listened;
dogs gazing up with rapt attention.
Finishing his speech, he looked down and began his own
        change.
Bunny watched through the wide rearview mirror,
nodded when Lark was back up on four paws, then hit the gas,
driving their big yellow beast of a bus up into the maze of waste.

When the exit door finally opened,
she jumped
crossing the first fifty yards at breakneck speed,
well ahead of the pack.
Surprise, Lark told them, it's all about surprise.
But anger helps too. The fury inside her fuels every step.
In no time her snapping teeth have found another dog's thigh.
And with that yelp, the enemy pack turns.
Now the engagement begins,
as the waves of dogs she leads

fall in behind her, aiming for the enemy's haunches
and necks.
She knows the smell of every wolf on the bus,
anyone else is fair game.
The dog she's attacked turns and lunges, but
he's not well trained, loose in his fighting,
and when one of her dogs intervenes, going for the throat,
it's over fast. She releases her bite and snaps to her left,
sinking her fangs into enemy hide,
but the tight flesh between her teeth won't give,
she gnashes again and as the flesh tears away,
warm blood fills her mouth, its familiar taste
flooding her tongue and throat.
Her heartbeat surges.
This is satisfaction.
Bite snap, go.

XV

Lark attacks, knowing this could be the end.
Back in the city, perched on the rooftop like a crow
watching the Econolines being loaded with serious muscle,
he had sensed the scale of what he was up against and
a yawning black hole of doubt opened up inside.
He had looked at Maria,
who read his mood and shook it off.
"Come on," she said. "We're ready for it."
He knew she was wrong, but he went anyway.
Perhaps that is what Tati spoke of,
the curse of the coyote,
how, hungry for the pack,
you try to fight your way back in,
only to be snapped up and
ground down into the dust.
He's planned, he's studied, he knows
now is no time

for the impulsive play.
But still, he's putting it all in motion.
Perhaps out of revenge,
perhaps out of nothing more than
love of the game.

There are two things that make
the conscious world move,
decision and desire.
And Lark has never felt more awake
than he feels leaping forward now.
He bites and snarls and drives in
as Maria, with Bunny behind her, leads a wing of the attack
off to the right, drawing the fight away from their target.
Lark and the rest of the dogs barrel on toward the hill,
where Baron stands
with a blond man, a little fellow, and a giant,
encircled by a protecting wall of dogs.
The men look more confounded than concerned,
more curious than afraid.
And with an anger alive in his chest,
a raw fury Lark has only rarely felt,
he finally becomes
the beast he is.
He charges toward the men, his ears back.
Growls, barks, and cries surround him.
Win or lose, all Lark wants to do
is eat that expression off their faces.

Mid fur-filled bite, while
shaking off an attack on his flank,
Lark sees one of the men,
the blond,
put his fingers to his mouth
and let out a low whistle.
And then Lark feels the night around him

begin to simmer with motion
and he can't tell
if he's been caught in a trap
or something even more
unpredictable.

XVI

At the whistle's mark,
Palo's wolves leap out
from behind the shadows of debris and the ridges of rusted
      waste
falling on both sides of the fighting pack and raising the volume
to something louder and more chaotic,
a shrieking, killing symphony of noise.
Anthony sticks close to Palo,
a dog protecting his master
from the unbridled violence that's closing in.
The little man speaks up. "This is most unexpected,
do you think we'll be all right?"
At which point Palo's glance catches Baron's,
for the first time they understand each another.
Baron pulls his shirt over his head, Palo shuts his eyes.
"What are you—" but then Venable screams.
For at the signal of the change,
the dogs at Palo's feet have leapt up on Goyo,
the man whose chain-link fence in Mexico
held certain dogs to the cruelest death.
Now Goyo is the one cornered, the one
trying to survive as the pistol he pulls out
falls away useless while leaping
fangs sink into veins on his wrist.
Three dogs take him down so fast his last moments
are mere motion and guttural groans.
Venable kicks at the dogs, shouting,
his attention divided between

the agony of Goyo's suffering, which he can't fight,
can barely look at,
and the rippling metamorphosis on his side
which he can't believe, and can't turn his eyes from.
The briefcase has fallen from his hands and burst open,
the cash spilling into the wind and mud.
Baron and Palo rise up, beasts themselves now,
and dive at each other without hesitation
while Venable is still screaming a high-pitched scream,
kicking at the dogs that draw near.
The dogs don't touch him,
letting him watch, helplessly, as his friend
is torn and rendered
into large and muddy chunks
of bone, meat, and tendon.
Sobbing now,
Venable doesn't hear
the helicopter descending
or the first bullets
raining down.

XVII

Samuels and Ryan, armed with night vision
and assault rifles, feel something akin to battle.
In a way, this is nothing, these
are just dogs after all, wild feral vermin,
target practice, though
an urgency does drive their efficiency,
as the distance of helicopter and
the wavering of human decision
have brought them in range too late for three men
who have now disappeared from their radar.
But the fourth still stands clearly at the center.
Perhaps they can save the fourth.

*   *   *

Peabody and Morrow watch as bullet after
    bullet
is squeezed off into the fray below,
the tip of each rifle moving in
small increments of sure precision,
as Samuels shoots at his next target,
as Ryan fires with
a certain calm.

XVIII

Dog and wolf packs usually fight bloodlessly,
a snarling for pecking order
or mere dominance,
but these packs come with blood that's tinged
with the more brutal violence of man,
making this battle something unique.

And just like that
Maria dies, a bullet
from above cutting through the bone of her skull
releasing her in one fell swoop from the vast blue sea of
    sorrow
she had only just learned to navigate.
Bunny sees her go, watches
the darkness pulled across her face like
the snapping of blinds,
and for him
and for the whole new pack, the battle
is done at that, ending with an abrupt metal punctuation.
He rears back on his haunches,
spinning away from the mass,
almost making it to the tires' shadows
when a bullet catches him as well

tucking between his ears,
sending his long snout crashing down
into the wet dirt.

He wouldn't have lived long
without Maria
anyway.

Spence, Russ, Griff, Stone, Cho, Pauley, Kato, Miguel, Ian, Marc,
Ali, Gus, Ice, Spike, Shel, Francis,
Jin, Craig, Zed, Tanner, Skip, Ben, Jon, Arturo
all go down in quick percussive beats,
one's teeth in another's skin, yelping as
bullets work and bodies spin, flip, are kicked down.
Soon the dogs are racing to run
away from this grim metal storm,
still with the war, though, as they pull their battles
out of the invasive light.
In twos or threes, they flee, chasing or chased,
their fights moving fast to the shadows
like spilled marbles running under the furniture,
or a school of fish darting to the hidden depths.
Lark pauses and measures the vanishing field, finally spotting
a dog he would know anywhere,
his great betrayer, his oldest friend, his simple destiny,
scampering off to nimbly duck behind a sagging column
of torn rubber and steel.
Lark pursues Baron full pace, tongue lagging,
with a passionate resolution
and a vengeful glee.
Dashing around the corner
he races into
waiting teeth.

Venable looks to the hovering helicopter, still screaming.
His shoes are soaked in blood and dirt,

a thousand muddy bills flutter loose in circles
a swarm in the wind around him.
His arms are open wide, his mouth agape,
begging the gods in the machine
to carry him away from this
unfathomable world.

XIX

"Look out for Palo," Annie had said
and a blind loyalty to the brother who brought him here
fills Anthony's body with keen light and brutal focus.
There is a kind of redemption he feels as he sends
searing jaws down into the enemy's muscle and fat.
Yes, this is it. Take it all down. Bite deep until its dead.
Palo fights at his back.
Anthony lashes out at the dogs coming at them,
the fire of universal aggression toward the unknown
propelling him forward until the moment arrives
when he hears
Palo collapse behind him.
Glancing back, he sees that two bullet holes have
sheared off the left side of the blond dog's head.
And so Anthony stops too, pants, ponders, and wonders
what next, watching as the dogs from his pack scurry off,
just as the other pack did when their Queen died.
Then he hears a bullet snap
and looks up to find
the only two left
are him
and one angry bitch.

XX

That dog there, the one in her sights, turns and
looks to his dead companion.

She notes the pause,
the chink of weakness and
in a flash she lunges.
As she crosses the ground,
another dog by her side is hit and goes down
with a piercing whine.
At this, her target turns his head
and sees her speeding at him.
So much for the element of surprise.
He rears back and races from the site,
fleeing either from the terror overhead
or the anger in her eyes.
Either way, she doesn't care,
there will be nothing to stop her.
She has chosen his fate.
She knows she will chase this certain dog
to his certain end.

XXI

Up in the helicopter,
Peabody watches on the radar as
orange lights one by one
go black like matchsticks blown out.
Samuels and Ryan are taking their toll.
"There's the guy there." Morrow aims a
      spotlight.
Peabody sees Venable standing
clearly insane in his hysteria.
"That's the guy," Peabody says to Morrow.
"The little fellow?"
"Yeah."
Venable is yelling and hopping around,
yelling like a fevered fool.
Peabody watches him, thinking about the soft self-assurance

he heard in Venable's voice
when they first spoke months ago,
recalling all the places that voice has led him since.
Peabody says, "Let's loop around and make sure everything's
    secure.
We can come back and pick him up later."
The helicopter crew is silent
knowing they're leaving this man
to the judgment of mad dogs.
But when the soldier Samuels speaks up,
all he says is, "Okay."
"Yeah." Ryan shrugs. "No point landing
till we know the ground is clear."
And the chopper heads off
leaving Venable
soiled and screaming
with a fresh and blossoming pain.

They arc the helicopter round in
widening circles above the landscape
fragments of orange popping on the screen
as dogs fight in the shelter of the dump's refuse,
impossible to target. So the helicopter flies on,
each man reading the earth carefully, eyeing the terrain,
until suddenly: "Fuck. What the hell is that?"
Ryan's pointing to something glistening in the mud.
"Get closer," says Samuels.
Ryan is on his walkie,
alerting unknown and distant voices
to the strange scene they are descending toward,
one which has everyone onboard,
even the battle-scarred soldiers,
staring wide-eyed
in dumb wonder.

* * *

XXII

She chases the dog,
her paws raw and torn from the rocks and loose glass,
her neck bleeding as she leaps over tires and through toxic mud.
The radial fibers tear into the tender flesh between each paw.
The pain fuels her anger as she eyes her prey hop nimbly
    from one pile to the next.
She keeps after him.
She will chase him until
he has been severed from time.

XXIII

Cutter hides at the edge
watching gravely as Blue,
pierced with a bullet
that must have touched his brain just so,
lies twisting in the mud with an epileptic fury.
Blue's contortions are worse than shock, electrical
crosscurrents inside his mind set the change
surging.
Cutter can barely watch as Blue's face
goes canine then human then canine again,
fur riding up and down his flesh like a bristled wave,
Blue's spasms squeeze an agonizing wet growl from his throat.
Cutter steps out gingerly, preparing
to end his friend's pain in the surest and hardest way.
But bright lights sweep the ground and he quickly jumps back
as the helicopter descends.
Three men, moving fast, grab
a shaking, bleeding Blue, lay him on a plastic sheet,
and lift him into the loud bird.

* * *

As it rises, Cutter steps into its wake,
looking up
as his friend disappears,
swallowed into the bed of the night's
low clouds.

XXIV

The helicopter never went back for Venable
he was left to wander, broken, back
to the limo that still sat waiting, just over the hill.
Getting in, the blood and mud
leaked from his clothes, staining the perfect
white leather.
"Go," he shrieked.
The driver, who'd been listening to his iPod
oblivious to the night's events,
looked around for the others.
He wouldn't budge without them, after all,
he was hired by Goyo.
He would wait.
"Goyo's dead! Goyo's dead!" Venable swung
for the back of the driver's head
through the open partition.

A weeping, thrashing Venable
was pulled kicking from the car.
The driver threw him to the dirt
and spat on him for good measure
before driving away.

The driver didn't care, fuck it,
Venable couldn't fire him, he quit.

Venable slapped his palms on the wet earth
and collapsed into sobs that shook
the world around him.

XXV

Fifteen miles away, as they cut across the night sky,
Ryan is still on the radio, calling in descriptions
of the dog man thing that's twitching on the tarp.
Peabody stares at it,
almost feeling the spasms and the agony in his own gut.
Whatever it is, the trembling flesh is swollen and pink,
thick strands of fur rising from patches
only to quickly recede again.
Even the bones seem agonized
as the cycle repeats itself.
Peabody can't bear to watch
and shifts his gaze to the landscape instead.
The darkness below
makes him suspect the helicopter is headed
away from the city,
and sure enough when they finally touch down
it's at a military base
way east and Sierra high.

A medevac team is waiting on the tarmac and within seconds
two men have jumped on board with
a needle full of something.
They dose the beast up and load it, still groaning,
onto a gurney, into an ambulance, and off they go,
taking Samuels and Ryan with them.
Morrow and Peabody are left staring
at the siren lights that disappear past a Quonset hut.
Just like that, the mystery
has vanished.

* * *

Peabody looks at Morrow. "Any idea what that was?"
"No. And the way these guys work,
I'm sure we'll never know."
They silently stand there,
letting their adrenaline cool.
Morrow jumps onto the tarmac
and offers a hand to Peabody.
"Come on, I've got a feeling we're going to
have to find our own ride home."
Peabody takes his hand and hops down
not saying anything as they head toward the base
their minds slightly blown
but their bodies intact.

XXVI

Anthony's vow to Annie ended
the minute Palo closed his eyes.
Just like that, his blood hunger died away
and all he wanted to do was flee the game.
But leaving has proved tricky,
that mad and vengeful cur is still close on his heels.
What a waste. To turn and bare teeth
would be to struggle for or against something
he no longer knows or feels. The war between life and death
goes on without him tonight,
now he simply runs.
The dog maintains her pursuit,
try as she might neither losing ground nor gaining it.
They have left the dump behind
and now race through the empty veins of the city
across barely lit neighborhoods
where the people living stretched-thin lives
clutch at the edge of civilization.
Anthony runs on, along the pocked and torn roads,
past trailers lying at loose and random angles.

He barely glances back, his pace feels sure.
Eventually he can escape this dog and then,
perhaps, he'll head back to the sea,
this strange chapter finished. But first
he just keeps running
from a dog he could take
if he even cared.

XXVII

Cutter wanders tail down back toward
the last thing he can think of as home.
It takes him longer, unsure of his way
mourning his lost friend with every step,
sniffing for traces of familiar dogs or familiar signs.
When he stops and curls up beneath the dry sagebrush,
a long, unbroken whine leaks out of him.
He remembers Blue in pale rooms full of cards,
a dog with a head full of hearts and spades and
fifty-two memories in every hand.
Cutter cries for his friend.
When the sun comes down
and our bodies rest,
our souls catch up.

Early the next morning, he rises to venture
out into the new pink light.
Chased by some kids through an abandoned lot
and slinking through alleyways eating
whatever an alley's got,
Cutter keeps heading south.

He reaches the bunker in four days' time.
The steel door is open, so he crosses the lot
and trots right in, his nose

up for trouble. But there are only
a handful of dogs and a couple of guys
all looking bruised, scarred, tired.
They had made it back in ones and twos,
and not many at that.
Finding a quiet corner, he lies down on the concrete floor
and changes, then searches through the warehouse
till he finds the pile of clothes he left behind.
He buttons his shirt
and nudges a guy
resting against the wall.
"What's the plan?" Cutter asks,
The guy doesn't even look at him as he answers.
"We wait."
"What do we wait for?"
"We wait for Baron."
"Is anyone sure he's coming back?"
The guy shrugs.
Somewhere back in the shadows
a lone dog sighs
a long sigh.

XXVIII

Her body is sore
with the plain truth of exhaustion.
Her anger has burned down to small coals
as thirst pulls at a throat
scratched raw from the grit and the grime,
but she's come so far
there's nothing for her to do but go on trailing.

A mile on ahead, he stops, lifts his leg,
pisses against a tree,
then moves on.

Paces later she barely pauses as she passes
but sniffs the wetness, and feels the heaviness sink in.
She can sense the strength buried in his scent.
And something about it
gives her chills.

She shakes it off with a snort
and keeps going.

There are another two miles of this.
He moves with a kind of assuredness,
his body swaying with cowdog hips.
She blinks
half-blinded by the dirt and salt from the roads
but can't quite see him clearly.
She watches though
with great wonder
as he slows, then pauses
at a small roadside puddle.
She approaches cautiously,
edges around him, feels nothing,
the fires inside her having
died down to smoke.
As he drinks
he steps gingerly to the side, making room.
Drops of oil paint, warped rainbows on the surface
but it's good enough for now.
Their cold noses
just barely
touch.

He turns then
and heads back the way they came.
Blinking,
she follows.

XXIX

Almost noon and Peabody's up to his elbows
down at the station.
The phone rings and,
expecting news on an abuse case,
he's surprised to hear a familiar lisp.
"Detective?"
"Ah," Peabody settles in. "I guess I was expecting
to hear from you."
Silence.
"You were there, I assume?" asks Venable.
"Yes." Peabody leafs through a stack of papers,
waiting for the conversation to move on.
"I was quite surprised by it all. By everything."
"Yep. Me too," says Peabody.
Silence, silence, silence.
"So, what are you doing about it?"
"Hmmm." Peabody leans back in his chair. "Well,
I had a partner once,
a long time ago, back when
I was young and he wasn't.
Anyway, you know what he would always say?"
"What was that."
"Well, Mr. Venable, he would say, 'You gotta remember, kid,
this universe was built by the low bidder.'"
Silence, silence, silence.
Peabody picks some dry skin on his knuckle.
"I'm not sure I see," says Venable.
"Well, that's all I've got. Good luck, Mr. Venable."
Peabody hangs up the phone.
He looks at the photo of his boy and his wife.
And, diving back into his papers, he reaches out

in an offhand way and touches the picture frame,
almost for luck, mostly for love.

XXX

When the time came,
when Anthony changed back
as they lay in the shade of a room
with rough lumber walls and a clay dirt floor
in a corner of the canyon ranch he had led them to,
she watched, still a beast,
as his flesh slid into its familiar shape.
Not believing, not trusting, but knowing and feeling
her eyes grew wider as
his muscles were reborn and his slender cheekbones
fell back into place.
Her heart surged, her breath lifting
to the top of her chest
as he emerged whole, like a gift from the gods.
Lying out before her on the floor naked and beautiful
softly breathing, he did not know her, not yet,
that would come soon,
but for now her tail was thumping on the soft earth
with the solid rhythm of joy.

And then
when she changed back
Anthony didn't say anything,
his whole body frozen in tense disbelief.
Again, he waited for the hand that would shake him,
wake him sleepy there on the beach of Venice,
but no hand came.
The dream reality kept unfolding, her taut stomach,
the line of her breasts,
the hair between her legs and
the curve of her thighs.

Even before her face was back,
he knew, his muscles clenched with joy.

As her eyes recast themselves,
he gently reached
across the floor with an open hand
which she seized and held.

He pulled her close, wrapped himself around her white skin,
kissing small pieces of her, salty and wet from the change
touching like a blind man
every mole he had memorized,
breathing the scent of her in.

They didn't speak, they didn't explain
their embrace said it all with
familiar tastes lips touching lips and neck and ear,
the perfect familiar nature rushed
like white water through their spinning minds,
muscles pulling shoulders and hips close
as the rough soil scratched against their skin.
Palms and fingers ran along chests and thighs.
They shook with something that was almost anger
or frustration but truly
only the violent reassurance
of lost things found
driving through them
like a stake.
Kiss embrace kiss shaking off and shivering
embracing in the nakedness of the noon day light.

Afterward, looking out a small window where the blue sky
        entered,
she listened to the sounds of the ranch,
metal clanging, a man's voice
a girl's voice, she heard all this

as Anthony held her still.
Then, like a knot
finally released
she exhaled.

A few moments later,
wearing a borrowed blue dress, she waited as
the girl named Annie talked to Anthony.
Behind them in the driveway, a scarred old man
sat idling in a pickup.
"We're going up the coast," the Annie girl said.
"What about the other dogs?" Anthony asked.
"You're the only one who came back."
Annie looked like she was pretty once,
sometime before
she was so infinitely sad.

XXXI

With the advertising money gone,
the once burgeoning drive to adopt dogs
in the county of Los Angeles withers,
the strays pile up in the kennels
and the short-lived reverse on putting them down
is, predictably, re-reversed
by a clearly regretful but pressured city council.
Dogs who have been passed over
are led to a room where the nurse holds the paw
and the veterinarian slips a thin needle into the living vein.
The dog breathes heavily and the lids flicker
dying down
to nothing.

There are three dogs playing in three separate yards
for whom the machinery of the pound
no longer matter, four months ago they were taken in

by the owner of a deli,
by the daughter of a gym coach,
and by an art teacher
up in the Valley.
These dogs have by now lost their memory of one another
as distant faces and shared scents have been rinsed away
by happier days.
They have forgotten too the man
who once quietly sheltered them
from the chemical jaws of the system.
But they never forget,
the taste
of those carne asada
tacos.

At the edge and the center of heaven,
coyote naps
in the prime mover's shade.

XXXII

Peabody's driving home,
he's blinking hard, pushing it all back,
the memory of the blonde
smiling at him in the San Pedro twilight,
Anthony kneeling, weeping
in the coals of his burnt-out house,
even the smell of the dogs that surrounded him
in the dry heat of the ranch that day.
He lifts each memory up to the light,
then buries them all.

Peabody learned long ago
that holding on to anything too tight, even the truth,
can drive you to places no one should see.

Peabody learned long ago
that having all the answers
was something quite different
from simply saying
case closed.

Case closed.

XXXIII

Moons slide by.

On the beaches of Santa Cruz
two dogs play,
watched over by Annie, the nice young lady
everyone knows, whose laughter
is all ice cream sweetness,
who befriends the homeless, bringing them
curried egg sandwiches and listening to their raspy tales
of who they were before they were this.
Annie takes in the sunset, sitting on benches
amid the lost carnival souls. The broken voices ramble on,
their sad pirate tales curling in the air, but she's silent now,
the rose color fading from her cheeks
her gaze as wide as the empty horizon
and an expression slipping to pebble hard
as if she's only waiting now
for the ocean to rise
and drown the pain.

On the beaches of Santa Cruz
two dogs play,
silently watched by a one-armed man
with lines on his face
hard as ridges on redwood bark.
He sits, never talking to passersby,

never offering his name,
simply chews on his lips and sighs through the days.
He lets the dogs play for hours
before limping after them
toward the soft light of home.

On the beaches of Santa Cruz
two lovers sit on a bench at night
curled up in their small
corner of the world.
She laughs, thinking
of the crooked path they tumbled down
to get here,
where the act of falling finds only
the assurance of another embrace,
where hands are held
with unthinking constancy.

Pointing up at the sky
their voices gild the perfect quiet
as they softly whisper names;
pearl moon,
skillet moon,
lemon moon,
cue ball moon.
Smiling at their own smiles and
leaning together like slender cedars,
with all the tenderness of foolish love.

Cats have been disappearing
from the neighborhood.

XXXIV

Her girlfriend is late for their Tuesday drink night,
so Bonnie orders another pinot grigio

and asks if maybe she can have some crackers.
It's been a tense week,
her allergist says it's the change of seasons
that leaves her feeling all shaky,
but she's not sure.
Maybe it's the Santa Anas.
A tall man comes through the door
and asks about the seat beside her.
"I'm waiting for a friend." She smiles.
"Oh, that's fine, I'll stand." He nods,
and orders a Pellegrino with lime.

Some polite conversation follows,
names, jobs, anecdotes from the day,
then for some reason, whether it's the wine
or the comforting way he listens,
she keeps going, telling him things
that come from deeper and deeper inside,
the loss of the dog, the fear of the future.
She says nothing of the loneliness,
but she knows it's there, she wears it like perfume.
She goes on and he sits listening,
with an expression that holds no judgment.
Finally, she pauses,
smiling with a slight blush.
He places his hand
on hers and says,
"Bonnie, have you ever felt
that you were somehow
different?"

When her friend finally shows,
late because her car wouldn't start,
she finds Bonnie long gone.
The bartender said she left with a fellow
oh, about thirty minutes ago.

Well, good for her, the friend thinks
as she orders herself a rusty nail.

Back at Bonnie's house
he takes the knife
and slowly cuts himself
along a well-worn
pink-and-yellow scar
running the length of his last finger.
She knows she should be frightened
but she isn't.
She trusts Lark.

XXXV

Now too,
resting throughout LA,
kneeling before our children,
lying beneath the broad and blond wood tables
where single moms
cut up wet apples and fresh pears.
Now too,
at the crest of the city's horizon,
trotting alongside runners in the hills
these dogs with their watchful eyes,
pricked-up ears and bristled skin,
are still tense with anticipation.
They move through the days
looking and longing for the once promised
and foretold sign of
Baron.
The new beginning.
An old promise.

They wait,
alert for the moment

when the light changes
and the world rears back
feeling the sharp teeth
of the plan
on its exposed
and waiting neck.
These dogs are ready
sitting patiently
at our feet.

Let us pause now
and close this sanguine song.
Let us cock our own ears and listen

to the random, ringing jangle
of the linked chain
and cool steel leash
dancing together
across the city's
ever looming twilight.

ACKNOWLEDGMENTS

Dedicated to Nora Montana and Carolina Rose. With gratitude to Jennifer Barth, Stephanie Cabot, and Keira Alexandra. Additional acknowledgment goes out to Chris Desser, Lindsey Stanberry, and Chris Parris-Lamb for their assistance. Thanks also to mom, for letting me get a dog.

ABOUT THE AUTHOR

Toby Barlow works in advertising and lives in Detroit and Brooklyn. Previously published by N+1 and *Gargoyle* magazine, he is a contributor to The Huffington Post. This is his first novel.

"If Ovid had been raised on a steady diet of Marvel Comics, Roger Corman, and MTV, he might've written something like Toby Barlow's *Sharp Teeth*. . . . It's everything you'd expect from such an odd and potent hybrid: highly addictive, enormously enjoyable, and unexpectedly moving."

—Scott Smith, author of *The Ruins* and *A Simple Plan*

"A hot-tongued, howling wolf of a book, strange and tender, luscious and cool, frisky as a pup but with a mouthful of fangs. Once bitten, I was smitten by its beauty."

—Joseph O'Connor, author of *The Star of the Sea*

"Forget any reservations you might have about werewolf stories or verse novels. This is great, engaging, wonderful stuff. Sondheim should make it his next musical."

—Michael Moorcock